Lock Down Publications and Ca$h Presents

PAPER, ROCK, SNAKES

Is Blood Thicker Than Water

Written By

Vincent "Vitto" Holloway

First Edition 2025

Printed in the United States of America

This is a work of fiction. Names, characters, places, and incidents either
are products of the author's imagination or are used fictitiously. Any
similarity to actual events or locales or persons, living or dead, is
entirely coincidental.

Lock Down Publications
P.O. Box 944
Stockbridge, GA 30281
www.lockdownpublications.com

Like our page on Facebook: Lock Down Publications
www.facebook.com/lockdownpublications.ldp

Stay Connected with Us!

Text **LOCKDOWN** to 22828 to stay up-to-date with new releases, sneak peaks, contests and more…

Like our page on Facebook:
Lock Down Publications

Join Lock Down Publications/The New Era Reading Group

Visit our website:
www.lockdownpublications.com

Follow us on Instagram:
Lock Down Publications

Email Us: We want to hear from you!

Prologue

Pastor Shapphire Stone was one of the most influential and well-connected people in the country. She regularly dined with the judges, police, chiefs, mayors, governors, and anyone else who could fast-track her agendas and those of her business associates. You were guaranteed to find a few of the top twenty on the Forbes list in her rolodex, along with those who preferred to keep their wealth a secret from the world. She was a mover and shaker, and she tended to get things done. Her opinion was sought after by people of importance, and numerous dignitaries kept her counsel. She was loved all over the country. She held keys to numerous cities because of her charitable work. She financed soup kitchens and homeless shelters. During the holidays she was a blessing to the less fortunate. She set up clothes drives during the winter, gave away turkeys during Thanksgiving, and toys during Christmas. Her name was gold to any charity she put her weight behind. People far and wide went out of their way to get her on board with any foundation or charity because they knew that where she went, the donations followed. She took care of her friends and destroyed her enemies in the city. In the City of Medicine, she was an angel in disguise to the population. The people loved her, especially the Black community. Wherever she appeared, crowds were going to show up. She wasn't afraid to congregate in the urban neighborhoods because she was always welcomed. Whenever she showed up in the projects, she could barely get out of the car because of the crowds surrounding her. She brought kids ice cream and candy. She helped pay bills and rent. She also helped the Bloods and Crips call a cease-fire. She was popular and revered, loved and liked. It would be a hazard to say anything against her in the wrong part of town. Some people thought she was the modern-day Mother Theresa, but they didn't see her for what she really was—a façade!

A greedy, conniving, and manipulative devil. She had two passions in life—money and young Black boys. She fed these passions whenever and however she could. She loved going to the projects, not because of the receptions she received every time she pulled up, but because she had her pick of young, virile Black boys to indulge her every whim and desire. Single mothers made is so easy for her because they basically begged her to take their sons off their hands. She made her choices based on a couple of different factors, but the main one was the situation at home. Most of the mothers were single parents with numerous kids, struggling to pay the bills. These were the ones who were easy to convince to let her take their sons for a few days. She paid a few bills, and it was smooth sailing. The boys who pleasured her like she instructed got college educations, money, shopping sprees, and anything else they desired. When she made appearance in the projects, little boys begged for her to pick them so they could cut her grass, rake her yard, or whatever else they could dream up. She loved the inexperience of the boys because she could shape and mold them to her liking. She liked them young and Black, and she had a wide selection to choose from.

Her love for money was a different story. She had to have it, and she would go to any length to get it. She owned numerous businesses where Black people spent their money instead of paying their bills. She just loved tax time because Black people went crazy with their spending when those checks came. She owned beauty salons, barbershops, liquor stores, beauty supply stores, corner stores, gun shops, and pawn shops. All were strategically placed in urban neighborhoods. Nobody could trace these companies back to her because she had used dummy corporations to purchase them under assumed names. She generated millions from these businesses, but her cash cow was her baby—her church. The A.M.E. Diamond Church of Christ. Her congregation was mostly Black despite her being a white woman. Her church held two thousand people, and could add five hundred more if she added chairs to the balcony. Every Sunday it was a packed house; she even had a waiting list of people wanting to join. She had two ATM machines set up in front of the church by the entrances. She passed the offering plates around twice, and sometimes three times, depending on how high the fervor was during the service. She passed them around twice during her bible study class on Monday and Wednesdays, and every time they came back to the front, they were full. Her more affluent parishioners regularly wrote checks for the church and her charitable endeavors. It amazed her how many people gave their hard-earned money in the name of the Lord. As long as people continued to believe in Jesus Christ, she would always be rich.

"Okay, kids, that's it for the day. Hopefully I'll see you all in next week's class," Shapphire said, standing up. "Who wants to stay back and help me clean up?" she asked with a smile on her face.

Every boy there raised his hand and raised it high as they could to get her attention.

"That bitch is a pervert," Keisha leaned over to whisper to her home girl.

"Mmm hmph." Her friend agreed, shaking her head at the boys' eagerness.

They both sat there with looks of disgust on their faces as they watched. Rumors of her sexcapades were whispered about, but nobody could prove anything or wanted to for that matter, so that's all they were. Rumors.

Shapphire saw the looks of disgust on the girls' faces and made a note to deal with it later on, but she put it out her mind as she studied who she was going to pick to help her. She already knew who she was going to choose, but if she didn't make a show of picking it would cause an uproar, so she went through the motions.

"Rosario, will you stay behind this week?" she asked sweetly to the boy she had been eyeing since he had started attending Bible study classes a few weeks ago.

"Yes, ma'am, I'll stay and help."

"Good," she said, smiling at all the moans and groans the other boys were issuing at not being picked.

She had to promise to pick them the next time before she could get them out the door. She made sure that the doors were locked because she didn't want any unexpected guests to walk in on her.

"Follow me to my office, Rosario," she told him as she eyed him.

"What do you need help with, Pastor Stone?" Rosario asked when they entered her office.

"There's no rush, Rosario," Shapphire said as she sat down behind her desk. "You're so well-spoken. I wanted to talk to you for a few minutes to find out your goals, dreams, and ambitions in life," she added as she studied him.

Rosario flushed with pride when he thought about who made sure he was educated. Shapphire saw him blush and thought it was cute. She looked into his eyes and saw a knowledge there that belied his age. Coming to a decision, she stood up and walked over to him. She reached behind her, unzipped the robe she was wearing, and let it fall around her ankles.

"I need you to help me with this," she said as she stood naked.

Rosario looked at her standing there in the suit she came into the world in and gulped. He had to admit that she had a body any woman would be proud of, and he couldn't stop his body from reacting to hers. He was nervous because he was fourteen years old, and she was his pastor.

"Pa...Pas...Pastor Stone...I...don't...think I can...do this," he said nervously.

Shapphire walked into his personal space until they were sharing breath.

"You can, and you will," she said huskily as she ran her hand down his pants and over the erection fighting for release.

She walked over to a stack of Bibles in her office, bent over, looked back at him, and said, "Fuck me."

Rosario looked at her shaved pussy and overcame his nervousness very quickly. He undressed and stood there waiting for her inspection. Shapphire saw his dick, and felt her pussy get even wetter at the size of it.

"Come put that in me now," she said impatiently.

Rosario wasted no time in walking over and sliding into her. He almost came as soon as he felt her warm pussy clutch his dick, but found his control and went to work. Youthful enthusiasm made up for his lack of skill and finesse.

"Oh God fuck me. Fuck me...harder, harder," Shapphire screamed as she threw her ass into him.

"Oh my God! I'm cumming."

She couldn't believe how fast he made her climax. That had never happened before, and she loved it.

Rosario felt his orgasm coming on and slowed down. He eventually stopped and pulled out of her. Shapphire was on the verge of another orgasm when she felt him pull out of her. Angry, she looked over her shoulder at him and saw that he had his eyes down with an embarrassed look on his face.

"What's wrong?" she asked softly, assuming he was feeling some type of way about what they were doing.

She opened her mouth to reassure him when he surprised her.

"I don't know how to say this without you looking at me different," he said, keeping his eyes on the floor.

"What if I say I wouldn't, would you tell me then?' she asked with faux patience.

"Yes," he answered quietly.

"Well, you can tell me anything because nothing will make me look at you differently," she said, not bothering to hide her impatience.

"I want to have sex on the pulpit where you give your sermons on Sundays," he blurted out.

Shapphire was stunned into silence. She couldn't believe he wanted to bring one of her darkest sexual fantasies to life. She knew that she had a keeper in this one, and she would do whatever she needed to do to make sure she kept him. She knew he was watching her, waiting for an answer, so she pretended to be thinking about it when she really wanted to jump with joy.

"To tell you the truth, that's a fantasy of mine also," she said, smiling at the look of relief on his face. "Come on," she said, grabbing his hand and basically dragging him to the front of the church. "I want you to fuck and cum in all three holes," she said, bending over the wooden stand that held her family Bible. "I hope you are up to the challenge," she added with a wicked smile.

Rosario smiled back at her before proceeding to show her he was indeed up to the challenge. For the next couple of hours, the only sounds heard in the sanctuary of her church were their moans, blasphemy being committed with every thrust of their bodies and a camera clicking as it caught them in all of their glory as they desecrated the Lord's house. Pastor Shapphire Stone had built her empire off of greed, the manipulation of young Black boys and their families. Now, because of that, a crack had been found in her armor. Didn't she know that all deeds in the dark would soon come to the light?

God Don't Like Ugly!

Chapter 1

Yero Owens was a true product of his environment. He grew up with the rats and roaches. He knew about wish sandwiches—two pieces of bread wishing you had something to put in between them.

He knew more about drug dealers and dope houses than he did teachers and schools. The streets raised him, and his mother's lessons were pivotal in his life. Whether you passed her tests or failed was the difference between life and death. His mother was a mom in name only. She was more in love with heroin than she was with her own kids. She was the woman who had taken his virginity and called it sexual education.

"Now you know what to do, so don't be bringing no nappy-headed kids home," she slurred as he slid off of her.

His sister Dynasty was left in his charge more often than not, and he made sure that she was all right. Even though he was just a child himself, he took on that responsibility. He had no choice but to make it. In the bowels of Bull City's ghettos, being poor was an affliction the government forced on you, but he refused to accept the status quo and did what he had to do. Education was important to him, but he couldn't afford to sit in a classroom all day for eighteen years, so he went ahead and studied for his G.E.D. By fifteen, he had completed his tests and was in the streets full force. He couldn't imagine working 9 to 5 for minimum wage. When he turned sixteen, his mother passed away from an overdose, but it bothered his sister more than it did him because he knew they were better off without her.

He was quiet—so quiet that people often forgot that he was around, and he used that to his advantage. He studied people, what they said, what they didn't say. How they moved and their reactions to adversity. An old head who noticed how observant he was told him, "Stay aware of your surroundings, and the people around you, or you'll never see the snake before it rises up and bites you."

Another thing he didn't have a problem with was girls. They stayed in his face trying to get his attention, but because of his experience with his mother, he didn't give them the time of day. When he was younger, his looks were a gift and a curse. He was quiet and shy, but it was the exact opposite. He just didn't like the spotlight his looks put him under, but the older he got, the more he learned to use what God gave him as a weapon to advance his agenda. Women always said, "Use what you got to get what you want," and he figured men could do the same, but he had no time for a girlfriend because loyalty and trustworthiness were foreign words to the girls he came into contact with. His wife—the streets—didn't give him the opportunity to cheat her. So he found his pleasure where he could and kept women where they belonged, on his peripheral. Durham was a cesspool of illegal activity, and he was soon to become the king of this concrete jungle.

***

The block was jumping. Product was getting moved, and money was being made. The atmosphere was that of an assembly line. The dealers, the fiends, and security all worked in unison with each other. Yero didn't tolerate foolishness. If it didn't make money, it didn't make sense.

"Yo, dog, check that whip comin' down the block," Puerto Rico said, pointing at the car.

"Damn, that shit hot," Casper shouted excitedly when he saw the car.

Yero looked at the car and frowned. He wondered why his lookout didn't radio in on the walkie-talkies they all carried, because he didn't allow luxury vehicles on his block. They drew unwanted attention to his operation. He watched, along with his team, as the car pulled to a stop across from them.

"What kind of whip is that?" Hollywood asked no one in particular.

"I don't know, but that shit some futuristic shit," Tonny said as he calculated how long it would take him to cop one for himself.

"That's the new Aston Martin," Yero said, watching the car with keen interest.

The team looked at him, but nobody was really surprised that he knew that. They had come to expect things like that from him.

"I'm about to go see who it is, 'cause they stopping business right now," Puerto Rico said seriously.

He started to move in that direction before Yero grabbed his arm, stopping him. He looked up at him with a question in his eyes.

"Chill, bro. All will be revealed soon, I think," Yero said quietly, never taking his eyes from the car.

Through the light tint on the car, he felt like the occupants were looking at him for some reason. He didn't see any disadvantage in waiting, so he did just that. He would make them reveal their hands first. Puerto Rico respected Yero's mind and did what he told him to do: wait.

***

"Gurl, why ye just sittin' there?" Aza asked teasingly.

"Yea, mem have never seen ye messed up over a bwoy," Light said, laughing from the back seat.

"Shut ye mouths," Suai said quietly as she stared out of her window, tryin' to get her courage up.

It had been ten years since she had laid eyes on him, and he still evoked the same emotions.

"Mem wish de gurls back home could see ye now, miss tough gurl," Aza teased as she joined in the laughter.

"Mem wish ye two stayed home," Suai said, fightin' her smile. She loved her cousins, but they were annoying sometimes.

"Uncle wouldn't have let ye come without us," Light said seriously.

"Ye lucky we came," Aza joked. "Ye should be grateful," she teased. It was only because they couldn't wait to leave the island and come to America.

Suai didn't respond to their comments because what they didn't know was that she was gonna come to America to find him whether her father allowed her to or not, but she kept that to herself.

"Come on," she said, opening her door and getting out of the car.

They all got out of the car and caused an uproar.

"Damn, she thick."

"Shorty got an ass on her."

"Come here, girl."

They were bombarded with catcalls as they walked across the street, but they never looked left or right. Suai's focus was on one man and one man only. Aza and Light followed her lead, even though they were lovin' the attention.

Yero saw the blood-red-tipped locs, and the feeling that she was familiar started form in his gut. He saw her face and knew that he knew her, but couldn't place her in his mind. Then he saw her eyes.

"It can't be," he whispered as his memories swept him away.

***

Yero was on his way home from another day in the trap when he heard a couple arguing in the alleyway. The streets had taught him to mind his business, so he was going to walk on by until he heard the female tell the man to get his hands off of her. She sounded young, too young to be outside this late, so against his better judgment, he slipped into the alley with his pistols in his hands to see if he could size up the situation. It was three in the morning, and he was ready to get some sleep. He slid behind a dumpster to listen to the conversation. He couldn't really understand them because they both had thick accents, but after listening for a few minutes, he surmised that the man was trying to rape the girl—something he couldn't allow.

"Hold still, ye little bitch," Black spat, tryin' to hold onto the struggling girl as he unzipped his pants. "Ye uncle promised ye ta mem, and mem gonna break ye in proper," he added as he finally released his dick.

"Wit' dat?" she asked sarcastically as she pointed at his shriveled dick.

"Ye little bitch," Black growled as he backhanded her across the face, knocking her to the ground.

"Ye will learn to respect mem," he added seriously. His pride was wounded, and his rage grew.

"Mem fada will kill ye fa putting ye hands on mem," she screamed, lookin' up at him as she held her busted lip.

"Little gurl, ye fada will be dead soon, and ye uncle will be bossman wit' mem as his right hand, and ye will be mine," Black laughed at the look on her face as he slowly stroked himself to hardness. "Now get up and do ye wifey duty," he said as he roughly snatched her up off the ground.

The girl was in a daze from hearing that her father might be in danger, but as soon as Black touched her, she started fighting. Black was surprised at the ferocity of her fighting. She almost broke away from him with her initial move, but he smacked her up a few times until she stopped struggling.

He grabbed her hand and used it to stroke himself back to hardness.

Yero saw what was happening and decided now was the best time to act. He crept from behind the dumpster, gripping his gun tightly in his hands. The man called Black had his back turned towards him, so he was able to get right up on him before he pulled the trigger. The impact from the shot knocked him off his feet. He thought he was going to have a hysterical girl on his hands from the gunshots and the dead body lying at their feet, but she was staring at him calmly with a look of curiosity in her eyes.

"Who are ye?" she asked with awe lacing every word.

He ignored her question as he checked her out. She was closer to his age of sixteen than he originally thought. She had dark chocolate skin with a budding body that gave you a glimpse of what she would be one day. She was a pretty girl, not beautiful in a traditional way, with her dimples and short locs. Honestly, she would be average-looking if it weren't for her eyes. They were the color of stormy skies—light grey, and hypnotic. He could feel himself falling into their depths, so he broke eye contact before turning to walk away.

"Wait, please," she said quickly.

Yero stopped but didn't turn around.

"Who are ye?" she asked quietly. "Who are ye?" she asked again when she saw that he wasn't going to walk away.

Yero turned around; he couldn't help himself. The way she talked sounded so good to him. Her accent made the simplest words sound melodic, like lyrics to a song. He stared at her, the way she was staring at him, and knew he just couldn't walk away from her.

"What's your name?" he asked, looking at her.

Suai felt an unfamiliar feeling making her heart flutter from the way he was looking at her. She put it in the back of her mind because her father was in trouble, and she didn't have any time to waste.

"My name is Suai," she said, returning his look. "Thank you fa killing dat bombaclot pussy bwoy," she added before spitting on the dead body.

"Speaking of which, we need to get away from this body before the pigs show up," he said, turning to leave. "There's no telling who heard the gunshot," he added, not wanting to see her fucked up over his body.

"Wait, can it be too much ta know ye name?" she asked, wanting to know who her knight in hoodie and Timbs was.

"You don't need my name, shorty. Just get out of this alley," he told her before walking off.

"Can mem have one of ye guns?" she asked, as what Black said about her father came rushing back.

Yero stopped and turned around, not sure if he had heard her right.

"What did you just say?" he asked, walking back over to her.

"Can mem have one of ye guns?" she asked again.

"Why?" he asked, curious about this girl, even though he felt like she was trouble.

"Mem have to kil' mem uncle," she said seriously.

"Why?" he asked again, just to see if she would break down.

He remembered the man called Black saying something about her uncle but didn't catch it all. He definitely didn't think she had it in her to kill her uncle, whoever he was. Suai looked at him, exasperated with the twenty questions, but she indulged him because he saved her.

"Mem need to kill mem uncle before he can kill mem fada," she said as she looked him in the eye.

Yero looked at her for a few seconds and came to a decision.

"Come on," he told her as he walked off. He was ready to get out of that alley.

"Ye gonna help mem kill mem uncle?" she asked excitedly.

"No," he stated bluntly.

He watched as her face fell and felt something tug inside of him. He shook his head to clear his mind.

"You're gonna kill your uncle," he added seriously.

"Give mem ye gun then," she said, ready to get it over with.

"Show me where your uncle stays," Yero said, walking off. He wanted to get far away from that dead body as possible. Suai led him three miles away from that alley to a section of row houses on a quiet residential street.

"What is your uncle's name?" he asked after watching the house for a few minutes.

"Bounty," she said with disgust.

"Bounty!" he exclaimed, looking at her like she had two heads. "You're talking about Bounty with the weed?" he asked seriously.

"Yes," she said simply, like it wasn't a big deal.

Yero shook his head. His respect for her had just skyrocketed. She wanted to kill one of the most ruthless Jamaicans in Bull City. He had the marijuana market locked down. He had any strain you wanted. No one but his workers sold weed inside the city limits. Violators usually washed up on the banks of Falls Lake if they were ever seen again. He didn't discriminate, and if you played with his business, you played with your life. And she wanted to kill him.

"Your uncle stays here?" he asked skeptically.

It was hard to believe a man who was so powerful and rich stayed in a spot like this, with no security around.

"Yea, he cocky. Think nobody would dare try him," she said seriously. "Only mem, Black, and mem uncle stayed here."

Yero figured that Black was the dead man in the alley.

"If you want to kill your uncle, you'll have to use your advantages," he told her seriously.

"Advantages?" she asked, looking at him with a puzzled look on her face.

"Bounty ain't gonna expect you to have a gun, let alone try to kill him," he said, schooling her. "So, you'll have to use that window of opportunity to lay him down."

Suai sat there, looking at him as she soaked in the knowledge he was giving her. Those feelings she'd stuffed in the recesses of her heart a little while ago reared their head again, but she snuffed them out because she had business to handle. She couldn't lie, though; she was feelin' this boy who wouldn't even tell her his name but yet saved her life.

"Here," Yero said, reaching into his waist and pulling out his other revolver before waving it to draw her attention to it. "This is a .38 revolver. It has five bullets in the chamber, so make them count," he added, handing her the gun.

"Mem will bring ye gun right back," she said before jogging across the street.

She slowly walked up the stairs leading to the front door of her uncle's house, wondering if she could really kill him. But then she remembered what Black had said about her father dying, and felt her resolve harden. She took a deep breath and knocked on the door. After a few seconds, she heard her uncle's footsteps.

"Suai, gurl, why did ye run off now?" Bounty asked as he grabbed her up in a hug. He didn't notice the gun she was holding tightly by her side as he looked over her shoulder.

"Where is Black, gurl?" he asked when he didn't see him with her.

"Mem don't know where Black is, uncle," Suai said as rage washed over her at his fake display of concern. "Mem just decided to come back. Mem was mad and needed to think," she added when he released her from his embrace.

"Well, come in, gurl. Mem will call ye fada and let him know ye are safe," Bounty said as he walked into the house, leaving her to close the door. His mind was occupied with making sure his brother attended the funeral he had planned for him.

The mention of her father sent her into action. She took a couple of steps into the house, raised the gun like the boy showed her, and squeezed the trigger until it was clicking on an empty chamber. She stood there frozen, not sure what to do until she saw the pool of blood forming under her uncle's body. Then she snapped out of her daze and ran back outside to give the gun back to the boy like she promised, but he was nowhere to be found. That saddened her more than she cared to admit because she didn't even know his name.

Yero saw her looking for him, but he was hiding behind some bushes, watching her. Until he had heard the gunshots, he had doubted that she was actually gonna do it, but she surprised him. He was still there because he wanted to make sure she was alright. Now that he was certain she would survive, he crept off without a plan to see her again. As much as he wanted to get to know her, they were from two different worlds, and he didn't have time for games.

Suai walked back into the house dejected because the boy who saved her life wasn't there, but she didn't have time to dwell on it. She walked over to her uncle's body and snatched his phone off of his hip. She sat down on the floor and dialed her father's number.

"Did you find mem daughter, Bounty?"

When she heard his voice, she immediately choked up, and all of her emotions bubbled to the surface as tears cascaded down her face.

"Fada."

***

Yero snapped out of his memories to find his team holding the women at bay with pistols pointed in their direction.

"Stand down," he ordered his men.

"Are you sure?" P.R. asked in Spanish.

"Yeah, I'm sure," Yero replied.

He turned his attention back to the woman with the blood-red locs and said, "Suai."

Chapter 2

When her name rolled off of his tongue, Suai felt herself getting emotional as tears welled in her eyes, but she fought them back. Her father was the only man who had the power to make her cry, but now it seemed as if there were two. Finally finding him after so many years was overwhelming. She had dreamed about this moment for so long, had played out the different scenarios in her mind over and over again, but nothing prepared her for the man in front of her.

"Ye remember," she said quietly, her eyes never leaving his.

"I make it my business to remember my accomplices," Yero said seriously as he held her gaze.

He knew his team was looking at him for an explanation, but he ignored them because he was suspicious about her just popping up in his life; especially since he never gave her his name. It had been over ten years since that night, and he didn't believe in coincidence.

"Ye didn't tell us he was a Mexican too," Aza joked when she heard him speaking Spanish.

Aza looked him up and down blatantly, and she had to admit he was fine. She could see why Suai caused such a fuss over the years on the island.

"Yea, mem didn't know ye did bwoys from de south of de border," Light said laughing.

Suai's face flushed with embarrassment as everybody laughed at her cousins' jokes.

"Shut ye mouths," she growled at them.

She looked at Yero, ready to profusely apologize for their comments but stopped when she saw that he was smiling along with everyone else. She shook her head and begrudgingly smiled also.

"Who do you have with you?" Yero asked, deciding to help her out with the embarrassment she was feeling. Plus, his question was twofold: one, he wanted to ease her predicament, and two, he needed to know everyone he came in contact with because everybody was a potential witness.

"Mem name is Aza and did mem sista Light," she said boldly before Suai could say anything.

"Mem name is Puerto Rico, and mem like what mem see." P.R. used her accent and dialect to introduce himself.

"And can you eat pussy, Puerto Rico?" Aza asked, stepping up into his face.

Suai and Light smirked because they knew Aza could handle any man.

Yero shook his head because he knew that P.R. wasn't used to women coming at him like that, but he put that out his mind because all of his attention was solely on the woman standing in front of him.

"We need to talk," Suai said seriously. She needed to get him alone. She had waited ten years to find him, and now that she had him, she wanted him all to herself.

"I'm waiting on someone to come through, but we'll handle that as soon as I'm done with that because I agree, we do need to talk," Yero said to her. He was about to expand on that but was interrupted by his name being called over the walkie-talkie on his hip.

"Talk to me."

"Black-on-black Dodge Charger turning onto the block," the lookout said.

"Got 'em," Yero said before bending down to pick up the duffle bag lying at his feet. He watched the Charger glide down the block until it slid to a stop in front of them. He walked over and got into the car.

"What's up, Y.O.?" Detective Jerome Davis asked as he pulled off to circle the block.

"Money, JD, always money," Yero said bluntly. He didn't like police, period, crooked or not. He had people on his payroll that he had to deal with. He paid very well to make sure no pressure, or attention, was put on his people. It was a necessary evil in his line of work.

"You got something for me?" the detective asked, ready to get his hands on the money.

"How are your wife and little J.D. doing?" Yero asked quietly, ignoring his question. "Family is the most important thing in a man's life, right?" he asked, turning his head to study the detective.

Detective Davis was quiet for a few minutes, clenching his jaw as he chewed on the warning Y.O. was giving gravely. He held the keys to their closets of skeletons, and even though he didn't like the subliminal message, there was nothing he could do about it. It was his lot in life, and he accepted that. As long as he didn't rock the boat and did his job, he could prosper.

"Everybody's good," he answered, shrugging.

"That's good, J.D., real good," Yero said, opening the door and getting out after they pulled to a stop where they started, leaving the duffle bag on the floor. He tapped the roof of the car, letting him know to get lost.

"Can you ride a bike?" he asked Suai after the Charger disappeared off the block.

"Only if me de one driving," she replied seriously.

"P.R., give her the keys to your bike."

Puerto Rico looked at him like he was crazy.

"Y.O., dog, you're tripping. Give her Hollywood or Towny's bike," P.R. said seriously.He wasn't feeling the idea of her riding his baby. He had a 2003 Kawasaki Ninja painted with the Superman theme.

"Dog, you're actually worried about that shit when you know I got you regardless?" Yero said with a smirk on his face.

"Take care of my baby, shorty," P.R. told Suai as he tossed her the keys.

"Mem got you, bwoy," she said with a smile. "Which bike is it?" she asked, looking at the assortment of bikes on the block.

"The Superman Ninja," P.R. pointed to his bike.

Suai tossed the keys to her car to Aza before walking over and swinging her leg over the bike. She grabbed the helmet off of the handlebars and tossed it to P.R. He looked at her like she was crazy but kept silent.

Yero watched her across the bike and liked what he saw. She caressed the bike like it was her lover. Everybody in his inner circle had bikes because it was easier to evade police when they were on blocks.

Suai cut the ignition on, and the engine roared to life. She eased into first gear, then fed the engine by hitting the throttle, making the bike rise up on its back wheel. She fed the gas until she was going almost thirty miles per hour. When she let the bike back down on both wheels, she hit the front tire brake, raising the back wheel into the air. As she jackknifed, she used her powerful thighs to swing the bike around like Tom Cruise did in the *Mission Impossible* movie. Everybody was going crazy at the stunts she was pulling off, but Aza and Light weren't impressed because all of them knew how to ride.

Suai cruised back up the block, smirking at the compliments she was getting, but she only wanted the praise of one man. Yero saw her looking at him and knew she was looking for praise, but he wouldn't give her what she wanted. He walked over to a black-on-black GSX Suzuki Bandit 1300, believed to be one of the fastest street bikes in production. The bike was low-key but powerful, which fit his personality perfectly. He climbed on, cut on the engine, revved the throttle, and took off down the block. He popped a wheelie and disappeared off the block. A few seconds later, Suai copied his maneuver and followed behind him.

"It look like she might have found she match," Light said to her sister as she watched the bikes disappear.

"Now mem gon find mem match," Aza said, walking off to kick it with the niggas on the block.Light shook her head and laughed as she followed after her twin. Their first trip to America was shaping up to be real interesting.

***

Tropicana's was jumpin'. It was Friday night, and all of the ballers were out, which brought out the material girls as well. Tangie was the owner, but she was behind the bar helping out because two of her girls had called out, and they were filled to capacity. Her job that night was twofold. She was in a bind because her sisters were putting pressure on her to find someone thorough enough to do business with. They were irate with her because the last niggas she sent to them were bitches and had to be dealt with. So, she had her eyes peeled as she served drinks, on the lookout for a certified gangsta. As the night wore on, she was starting to get discouraged with the prospects she was coming in contact with until she found the perfect solution to her problems, and they weren't even a man.

"Dynasty," she yelled out over the music. She even waved her hand to make sure she got her attention.

Dynasty walked into the club on the arm of Low, a local hustler from the west end of Durham who was on the rise, looking like a million bucks. Her Christian Dior wrap-around dress hugged her curves like a glove. The chocolate brown color of the dress matched well with her olive skin tone. Her Prada-stamped crocodile leather pumps of the same color cost more than most people's car notes, and her diamond accessories were catching the lights of the club, giving off the rainbow hues only true VVS's could. She knew she was the shit, and everybody else was her toilet. Bad bitch in the building, stand up and clap, mu'fucka!

She heard her name being called and quickly found the source.

What the fuck this stupid bitch want? she questioned in her mind as she watched Tangie wave her down. She was gonna ignore her, but the bitch was putting her on blast, and it was rubbing her the wrong way. So, she decided to go check her about that loud shit.

"Baby, go find a booth while I go see what the owner callin' me for," she told him before gliding over to the bar. And glide she did because her strut was so effortless it hardly looked like she was moving her legs at all. "Bitch, why the fuck you calling me all loud and shit when you know I don't fuck with your bird ass?" she asked with a frown on her face.

"Hello to you too, Dynasty," Tangie said, rolling her eyes at her. "Why are you rolling with Low when your brother is beefing with him?" she asked curiously.

Dynasty looked at her like she was crazy. She couldn't believe she had been called over for some bird shit.

"Bitch, mind your fucking business," she gritted at her. "If you called me over here to gossip, miss me with that shit. Fuck is wrong with you?" She turned to leave, but Tangie stopped her.

"Dynasty, wait," Tangie needed her, but she didn't want her to know it. "I need to talk some business with you," she added seriously.

Dynasty stopped and turned around. She was wondering what Tangie could possibly want business-wise with her. This bitch was a bird, and she was a thoroughbred—two different worlds.

"I'm listening," she said, more out of curiosity than interest.

"I need to get at Yero," Tangie said, trying to keep the desperation out of her voice.She had been hearing about Y.O.

for a minute now and knew he was the type of man her sisters were looking for. Dynasty started laughing; she couldn't help it.

This bitch is too much, she thought. "My brother don't do birds," she said, sneering at her.

Tangie let the insult roll over her because she knew the real reason Dynasty didn't like her was because people said they looked alike.

"I don't want to fuck him. I need to talk to him about those t-shirts he was looking for. I know a vendor who has them by the truckload," she said in a stage whisper.

Dynasty stood there, wondering if she heard what she thought she heard. The bitch said t-shirts, but it was no doubt what she was referring to.

Is this bitch trying to set me up? she questioned herself. She thought about it and figured the bitch was stupid to set her up.

"I don't know what you're talking about," she answered, just to see her reaction.

"Look, you know I got plenty of people in here bumping their gums after a few drinks. We both have a need . . . I need a certified gangsta, and y'all need a t-shirt supplier. Fair exchange is no robbery," Tangie said, selling her idea.

Dynasty was still looking at her skeptically.

"If you tell your brother to get at me, I'll give you and your date free drinks all night," Tangie said, throwing the incentives into the pot.

Dynasty couldn't believe this bitch tried her on some bird shit.

"Listen to me and listen good, bitch. If I do decide to give my brother your message and it turns out you are bullshitting, I will peel your wig back and send it rotting to your mother," she said seriously. "And don't even try me on some free lunch shit." She reached into her purse and pulled out a big knot of money. "I get money, bitch. I'm buying the bar. Fuck your free drinks."She tossed her the money and walked away to the cheers of people happy for free drinks.

Tangie watched her walk away with her head held high like she was a queen and smirked. She was happy because she had accomplished what she had set out to do that night. She knew Dynasty was going to pass on her message to her brother and got her to buy the bar out by playing to her pride. It was easy to do because she was just like her sister Loca. She soon forgot about her encounter with Dynasty as she ran around making free drinks for her patrons.

Chapter 3

Yero and Suai turned onto a block filled with abandoned cars and boarded-up houses. Suai was curious about where they were going, but she kept her tongue because she was content to just be with him. She would follow him anywhere. Yero pulled into a driveway and coasted around to the back of the house. Suai followed and parked her bike beside his. She looked at the rundown house with the boarded-up windows, the peeling paint, the trash-filled gutters, and frowned as she followed him up the steps to the back door. Yero looked over his shoulder as he put the key into the lock, saw her frown, and smirked at her.

"What? Daddy's princess too good to get dirty?" he asked jokingly.

Suai looked at him and noticed that he was leaving her behind, but she didn't like what he was insinuating.

"Mem will go anywhere wit' ye," she said seriously.

Yero looked into her eyes and saw that she was serious, but he was still skeptical until he found out her reasons for popping back into his life. She would remain a suspect in his eyes. He unlocked the door and pushed it open. He stood to the side and motioned for her to go in first. She walked in, then he closed and locked the door behind them. He waited a few seconds before turning on the lights. He smirked when he heard her gasp.

Suai stood there amazed at what she was seeing. They were standing in the kitchen, but it was the kitchen you would expect to see in *Architectural Digest*. The countertops were black granite. The cherry wood cabinets gleamed everywhere. A big Sub-Zero refrigerator was sitting in the corner, humming. She walked into the living room and again, she was rendered speechless. The furniture was butter-colored leather, and the walls were filled with prints of famous African Americans: Martin Luther King Jr., Malcolm X, Harriet Tubman, Marcus Garvey, Nat Turner, and many more. She saw the flat-screen TV with the game system attached to it. She wondered what the bedroom looked like, but in due time. Right now, they needed to talk. She knew he was suspicious of her, and she needed to ease his heart. She turned and saw that he was smirking at her. She rolled her eyes and sat down on the couch.

"Ten years, and ye are still amazing, mem," she said humbly as he sat down on the loveseat across from her. She was feeling some type of way because he chose to sit so far away from her, but she understood and kept her peace about it.

"Ten years, and you just pop up outta nowhere," he said, getting straight to the point. "I didn't even tell you my name. So how did you find me?" he asked as his eyes locked onto hers.

"Mem know ye are suspicious of mem, but dere's no reason to be," Suai said sincerely as she thought about all of the things she had to go through with her father over the last decade because of her obsession with him. "De day ye saved mem from dat mon, mem heart belonged to ye. Mem was crushed when mem couldn't find ye dat night. Mem fada came and took mem home, but mem couldn't get ye off of mem mind or heart . . ." She paused and took a deep breath before continuing. "Mem drove mem fada crazy begging him to find ye. For years, he refused ta give mem what mem wanted."

She frowned as she thought about how stubborn her father was.

"Mem think he didn't want ta let mem go. Every birthday he would ask mem what mem wanted, and mem would always ask fa ye. Every year, he refused. He forbade mem ta ever step foot in de Americas again after what happened dat night, but mem told him dat mem had ta find ye. He finally gave in when he saw mem was serious and would defy his wishes if he didn't give mem what mem heart desired. Crazy part about it is, he knew who ye were de whole time. After mem told him everything that happened that night, he used his resources to find ye. Mem his only child and ye saved mem. De day he told me ya name, mem made plans to come ta ye. He forbade mem coming by meself, hence mem cousins, but mem here now, and mem here forever." She looked at him with tears in her eyes because her emotions were threatening to overwhelm her.

She knew without a doubt that she loved him and was his forever, but did he want her?

Yero sat there and digested everything she told him without a word. He wondered how her father found him. He knew he wasn't untouchable, and he looked forward to finding that weakness and transforming it into a strength. He thought back to that night in the alley and the body he had caught all because he knew it was the right thing to do. He remembered her determination to kill her uncle because her father was in danger. He remembered her calm demeanor despite the fact she had just witnessed him kill a man, but more importantly, he remembered how she made him feel, the same way he was feeling now. But he wasn't sixteen anymore. He was a man with a mission to accomplish, and anybody around him had to be vetted and tested by fire.

"How do you know I don't already have someone in my life?" he asked seriously, watching her reaction.

Suai felt her breath catch and her chest constrict at the thought that someone was already occupying the spot she had claimed as her own for so long. The thought never once crossed her mind, but here it was, front and center. She looked into his eyes to see if he was playing with her, but he wasn't giving her anything with his stoicism. She took a deep breath and answered his question.

"Mem don't know if ye have a gurl, but she must not be doing she job if mem here wit' ye," she said seriously.

"How did you spot my lookout, and how did you get him to remain silent?" he asked, the question that had been on his mind since she showed up.

He didn't let her know that her last answer pleased him.

Suai stood up and performed a slow pirouette.

"Look at mem and tell mem how mem did it," she said with a smirk. "Ta answer ye udda question, mem fada taught mem everything, so mem know a lookout when mem see one," she added as she walked over to stand in front of him.

She wanted so badly to touch him; it was driving her crazy, but she wouldn't unless she was allowed to. She couldn't take him rejecting them being together.

Yero took everything she told him and stored it in his mind. She didn't know that she had just signed the lookout's death certificate, or maybe she did. He wouldn't put it past her to try and school him to show him her worth. He was humble enough to appreciate the lesson because he would rather it cost him nothing now instead of everything later. He put that out of his mind, though, as he focused on the body in front of him. He was a man, so he appreciated the curves, but he was in complete control of himself because he wasn't handcuffed to his lower self. He studied history, and many empires were toppled because of pussy. He was taught at a young age to admire beauty, and he was definitely admiring what was in front of him. Her Amiri jeans looked painted on the way they hugged her ass and hips. Her waist was so small it was almost nonexistent, but it was there, holding everything together nicely. As his eyes continued to travel upward, her body spread back out to give her the perfect coke-bottle shape. Her breasts were straining against her Amiri bone t-shirt. Her body was on point, but it paled in comparison to her best feature: her eyes. Her blood-red locs set off her chocolate skin tone, but her steel-grey eyes were hypnotic. He remembered her eyes from that night; he would never forget. His eyes found hers, and he could see the yearning inside of them for the feeling she felt only he could give her, but she would have to wait because business before pleasure, always.

"Ye like what ye see, Mr. Owens?" she asked quietly.

She was embarrassed by how wet her panties were.

"You look good, ma, no doubt about that, but if you want to be the queen of my chessboard, I need more than looks. I need to know you are down for me and only me, regardless of the pressure or circumstances. I have to know that I can count on you," he said seriously. "You have to get baptized by fire. I need something done."

Suai let out the breath she had been holding because he wasn't rejecting her. She smiled at him because she knew that she would do whatever he needed her to do. She knew beforehand that he would test her loyalty, so his request wasn't a surprise.

"Mem will do what mem need ta do ta show mem loyalty," she said seriously. "Can mem touch ye?" she blurted out, not being able to stop herself.

She cringed because even to her own ears, she sounded like a schoolgirl.

"Let me tell you about this nigga I need you to holla at," Yero said seriously, ignoring her request.

Suai let out a frustrated sigh and glared at him. He knew what he was doing, and the smirk ghosting around his lips let her know that he knew she would play his game for now. But she didn't come to America to lose.

"When mem handle dis pussy bwoy, mem get what mem want?" she questioned after he finished running the job down to her.

"You will get what you want, Suai, but let me warn you . . ." he said, his voice hardening. "When I touch you, it belongs to me and only me." He let her know he didn't play seconds.

Suai stood up and smirked at him.

"Bwoy, mem belonged ta ye dat night in de alley. Ye just didn't know it yet," she said before walking out the house to go do what she needed to do.

Yero finally allowed himself to smile when he heard the bike start up outside. It seemed as if fate was shining on him. Ten years since he had seen her, and now she was back in his life like she never left. He had seen her strength that night, so he knew that she was capable of doing what he asked her to do. But ten years could change anyone. He needed to be sure of everybody around him, especially if they were going to sleep beside him every night. He got up to leave when his phone started ringing. He looked at the screen and saw that it was his sister. He answered.

"Talk to me."

"Big bro, look, this bird bitch Tangie needs you to get at her about them t-shirts we been trying to find a vendor for," Dynasty said.

"You still got that nigga with you?" he asked her.He knew Tangie to be a gossip, but he didn't think she knew anybody with what he was looking for.

"No, I got rid of him when the club closed," she said, with disgust lacing every word. "How much longer do I have to chill with this goofy?" she asked, ready to get shit poppin'.

"Till I tell you," Yero said seriously. He knew how hotheaded his sister could be and needed to keep a short leash on her.

"Who does Tangie know with t-shirts?" he asked seriously.

"I don't know, but the bitch told me to pass a message to get at her about it. She seemed desperate, so be on your shit. If I didn't know you were looking, I would've never entertained that duck, but who knows? She might be good for something. I'm gone. I love you," she said before hanging up on him.

Yero didn't have her personal number, so he called the club and waited for someone to pick up.

**

Tangie was in her office, nestling her feet after being up all night, hoping Dynasty passed on her message to her brother when her phone rang.

"Tropicana, Tangie speaking," she answered.

"You looking for me?"

Tangie froze when she heard his voice. She would recognize his baritone anywhere, but she wanted to be sure.

"Y.O.?"

"You told me to get at you, right?" he asked seriously. He didn't have time for games.

"Yes, I did, but I'm surprised you reached out so soon," she said, gathering herself.

"I heard you're looking for those t-shirts," she said like she was in the know.

"I'm not even going to ask how you know my business because all you bitches do is gossip," he said seriously. He didn't usually disrespect women, but he was upset that she knew his business. Another leak to deal with. He would get her to tell him the source later, but now he needed to know about these t-shirts she was talking about.

"Just tell me who you know that can fill my stores up with t-shirts," he added, cutting straight to the chase.

Tangie usually checked niggas for calling her out her name, but she heard the anger in his voice and decided to leave it alone.

"My sisters are vendors for t-shirts in bulk," she said.

"Who are your sisters?" he asked, tired of beating around the bush.

"Tiphany and Precious," Tangie said, sensing his impatience.

***

Yero took the phone away from his ear and looked at it strangely. Did he just hear her right? Did she say Tiphany and Precious?

"You're talking about the Alvarez twins? Those your sisters?" he asked rapidly, trying to temper his excitement.Everyone had heard of the Alvarez twins. Their reputations preceded them; they were big dogs when it came to the drug game in the South.

"Yes, they are my sisters, and they want to meet you," Tangie said, rolling her eyes.She knew that her sisters were known, but so what? Them bitches weren't all that.

"You interested?" she asked.

"Set it up for next week," Yero said, more than interested. Today was turning into a good day.

"And Tangie . . ."

"Yes?" she answered, happy he agreed to meet with her sisters.

"If this turns out to be some bullshit, I promise you they will find you floating in Falls Lake," he warned her before hanging up.

Tangie looked at her phone with disbelief on her face. When the dial tone started beeping, she hung it up. Even though she knew that she was telling the truth, she couldn't stop the goosebumps from forming all over her body. She picked the phone back up and called her sisters.

***

Bread and Lite were sitting in the parking lot of an abandoned warehouse in Georgia, waiting on the twins.

35

They were both spooked, but they wouldn't let each other know it.

"Where the fuck these bitches at?" Bread asked, wondering how much longer they were going to sit in the dark in the middle of nowhere.

"Nigga, they're going to be here," Lite said, looking over at his homeboy. He was acting real jumpy, peering into the dark like he was expecting something to jump out and get him. He had been noticing for a couple of weeks that he was acting different, scary almost, but he chalked it up to stress.

"What? You scared or something?" he asked, knowing just which buttons to push.

"What!" Bread shouted, looking over at his best friend, who was smirking at him. "You know I don't play games when it comes to these sticks." He picked his pistol up off of his lap and waved it around. "Shit, don't try me," he added, grilling Lite.

"Whatever, nigga," Lite said, pushing in the car lighter to light a cigarette. He couldn't front; he was jumpy too, and he needed some nicotine to calm his nerves. The lighter popped out. He grabbed it and was about to light his Newport when somebody tapped on his window. He jumped and screamed, "What the fuck!" He also dropped the lighter in his lap, burning a hole through his chrome heart jeans. He grabbed the lighter and looked over to find the twins standing there, smirking at them.

How the fuck these bitches creep up on us like that? he thought as he rolled down his window.

"Damn, nigga, what are you scared of?" Tiphany asked sarcastically as she stared at them.

"Nah, you just surprised me, that's all," Lite said as he got himself under control. He chanced a quick glance over at Bread, and he looked like he was frozen in a block of ice. He turned back to the twins and said, "We got the money, so let's handle business so we can get back on the highway."

"Before we conclude our business, we want you two to listen to something we've come in possession of," Precious said, holding out a CD for him to take.

"What's this?" Lite asked with a confused look on his face as he took the CD from her. The gloves she had on escaped his notice.

"Just pop the CD in, nigga, because I got shit to do," Tiphany said seriously.

Lite was about to check her about her tone, but the look on her face let him know that she wasn't playing. He never liked dealing with her anyway because she was more hot-headed than Precious. He slid the CD in and hit *play*. Bread started sweating heavily because he suspected what was on the CD. He gripped his gun and prepared for war.

"Who sold you the drugs?" One could hear the anticipation and eagerness in the questioner's voice.

"Tiphany and Precious Alvarez and Jeremy Lite. I'm not built for prison. So if it's them or me, I'm picking me. Fuck them."

Lite was so shocked to hear Bread's voice on recording snitching on them. He snatched his gun out of his waist and prepared to kill the nigga trying to sink the ship. He looked over at his snake-ass homeboy and got another shock that night.

Boom!

You bitch-ass nigga, Lite thought when he saw Bread kill himself. He pumped a few more hot ones into his ass for good measure. He couldn't believe this shit. He turned to the twins and tried to explain.

"I didn't know shit about this. You have to believe me . . ."

Blomb! Blomb! Blomb!

"Shut your bitch-ass up," Tiphany said after she put three slugs into his face. "Association breeds assimilation," she told his corpse before opening the back door and grabbing the black duffle bag sitting on the back seat. She popped it open to make sure it held their money.

"I can't believe he killed himself," Precious said incredulously. She was mad she lost fifty stacks betting on that clown.

"Bitch, shut up and set my money out," Tiphany said, laughing at the look on her twin's face. "Bitch niggas will always do bitch things," she added seriously as she tossed the duffle bag onto the back seat and hopped into the driver's seat.

Precious got in and kept silent. What could she say to that? She had just lost fifty stacks thinking a nigga had some heart. As they pulled off, she tried to figure out a way to get her money back. Atlanta was full of bitch-ass niggas, so she would get plenty of opportunities to get her money back.

Chapter 4
(One week later)

"What do you know about this nigga Y.O.?" Tiphany asked, looking at her twin.

Precious was standing at the two-way mirror, watching the dance floor of their club, *The Pretty Flower*, waiting for Yero and his team to make an appearance. She looked over her shoulder at her sister and imitated their half-sister Tangie.

"He's about 6'2", toffee-colored shin, brown eyes, keeps his hair done up in cornrows, and he works out. All around he's a thoroughbred nigga."

She laughed after she finished describing him, using the voice of their valley girl acting sister.

"Bitch, I don't give a fuck about his looks because this cat stays licked," Tiphany said, patting the crotch of her Artik jeans. "All I need to know is if he can move these birds," she added seriously.

"According to Tangie he's official in his city, and he's making noise," Precious told her, repeating the info she was given.

"Yeah, she said that about Bone and his people too," Tiphany scoffed as she rolled her eyes. "That bitch good for sucking dick and spending money," she added seriously.

"That's still our sister," Precious said, eyeing her twin.

She believed that blood was thicker than water any day, and the world was the ocean in her eyes when it came to her family.

"Only because Papi cheated on Mama before she died," Tiphany said angrily.

"Papi wants us to establish a foothold on the East Coast, and we need North Carolina in order to do that," Precious said, changing the subject before her sister could go on over her usual tirade about their father's infidelity.

Tiphany knew what she was trying to do and let it go.

"When is this nigga supposed to be here?" she asked, ready to meet the man.

"It should be any time now," Precious said, looking at her watch before turning her attention back to the dance floor. "Oh, by the way, Greg is set to testify before the grand jury next week," she added nonchalantly.

"What!" Tiphany shouted as she sat up on the leather sofa she was reclining on and grabbed her phone to call up some of her shooters. "Why are you just now telling me this shit, P?" she asked angrily.

"Because I have things under control, sister dear," Precious said, smiling at her twin wickedly.

"You sure?" Loca asked skeptically as she paused in dialing her people up.

"Trust me, Loca." Precious said before turning back to the dance floor. "Oh my God, come look at these niggas that just walked in," she said, fanning herself.

"Which one is the infamous Y.O.?" Tiphany asked when she spotted the niggas on the floor.

"Do you even have to ask?" Precious asked sarcastically.

Tiphany didn't respond because it was obvious who Y.O. was. With Tangie's description on their minds, it was easy to pick him out. He stood out like a Ferrari in a lot full of Honda Accords.

"You see what he has on?" she asked, feeling his style.

"A black and grey short sleeve Gucci sweater with black stone-washed purple jeans and a pair of Gucci runners on his feet," Precious said, showing her eye for fashion.

"Damn he got my pussy wet," Loca said seductively.

She was doing something she hasn't done since Denzel played a crooked cop on *Training Day*, sweat a man.

"Bitch, I know you're not star-struck?" Precious jokingly asked as she walked over to her desk.

She couldn't lie though; the boy was fine.

"Don't front on me, P, like you don't want none of that dick," Loca laughed because she knew her twin was faking.

They were identical after all.

Precious tried to hide her smile, but she couldn't.

"Yeah, you're right, but only if it's big enough," she said with a laugh as they slapped hands.

She hit the button on her desk for the intercom.

"Kim, send those gentlemen up to our office," she told her cousin, who was working as a bartender that night.

"Some of his homeboys are cute too," Tiphany said as she put on another coat of lip gloss.

"Let's get these bricks moved, then we can see about some dick," Precious said seriously, but she cracked a smiled and grabbed her makeup out of her purse while her sister rolled her eyes at her.

***

"Damn, that bitch turning tricks," Hollywood said, staring at the stripper working the pole up on the stage.

"These ATL bitches serious," Towny said as he grabbed his crotch at all the ass in the building.

"Why the fuck these bitches want to meet in a fuckin' strip club?" Jah asked, looking around at all the people crowding him.

Prison made him wary of crowds, and he felt naked without his gun, but his box cutter was in his pocket. It would have to do in close quarters.

Yero looked at Jah for a few seconds before saying anything, silently letting him know to watch his mouth. Jah smirked at him, so Yero checked him.

"Yo, y'all watch that bitch shit around these females. We're dealing with women who are a different breed, and that shit is not gonna fly," he said as he looked around the club, scoping the scene out.

Jah didn't like being checked, but he kept his mouth shut for the time being.

"Jay-O, Hollywood, PR, and Casper, y'all post up around the club and be ready for whatever."

Yero gave out the instructions and watched as his team moved through the crowd, stuffing money into the strippers' thongs and G-strings, shaking his head. He didn't like the meeting place any more than Jah did, but he kept his feelings to himself because he saw the advantages it brought to the twins. If anything went wrong, they were expecting his team to be preoccupied with all the ass and titties in their faces. He continued to scan the club until he spotted the mirrors on the second floor. He figured they were mirrors because they were the only mirrors in that section of the club. Plus, he saw the silhouettes of two people standing on the other side, watching the happenings on the floor. He took note and kept it moving because he didn't want to let on that he knew what he was looking at. He might need that information later on. He also hoped that Towny was alert outside.

"We gon' stand here all night?" Jah asked sarcastically as he watched the asses pass him by.

"Let's go get a table because they already know we are here," Yero said, sparing the mirrors another glance before moving through the crowd.

***

"That nigga know we up here looking at him too," Precious said, respecting his military. Most niggas would be caught up in the ass and titties being paraded around them, checking for the exits, scoping the scene.

"Or maybe he just likes looking at himself," Loca said dismissively.

She didn't like giving dope boys too much credit because all they did was sell dope. Some could do it better than others, but rarely did one show her enough to reach the upper echelon of dope boys.

"He's just a hood nigga like all the rest. A fine one, I give you that, but a hood nigga, nonetheless. His aspirations probably started with big rims and ended with useless jewelry," she added, letting her sister know not to get her hopes up too high.

Tangie's track record was spotty at best, and more than likely, they would have to clean up her mess again because the niggas she usually sent their way were certified lames.

"We'll see, Loca, we'll see," Precious said, with a feeling that Tangie might have hit the jackpot with this one.

***

Yero spotted the Latina headed their way before Jah did because he was caught up in watching a snow bunny with an ass any woman would envy. He caught her eye and noticed that she didn't try to look away. He also noticed that she didn't move like a typical employee despite the fact that she was dressed like a stripper. She moved with authority, like she was used to giving orders. Probably a part of the invisible army he knew was floating around the club.

"Gentlemen, my name is Kim, and management would like to see you," she said as she stood there in a red thong with red strawberry-shaped pasties on her nipples, looking seductive and fierce at the same time.

"What the fuck for?" Jah barked before Yero could say anything.

He reached into his pocket and palmed his box cutter, ready for whatever.

"Puto, who the fuck are you talking to?" Kim barked right back.

She was only 5'3", but she didn't back down from anyone, no matter how big they were. The razor she carried around in her mouth was always a great equalizer. Yero grabbed Jah by his arm before he could say anything else and fuck up the play.

"My apologies, Queen. Please forgive us for our lack of manners. Please lead the way."

He was hoping that his conciliating tone smoothed any ruffled feathers from Jah's disrespectful mouth.

Kim wanted to turn up even more, but she calmed down because she didn't know how important they were to the twins. Either way, she wouldn't tolerate any disrespect at all. She tossed one last screw face at his homeboy before turning on her heels and walking off. Jah didn't notice because he was too busy watching her ass bounce as they followed behind her. Yero looked at him in irritation and shook his head. It was very easy to see why he was the head and Jah was just a cog in the machine. They followed her up a set of stairs tucked away in the back of the club. Yero noticed the mirrors as they passed under them and knew that his assumption was correct. They probably concealed the twins' office so they could watch their money without being seen. When they reached the top of the steps, they were met by a massive bodyguard. Kim walked up and spoke to him in Spanish.

"Precious and Tiphany sent for them," she said rapidly.

"They have to be searched," the bodyguard responded seriously.

Jah couldn't understand what was being said, and that had him feeling some type of way.

"The twins sent for them," Kim said, trying to avoid problems.

"They have to be searched," the bodyguard stated again, even more adamantly.

Kim sighed and knew that there was no use in arguing. She walked over to Yero and Jah to tell them they had to be searched.

"Fuck that," Jah exploded.

He wasn't feeling this shit. He was already without his pistol, so he wasn't giving up his box cutter.

"Fuck getting searched," he added, grilling her.

Kim bristled and was about to respond, but Yero stepped in and diffused the situation before it got out of hand.

"Give up the box cutter and chill the fuck out," he told Jah sternly.

Jah wanted to say something, but the look on Yero's face made him change his mind. He took the box cutter out of his pocket and gave it to Yero.

"Come search us," Yero told her in Spanish.

"You speak Spanish?" she asked, surprise etched all over her face.

She looked at him with new interest. Yero remained silent because he didn't answer stupid questions. Kim saw how he was looking at her and realized her question was rhetorical. Embarrassed, she told the bodyguard to conduct the search. After retrieving the box cutter, she knocked on the steel door.

"Come in," a voice from the other side called out.

Kim opened the door and stood to the side to let them enter. Yero walked in and saw two beautiful Latinas sitting on one of the two sofas located in the office. He noticed after a few seconds that they were identical twins. He had heard so much about them, but it was hard to match the reputations to the faces in front of him. He erased that thought from his mind and focused because he knew better than anyone that looks could be deceiving.

"Damn, these bitches bad," Jah shouted excitedly when he spotted the twins.

Before Yero could even blink, the situation spiraled out of control. Kim spit the razor out of her mouth, grabbed Jah, and put it to his neck.

"Give me the word, cousin, and I will open him up," she said seriously in Spanish.

The twins got off the sofas and walked over to Jah. Tiphany pulled out her .357 snub-nosed revolver and put it under his chin.

"Who are you calling a bitch? Me, or my sister?" she asked seriously.

Yero stepped in between Jah and the gun, backing Tiphany up in the process. Regardless of his actions, Jah was family, and he was gonna ride with him, right or wrong.

"Oh, you loyal enough to your homeboy to die for his disrespectful mouth?" Precious asked as she studied him up close. *Damn, this nigga fine*, she thought.

Yero didn't even bother to respond because his actions spoke for themselves.

"I guess you are," she said sardonically. "Cousin, let him go."

Kim was aggravated, but she obeyed. Jah wanted to flash out but knew he didn't have any wins right now. He would fall back for the time being, but he wouldn't forget.

"My man didn't mean anything by what he said. Where we're from, it's used as a term of endearment. Granted, it's disrespectful, but it wasn't intended to be," Yero said seriously.

"Tell ya man to watch his mouth because we are grown ass women, and we don't take kindly to disrespect. This is the only warning you will get. The next time, you both die," Tiphany said, grilling Jah.

"You got that," Yero said. He was angry, but he didn't let it show on his face.

Jah was heated, but he still kept his peace because he was smart enough to realize the severity of the situation, but the shorty who put the razor to his neck would die. He put his word on that.

"Loca, put the pistol up. I'm sure this nigga knows that we have a zero-tolerance policy for that disrespect shit," Precious said as she also grilled Jah.

Jah smirked and grilled her back but remained silent. He wasn't feeling how they were talking about him like he was a puppy or something.

"Since we've come to an understanding, let's sit down and discuss business," Precious said, motioning to the two sofas in the office.

The twins sat on one while Yero and Jah sat down across from them.

"My name is Precious, and this is my sister Loca." She made introductions like the last five minutes didn't happen.

"I'm sure Tangie had given you the rundown on me and mines, but I'm Y.O., and this is Jah."

"I see you have good judgment," Loca said, chuckling at his reference to Tangie and her big mouth. "What is your ethnicity?" she asked bluntly.

She was intrigued by him and didn't bother trying to hide it.

Yero wasn't surprised by the question because his looks always came up with women, but he was surprised that the twins were being women in this moment. He put it in the back of his mind as something that could be exploited later down the line.

"My mother was Dominican and Black. She told me that my father was also Dominican and Black, even though I've never met him."

"Can you speak Spanish?" Precious asked him.

For some reason his face seemed familiar to her, but she was positive she had never seen him before.

"Of course, beautiful," he responded in the language he learned from his mother.

It was one of the positive things she had taught her children.

47

Precious felt herself blushing and was embarrassed because she was feeling like a schoolgirl. She couldn't help it. She was feeling him. Tiphany was feeling him also, but money was first and foremost on her mind.

"How many are you moving a week?" she asked bluntly.

"Five a week," Jah blurted out. He was tired of them talking around him like he wasn't there.

Yero saw the dirty looks the twins shot Jah's way when he opened his mouth and took the conversation back over before they lost ground.

"We are only moving five right now, but we are in the process of expanding our territory, and I predict we'll be able to move over two hundred a month very soon. North Carolina is territorial, but we get money. As long as it makes sense, the big dogs will all play together," he said.

"I know a few guys in Durham, and they go hard. So what makes you think that you and your team are strong enough to even run your own city, let alone the whole state?" Precious asked as she looked into his eyes.

She had a feeling he was capable of more than they knew.

"You must've not heard about us," Jah said, smirking at them. He knew that their team put the fear of God in niggas in the city.

"Honestly, I'm questioning y'all's whole set up because I'm wondering why Y.O. would bring you to a meeting of such importance when it's obvious you're nothing more than a goon trying to act gangsta," Tiphany snapped. She was fed up with his disrespect.

Jah was about to respond when Yero held up his hand, stopping him in his tracks.

"Trust me when I tell you that the city will be mine without any problems. I'm also in the process of aligning my connections in order to ensure longevity for me and mine," Yero said.

He had to lock this deal in before Jah sank the ship with his childish pride and misogynistic attitude towards the twins.

"Connections?" Precious questioned dubiously.

"Yeah, we're not corner hustlers," Jah said seriously.

"Are we talking to you?" Tiphany asked calmly.

Anyone who knew her knew that this was the calm before the storm. She wanted to make Jah beg for his life. Jah just smirked at her. Yero saw what was unfolding and made an executive decision.

"Jah, let me have the room," he said, looking in his eyes.

His voice was calm, but no one in the room misunderstood the situation. This wasn't him asking; this was him flexing muscles he rarely had to use. This was him letting it be known who the Alpha and Omega was.

Jah bristled because he also recognized what it was. He normally wouldn't feel any type of way because you don't bite the hand that fed you, but he was doing it in front of two women who was disregarding him openly like he was a peon, and to him that was unforgivable. He stood up and scowled at Yero and the twins before unceremoniously exiting the room.

"He's very disrespectful," Precious said with disdain.

Yero wouldn't discuss his team with anyone outside of his team because it wasn't anyone's business what the inner workings of his organization were. He would deal with Jah later, but it would be in private and away from prying eyes. His sole focus was securing their future.

"We are beyond corner hustlers, as my associate so eloquently pointed out. We make money, and everyone eats. Greedy people usually get swallowed up by bigger prey. Me and mine are trying to build an empire. We're trying to become sustainable because this field is not built for longevity. We're trying to become a conglomerate," he said seriously.

He knew that they thought he was your average dope boy, but nothing could be further from the truth.

Precious and Tiphany sat there stunned for numerous reasons. One, they respected the way he handled his homeboy with grace despite how volatile of a situation it was turning into, and two, he was smarter than they gave him credit for. He was sitting in front of them talking about drug dealing like a CEO of a Fortune 500 company. They had seriously underestimated him.

"So you think that the great people of Durham will let you into the circle?" Tiphany asked, expressing serious doubt about a street nigga moving in the same circles as the upper echelon of Durham society.

"I have my ways, ladies. Believe me, they won't have a choice but to let me in, us in," Yero said with a smirk ghosting around his lips.

"I'm sure there will be a lot of bloodshed when you take over the city. So tell me how you plan on keeping the alphabet boys off of your ass while you accomplish this coup," Precious said, ready to hear more of his plans because he was exceeding her expectations, and she loved to hear him talk.

Yero could tell they still had a lot of doubts, and he needed this connect if his plans were to succeed. So he decided to put the doubts and worries to rest. He switched to their native tongue.

"Everybody has weaknesses. You just have to find them and exploit them. Humans by nature are greedy for money, sex, or power. Give them what you want, and they will give you the keys to their closets. Life is about balance, fear, and respect. When to forgive and when to forget. Peace and war. Few find that balance. It's not about what you know, but about what you do with what you know."

The twins were both fascinated and turned on by the passion in his voice. He had a look in his eyes that let them know that he would do everything he said he would do and more.

"What are your weaknesses?" Tiphany asked slyly in Spanish as she smiled at him.

"Do you really expect me to hand you the keys to my closet?" he asked, returning her smile.

Precious got up and walked to their desk. She grabbed two sets of keys and walked back over to them.

"These are the keys to a 1969 Ford Mustang Boss 302 and a 1969 Chevrolet Camaro RS 55. They both contain stash spots that have ten bricks apiece inside of them. You can get these keys, and we become your connect under two conditions. One, you have five days to move these twenty bricks. We don't fuck with small numbers, and we need to know you can handle our product. The second is you have to eliminate a nigga named Greg and his team because they have become liabilities. If you accept and complete both tasks within five days, we're locked in," she said seriously.

She knew that five days were harsh, but she wanted to see if he could handle the pressure.

"How much for each brick?" he asked with money on his mind.

"15 bands apiece," Tiphany said, knowing that only ones beating their prices were the cartels.

Yero stared at her as he calculated the numbers in his head. She was forcing him to move his plans up faster than he wanted to, but it wasn't anything he couldn't handle. If push came to shove, he would dig into his stash and pay for the bricks himself; something he was loath to do but would do nonetheless. As far as the liabilities, they wouldn't be a problem either. He admired their boss tactics. If Moses could part the Red Sea, and God could make it rain for forty days and forty nights, then he could make the clouds bleed and the streets flood.

"I accept your terms, and you'll have your money in the allotted time," he said before grabbing the keys from her hand. "Thank you for the opportunity again," he added before leaving the room to get to work.

"Five days, P," Tiphany said incredulously when they were alone. "What are you going to do when he can't meet your terms?" she asked seriously, watching her sister.

She knew Precious was feeling him. Shit, so was she, but money came before anything. Precious looked at her sister and knew what she was thinking.

"If he doesn't come through, then we will wipe him and his team off the map after we handle Greg and his people," she said seriously.

She was feeling his swagger, but she would make him disappear if he fucked up her paper. Tiphany looked at her sister for a few minutes, then broke into a smile.

"We'll see, P. We'll see," she said before sparking up a blunt.

Chapter 5

Skittles was super gay. He was 5'11" with a slim frame, light skin with brown eyes. He was a fly guy, considered a fashion connoisseur by most because he stayed draped in the latest designer, kept the hottest kicks on his feet, and the most expensive jewelry around his neck, wrist, and in his ears. He knew he was a fly mu'fucka and made sure that everybody else knew it too. He kept his hair cut to make sure his waves received maximum exposure. Facials, pedicures, and manicures were a weekly occurrence. Eyebrows stayed arched, and his eyes hypnotized both sexes. When he stepped out of the house, he was put together from head to toe, but he was best known for his most prized possession—his grille. It was rose gold with all types of precious jewels embedded in each tooth.

When he opened his mouth, it looked like a bag of Skittles, hence his name. He had canary yellow diamonds, sapphires, emeralds, onyx, rubies, pink diamonds, and diamonds. He had ten on top and ten on bottom, buss down, and it cost more than most people paid for their homes. He was flamboyantly gay, but he never had a problem attracting either sex. The problem was getting rid of them after the fact. People had a tendency to fall in love with him and wouldn't accept that it was over when it was indeed over. To men, he was the forbidden fruit. It would amaze people how many hustlers tried to holla at him whenever he came through the hood. He was late creep action, but he didn't mind because he got what he wanted and paid for it on top of that. To women, he was the best of both worlds.

He was the shoulder to cry on and ear to vent to when their men were dogging them out. Then he had a big dick to make them forget their problems for a little while. Nine times out of ten, he was fucking *her* and her man, so he was indeed the best of both worlds. Despite being homosexual, he was a natural killer. Niggas assumed that because he was gay they could never be caught slipping by him, but he took his craft seriously. He used that confidence against them though. Anybody with an ear to the street knew that he wasn't one to be slept on. He loved putting in work because it was so easy. Men looked at him and saw a bitch. They played him for pussy and got fucked, literally and figuratively. If you made the mistake of thinking him soft, it usually was the last mistake you ever made.

"Come on, Skittles, I need to see you," Rico begged over the phone.

Skittles smiled and wrapped the phone cord around his finger, loving the attention.

"We just saw each other last weekend, Rico," he said sweetly.

"I know, but my wife took a trip out of town and will be gone all weekend. So I want to see you. I know you are busy, but I promise I'll make it worth your time," Rico said desperately.

Skittles was about to tease him for a few more minutes, then turn him down again, but his phone beeped, letting him know that he had another call coming in.

"Rico, baby, hold on, I have another call." He clicked over. "Hello?" he asked, wondering who was calling him.

"Dead that issue," the voice on the other end said before hanging up.

Skittles started smiling as he clicked back over.

"Rico, baby, there's been a change of plans. I'm on my way over," he purred into the phone.

***

"Oh God fuck me, harder, harder!" Dynasty screamed as Low pounded her pussy from the back.

"Whose pussy is this?" Low growled as he drilled into her tight wet pussy.

"Yours, baby . . . oh, God . . . you . . . are . . . fucking me," Dynasty yelled as she felt another orgasm building. "I'm cumming. I'm cumming," she moaned as her body shook with the force of her climax.

Low felt his orgasm fast approaching, pulled out her pussy, grabbed her by the hair, and slid his dick into her mouth. Dynasty latched onto his dick and swallowed every drop of sperm that hit her tongue.

"Damn, you're a beast," he said, falling onto the bed as he tried to catch his breath.

Dynasty just smirked as she got up and made her way towards the bathroom. In her mind, she was cursing out her brother because he had her fucking with this lame. She was ready to dismiss this clown and make moves, but she had to wait for her brother to give her the word. The only thing making the whole ordeal worth it was the dick. The boy could fuck a pussy. Before entering the bathroom, she grabbed her iPhone and closed the door behind her. She sat down on the toilet to push his cum out of her as she checked messages. She erased all of them except one, the one she had been waiting on. Suddenly re-energized, she wiped herself and flushed the toilet.

"Baby, I want to try some freaky shit," she yelled out as she erased the most important message she had received to date.

'Dead that issue.'

***

Tyga tugged at his restraints again and wondered how in the hell he let himself get into this predicament. Then he looked over into the corner of the room at the woman sitting there smoking a blunt as she stared at him and knew exactly how he ended up tied to a bed in a seedy motel room on the edge of town.

"Bitch, if you let me go now, I promise I'll let you live," he said seriously as he gave her his most menacing stare. "You think that bitch-ass nigga Y.O. gon' do you better than I can?" he asked rhetorically.

His anger grew when the only response he received from her was laughter. He swallowed his anger along with his pride and tried a different tactic.

"Suai, baby, it doesn't have to be like this. We were good together, and we still can be if you let me go. We can turn the tables on Y.O. and put his ass on the midnight train to Georgia. The city will be ours."

He hated to admit it, but he was begging, and honestly, he didn't care because his life was hanging in the balance. He would suck a dog dick if he got to keep his life. He watched her for a few minutes and felt his hopes soar when she got up and walked over to him. The smile on her face let him see a light at the end of his tunnel. He was starting to feel some hope that he would make it out of the situation.

Yeah, this bitch can't outthink me, he thought gleefully as he watched her.

He couldn't help but notice her standing there naked as the day she was born. She had one of the best bodies he had ever seen on a woman. As images of her ass waving at him as he pounded into her from the back flashed through his mind, he felt his dick get hard. His sense of anticipation heightened as he watched her crawl between his legs and grab his dick in her hand. She slowly jacked his dick until the veins were bulging and his precum was oozing. When she slid him into her wet, warm mouth, he closed his eyes and moaned in ecstasy. In no time, she had him on the verge of climax, but suddenly she stopped and stood back up.

"Come on, baby, don't leave me like that. Let daddy come in your mouth," he begged as he tried to catch his breath.

"Ye see de difference between ye and Y.O. is he a boss bwoy, and ye a pussy bwoy," Suai said, smirking at him.

Her words were like a cold glass of water in his face. He glared at her as his dick deflated. He knew in that moment that he was going to die. He closed his eyes and thought back to the day he first met the devil reincarnate . . .

"Damn, look at this bitch riding that bike," Junior said when he spotted her.

Tyga watched the bike as it pulled to a stop in front of them. He couldn't front, the body riding it was one of the most stacked he had ever seen. She had the block on standby as they stared at her. He noticed the red dreads hanging out of her helmet and wondered what her face looked like. *This bitch probably look like Bruce Bruce in the face*, he thought wryly. She took the helmet off and shook her locks out as she smiled at him. Damn, this bitch bad, he thought as he smiled back at her.

"Damn, this bitch raw," Junior exclaimed when he noticed her face and grey eyes.

Tyga saw her shoot Junior a mean look and cringed. He wasn't about to let anyone mess up his chance to get in between her thighs.

"Junior, go count the money up in the dope house," he told his right-hand man.

Junior looked at Tyga and shook his head. He couldn't believe he was being shined on for a bitch. He wanted to say something slick, but he kept silent. he knew an order when he heard one, so he walked off to do as he was told.

"What's up, ma, what you need?" Tyga asked her when they were alone.

He saw her scoping his block out, but he didn't pay attention to that as he imagined himself fucking her brains out.

Suai looked at him as she climbed off of her bike. The jeans she had on looked like a second skin, and she had the attention of the whole block focused on her. Regardless of how good she looked, she was stopping his money flow, and that couldn't happen.

"Yo, mind y'all fuckin' business and get back to work," Tyga yelled at his workers.

He looked back at the woman standing in front of him, hoping she was impressed with his boss tactics, only to find her again scoping out his block, and again he didn't pay any attention to that as he stared at her body. He looked at her bike and thought it looked familiar, but he put that out of his mind.

"What you need, ma?" he asked again, hoping it was a man.

"Mem need some ganga," Suai said with a smirk.

She could tell he was mesmerized by her looks, and it gave her a sense of power over him.

"What kind, because I have all different flavors," Tyga found himself wanting to impress her, and the less she seemed to be impressed, the harder he tried.

"Mem only smoke de best," she said, licking her lips seductively.

"I have Pink Runtz and White Widow," Tyga said as he felt his dick getting hard as he watched her lips. "What's your name, ma?" he asked.

"Mem wan two zones of de Runtz and two of de Widow," Suai said seriously. "And mem name is Suai bwoy," she added seductively.

"Wallace," Tyga yelled to one of his workers. "Go grab me two ounces of Runtz and two ounces of the Widow," he ordered when the young boy was standing in front of him.

"A'ight, Boss," Wallace said before running off to do his bidding.

"My name Tyga, ma," he said when they were alone again.

"Nice to meet ye, Tyga," Suai said with a smirk. "And mem not ye mudda bwoy," she added sarcastically.

"You got a man, Suai?" he asked with an embarrassed smile on his face.

"Mem haven't found de man dat can handle mem," she said with a smirk.

"You been running with the wrong crowds, love," Tyga said, wondering what lames let her get by them.

"And ye de right crowd?" she asked, looking him up and down.

"It's only one way to find out."

Tyga said, knowing she would be impressed with his gear because he knew he was saucy.

"Give mem ye phone," Suai said, wondering if niggas in Bull City were this weak in general.

Tyga handed her his phone, feeling like he just hit the lotto. Wallace ran up and handed him the package he had requested. After realizing he wouldn't be needed again, he ran back to his post.

"This gas usually runs $500 an ounce, but I'ma let you get these on me," Tyga said, handing her the package at the same time she handed him his phone back.

"No mon, mem don't need ye charity. Mem pay mem own way," Suai said as she pulled out a knot of money from the fanny pack she had strapped across her chest and placed the weed inside. "Mem don't need no man ta take care of mem." She peeled off two bands in blue faces and handed it to him.

She hopped back onto her bike and cut on the ignition.

"If ye tink ye de man mem looking for, give mem a ring," she told him before throwing on her helmet, popping the clutch, and disappearing off the block.

Tyga was snapped out of his reverie by the ringing of a phone. He kept his eyes on Suai's face as she talked to whoever was on the other end. He had a horrible feeling that the call was about him.

"Mem pissed at ye . . . Ye left mem wit' no word fa days . . . mem gonna see ye soon, and ye betta not say shit, or mem got something fa ye." Suai was livid, and she let whoever was on her line know it.

"Dead that issue," the voice on the other end told her with a chuckle before hanging up.

Suai tossed her phone back onto the nightstand angrily.

Tyga watched as she walked towards the corner of the room and picked up a gallon milk jug that he never noticed sitting there before. She walked to the foot of the bed and stood there watching him.

"Mem gon' do ye a favor before ye burn," she said as she smirked at him.

He was almost too terrified to ask her what the favor was, but he made himself ask anyway.

"What is it?"

"Mem gon let ye cum one last time, pussy bwoy," she said as she set the milk jug on the floor before crawling onto the bed.

She grabbed his dick and stroked him back to hardness. She teased the head with her tongue until he was moaning for more.

"What's in the jug, Suai?" he asked as he tried to focus, but he was finding it hard to concentrate with her tongue lapping up his dick. His mind wanted to lock onto the word 'burn' she uttered earlier, but despite how detrimental his situation seemed, he couldn't focus.

"Don't ye worry," she said before making his dick disappear into her mouth.

"Oh, shit," Tyga squeaked like a little bitch as she deep-throated him.

Suai put all of her anger at Y.O. into sucking Tyga's dick. She was bobbing up and down like she was trying to catch the fattest apple. In no time, she felt his dick jerking, indicating his oncoming orgasm.

"Oh shit, baby, I'm cumming," he yelled as he erupted.

Suai pulled her mouth off of him in time and let his sperm land on his stomach and chest. Only one man's kids would slide down her throat. She got up and grabbed the milk jug from the foot of the bed.

Tyga was still trying to recover from the best blow job of his life. He had never felt like that in his life. Suai had the best head game in the city. He closed his eyes and tried to catch his breath until he felt something wet splash onto his body a few seconds later and opened them again. Before he could say anything, the pungent smell of gasoline hit his nose. His nostrils flared, and he started bucking against the restraints, trying to get free as the implications of what was about to happen to him hit his brain. Suai just stared at him with dead eyes as she continued to pour until the jug was empty. She knew that he would have to turn into Superman to break free of his restraints.

"Please, Suai, don't do this. Just let me go, and I'll leave town. You don't have to kill me. Please, not like this," Tyga begged as tears rolled down his face.

He would rather be shot in his head than to be burned alive. Suai struck a match and tossed it onto his body. Flames instantly engulfed him. He screamed like a banshee, but that didn't seem to faze her. She watched him until his screams died out. She wasn't worried about being discovered because the run-down, seedy motel was isolated and out of the city limits. If anyone came to investigate, she would add bodies to the funeral pyre. She got dressed and pulled out a freshly rolled blunt. She stuck the tip into the flames to light it. She turned and left the room with the smell of Pink Runtz and the sickly sweet smell of burnt flesh in her wake.

Chapter 6

Captain Henderson arrived on the crime scene in his squad car, trying to control his anger. He had been notified at his home that two bodies had been found in the parking lot of an abandoned warehouse, and one of them was connected to him. He threw his car into park and got out, to all eyes on him. Everyone on the scene knew who he was because his career was legendary in the state of Georgia. His arrest record was impeccable. Bad guys had come to fear his name in the streets. When he was a beat cop, he led the city of Atlanta in arrests his first five years on the streets. When he went after a perp, he got his man nine times out of ten. He was so good his superiors started calling him D.O.C. for all the inmates he put in prison. His career was cemented when he stopped the assassination attempt on the then mayor. Promotions came fast, and it was rumored that he would one day become commissioner. So far, he was satisfied with his career, but the one thing that he felt like would be the ultimate feather in his cap would be the arrest of the most conniving, murdering drug dealers Atlanta had ever seen— the Alvarez twins. Precious and Tiphany Alvarez had the big wigs in Atlanta fooled with their faux charity works, but he saw right through the veneer, the lacquer, the Prada, and the Gucci. He saw them for what they were, monsters, and he wouldn't be content until they were both rotting in a maximum security prison. He studied the people working the crime scene until he spotted who he was looking for. He stomped over, hoping he hadn't been called in for no reason.

"What do you have for me, Douglas?" he asked the forensic scientist working the scene.

"First off, I want you to take a look at these bodies to see if you recognize either one of them," Douglas said, leading him over to the two shrouded bodies. He lifted the sheets back off of their faces and stood back so that he could get a good look at them.

"Son of a bitch," Captain Henderson cursed when he recognized one of his snitches.

Even though there was a hole in the side of his head, he still saw enough to recognize him.

"What happened to this one?" he asked, pointing to his snitch.

He could guess from his wounds, but he wanted to be absolutely sure.

"Without an autopsy, I can't be a hundred percent sure, but the wound to the head seems to be self-inflicted, and the one I'm sure killed him. The other wounds seemed to be done after he was already dead, but we won't know for sure until we get them back to the lab," Douglas said seriously. "Do you recognize one of them?" he asked.

"Yes, he was one of my C.I.'s on the Alvarez case," Captain Henderson said painfully as he fought the bile rising in his throat back down.

"Yeah, I thought so. Follow me," Douglas said, leading him back to the car where the bodies were found. "Listen to this." He pressed play on the car stereo.

". . . who sold you drugs?"

Captain Henderson grimaced when he recognized his voice and felt his stomach clench.

". . . Tiphany and Precious Alvarez and Jeremy Lite. I'm not built for prison. So if it's me or them, I'm picking me. Fuck them."

Captain Henderson had never felt so disrespected in his life. The twins were blatantly showcasing their power and money. Their disdain for authority was evident. They were flipping them off figuratively and literally by leaving the CD of a private interrogation for them to find. He was starting to feel like he would never get them off the street. The pressure was building in him. The fact that there was a mole in his department added to that pressure. He looked around at the people working the crime scene and wondered who was dirty. He knew that it could be any one of them.

"Are you all right, Captain?" Douglas asked with concern.

Captain Henderson looked at him and felt his nostrils flare in anger like a bull seeing red. His eyes narrowed because now everybody was a suspect. Douglas almost shrank back at that look because it had so much disgust in it. Captain Henderson let out a primal scream that held so much anger it captured the attention of everyone working the crime scene. Everyone knew about his personal vendetta against the Alvarez twins, and they knew that the pressure was becoming immense. They watched him stalk off, mumbling to himself, wondering if the pressure had finally become too much.

***

"Where the fuck this bitch nigga at?" Jah whispered to no one in particular.

Yero didn't answer because he knew that Jah was just anxious to release some of the anger he was feeling for the situation at the club. He was still angry with Jah because he didn't know how to control his mouth, but he would deal with that later because now he had to be focused on the task at hand. They were sitting in the dark inside of Grey's house, waiting on him to come home. When they left the club, the cars were sitting in the parking lot like the twins said they would be. Inside each glove compartment, they found instructions for the stash spots and the information on Grey and his team, and the instructions to open the stash spots.

After making sure that the instructions for the stash spots worked and indeed held the bricks, he sent Towny and Hollywood back to North Carolina in the cars because they were his best drivers. He needed the bricks broken down and in the streets as soon as possible because he needed to make this money. When they studied the information on Grey and his team, he was impressed with the thoroughness and depth of the information gathered. They had addresses and security codes for everyone involved. He knew that the twins were powerful, and he would do well not to underestimate them just because they were women. He sent Jay-O, P.R., and Casper to handle the body of the team while him and Jah decided to cut the head off the snake. Now they were sitting in the dark waiting on the reptile to slither his way through his front door.

"Where the fuck these niggas at?" Grey mumbled to himself after getting the voicemail of one of his team members for the fifth time.

He had been trying to reach his people for a few hours, but they were incognito. He was driving through Atlanta on his way home with a lot on his mind. The last six hours had been bad. He and his team were the talk of the town until it started going downhill. They had the connect, and money was coming in faster than pussy to a pimp. They had Kimberly Court, Bankhead Projects, Kirkwood, Hollywood Court, and Herndon Homes on smash. If you were buying work, you were buying it from them. They were doing numbers like H&R Block during tax time, but then he received that fated phone call from the twins.

". . . Grey, you are drawing too much attention with all that flashy shit you and your boys doing. You are spending too much money with no proof of income," he remembered Precious calmly telling him.

". . . Precious, we good, baby, we got this. We are making you a lot of money, right?" he bragged to her.

". . . Grey, fall back, or we're gonna cut you off," Precious threatened before hanging up.

He didn't take heed to her warning, and she kept her word. She cut the water off for him and his team. He tried calling Tiphany, but she wasn't trying to hear him. For all intents and purposes, they distanced themselves and left them high and dry. In a forty-eight-hour span, they went from making money hand over fist to scrambling just to keep up pretenses. They went from moving fifty bricks a week to robbing people for their work to supply their customers. That worked for a while, but then they got indicted. In order to save his people, he agreed with the Feds to testify for a grand jury, but now he was regretting his decision. He was trying to get in contact with his team to let them know that he was leaving town, and that they needed to do the same. He still couldn't believe the way things had turned out. If only he had listened to the twins when they warned him about being flashy, but hindsight was twenty-twenty. He remembered the day he met Tiphany. He remembered the day she told him she could put him on his feet. He remembered setting the city on fire with the best dope on the East Coast. He remembered buying his cocaine-white Audi R8, and he remembered fucking Tiphany on top of the hood in the rain, but those memories were all he had left because his run was over. He had decided to run. All he had left to his name was his car, his house, and a couple hundred stacks. He would choose a town where he could lay back and make money; maybe find a wifey or two. He pulled up into his driveway and parked his car. He sat there for a few minutes and stared at his house. His home was a testament to his hustle. The day he bought it was the day he knew he made it. He hated the fact that he would have to leave it, but there really was no option for him. He wasn't going to nobody's jail, and he wasn't nobody's snitch, so he was leaving town. He had already called his realtor and put the house on the market. He got out of the car and hit the button on his keychain to make sure his doors were locked. He pulled his gun out of his waist and walked up the pathway to his front door. When he had his door unlocked and opened, he tucked his pistol. He pushed open the door and was instantly confronted by the familiar smells of his house. After closing the door, he walked over to the alarm panel to deactivate it before he had to explain to the police that he was indeed the owner of the house. Before he punched the code in, he saw that the alarm was already deactivated. Puzzled, he tried to remember if he had set the alarm that morning before he left, but he knew he had set it because it made him feel rich. In the projects, he never had an alarm to set, so he made sure to set it whenever he left the house. So if he had set it that morning, then who deactivated it, but before he could put it together, he felt a gun pressed into the back of his neck, bringing his worst nightmare to life.

"Damn, bitch-ass nigga, I been waiting on you," Jah said as he reached around and grabbed the pistol out of his waist.

He drew back and hit him with the butt of his gun, knocking him to the floor.

"What . . . what's going on?" Grey questioned as he grabbed his bleeding head.

"You already know what it is, playboy," Yero said as he stepped out of the shadows.

The first thing that came to Grey's mind was that the twins had found out about him agreeing to testify in front of a grand jury and sent some killers to take him out.

"Wait, wait, don't kill me. I got some money upstairs. Y'all can take that and let me leave town," he said, talking fast as he came up with ways to live.

The mention of money caught Yero's attention.

"How much money you holding?" he asked seriously.

"Six hundred bands," Grey said quickly.

He knew niggas weren't used to that type of money, so he hoped it was enough to buy his life or at least enough to make a move.

"A'ight, get up and lead the way," Yero ordered, already knowing what he was going to do with the money.

Sometimes the pieces just fell into place. Grey got up and led them upstairs. He took a painting of Malcolm X off of his wall to reveal a steel safe. It could only be opened by scanning the thumb print of the owner. He stood there looking at the safe, thinking about his life, and how he ended up where he was. Yero saw the hesitation and knew what it was about.

"Let me guess. You have a pistol lying in there, and you're wondering if you open that safe, will you have enough time to grab it and shoot us before we light your ass up. Life is about decisions, and you're facing one now."

He knew warfare was more mental than physical, and you could beat a man without laying one finger on him. He watched Grey turn over in his mind what he had just said and knew what his decision would be.

Grey thought about his options and knew that he would never be able to get to his pistol before he died. So he decided to take a chance and hoped they let him live once they got his money. He took a deep breath and opened the safe. After it was opened, he stared at the nickel-plated .9mm Beretta for a few seconds before deciding to take his chances. He stood to the side and looked at his captors.

Yero smirked at him. He knew that nigga didn't have what it took to be a lion in the concrete jungle.

"You should've went with your first instinct, Grey, because now you're gonna die a bitch nigga."

Grey tried to lunge at him, but the angels of death Jah pumped into his body stopped him midair. Yero looked down at his body and smirked.

Bitch-ass niggas were predictable and easy to manipulate. Niggas wanted all of these muscles to flex with, but most forgot about the most important muscle of all, the mind. If you can outthink a man, you could beat a man every time. They bagged up all of the money and wiped down any surface they might've touched while in the house. Before they left, a message was sent to all rats, and to make sure the message was received, they placed an anonymous call to the authorities and reported a murder.

***

"Loca, that nigga Y.O. is fine as fuck," Precious said, getting wet just remembering him talking to them in Spanish.

"Yeah, he can get this pussy whenever he wants it. I was so turned on when he was talking, I thought I would have to change my panties," Tiphany said, fanning herself. "His man Jah can get it too with his disrespectful ass," she added.

"Bitch, stop fronting like you don't like that shit. You love a thug," Precious said, laughing as they walked to their parked cars.

"He did turn me on too," Tiphany said, laughing along with her.

She couldn't stand a pussy-ass nigga, and Jah definitely had heart.

"What the fuck is this?" Precious shouted when she spotted two duffle bags sitting on the trunks of their cars.

Tiphany noticed the two bags and pulled out her pistol. She started looking around, wondering who put the bags there.

Precious cautiously walked over to the bags because she didn't know if they were booby-trapped. When she didn't hear anything ticking or any other odd noises, she opened the bags and saw that both of them were full of money. She saw a note sitting on top of the money in one of the bags and pulled it out. When she read it, she had to reread it to make sure she wasn't tripping.

"Loca, come listen to this," she called out to her twin.

She knew they had seriously underestimated Yero. Tiphany walked over and snatched the note out of her hand.

"Loyalty can never be bought, only given, and I give you mine for giving me a chance to better the circumstances for me and mine. I'm with you. Here's your money for the work. Never underestimate a man you don't know. You both are Queens, but I'm a King, and we control the board. I'll be seeing you soon, so be easy. Oh, and make sure to grab the Atlanta Journal-Constitution in the morning," she read aloud.

She walked over to the bags and looked inside.

"This is more than three hundred bands," she said, eyeballing the money.

They were full of blue faces, so it wasn't hard to guess.

"That nigga got me so turned on, I need to go get some dick," Precious said as she grabbed one of the bags before getting into her car.

"You better fall back because once I give him this pussy, it's over for you," Tiphany said, laughing as she gathered the other bag and hopped into her own ride.

Neither of them noticed the car that pulled off before they got into their cars. They were too focused on irrelevant things.

Chapter 7

Shapphire Stone was living on cloud nine these days. She was making money at an astonishing rate, and she was getting fucked better than she ever had in her life. She started sexing Rosario and getting all of her erotic fantasies fulfilled. She was a freak and a nymph, but Rosario surpassed her in both of those areas. He woke her up with the dick and fucked her back to sleep. The best part was that she didn't have to deal with any parents. Rosario had one aunt who was a drug addict and only took him in to get his checks. So as long as she had money, she didn't give a damn if he came home or not, and Shapphire made sure she had more than enough money for her habits. To her, Rosario was worth whatever she spent on him as long as he kept her satisfied sexually. He was becoming a huge part of her everyday life. He was with her at the church every day and was her de facto assistant. She was even contemplating adopting him. There wasn't any doubt she could get his aunt to sign the paperwork, and with her connections, they would get processed expeditiously. She was coming to trust him explicitly, so it was a strong consideration for her. Her next appointment was because of him. She remembered when he asked her to meet someone very dear to him. It was one of her fondest memories.

"Oh my God Rosé you are hitting my spot," she screamed as he plunged into her soaking wet pussy from the back as they floated in her indoor swimming pool.

"Will you do anything for me?" he asked as he concentrated on her spot.

"You know I will Rosé . . . oh my God, right there," she moaned as her orgasm built.

"I want you to meet someone who has been instrumental in my life." He moaned.

He loved fucking her because she knew how to fuck back, and her pussy was good.

"Set it up, Rosé . . . I'm cumming baby." She screamed as her climax took her to another atmosphere.

She was snatched out of her memories by the sound of her office door being opened. She looked up just as Rosario was leading a man into her office. She studied the man and had to admit that he was good-looking—a little out of her age range, but good-looking, nonetheless. She also noticed that he was expensively dressed in a dark blue Brioni suit, a handmade Ascot Chang dress shirt with a blue silk Hermès tie, and a pair of black Salvatore Ferragamo adorning his feet. She was impressed, to say the least. In her world, you had to look like money to make money, and he was certainly dressed the part. She stood up and extended her hand.

"Pastor Shapphire Stone, and you are?"

Yero shook her hand and saw the curiosity in her eyes.

"My name is Yero Owens. It's nice to meet you, Pastor Stone," he said sincerely.

He had heard about her through the grapevine, but he had never met her before. He respected her hustle, though, that's why he was there.

"Any friend of Rosé's is a friend of mine. Now, what can I help with?" She looked at him expectantly, wondering what he wanted. "Rosé, you can wait outside for us to finish," she added with a look.

"Nah, he good. He is a part of what is about to happen. He played a pivotal part in actually getting us to this point," Yero said as he watched the various emotions—anger, surprise, curiosity—flash across her face. She would make a poor poker player.

Shapphire continued to look at Rosario for some sign of what's going on, but he returned her look with an expressionless face. She decided to get this meeting over with quickly, then deal with Rosario. She turned back to the man sitting across from her with a smug look on his face.

"What is exactly about to happen?" she asked as she narrowed her eyes.

"We're about to become business partners," Yero said seriously.

"Business partners?" she asked with a look of pure disdain on her face.

He was so serious, it was almost laughable to her, but she let the drama unfold.

"Yes, business partners," he said as he tossed a thick manila envelope onto her desk.

Shapphire stared at the envelope with a look of trepidation. She was feeling sick in the pit of her stomach as she picked up the envelope and opened it. When her eyes landed on the pictures inside, that sick feeling turned into despair. She didn't even bother to look at Rosario as she flipped through the pictures of their sexcapade on the pulpit in her church. When she saw the picture of Rosario cumming on her face and her licking it up like a puppy, she put the pictures back into the envelope, closed her eyes, and took a deep breath. When she opened them again, she was calm and ready to deal with the situation.

"What exactly do you want?" she asked as her eyes found his.

Yero didn't gloat at his victory because he knew what the outcome would be before he even set the meeting up. A wise man told him to always stay ten steps ahead of the competition.

"I want us to become business partners. I know that you love money. All of the ventures you are currently running under dummy corporations are currently bringing in millions for you, and we all know how much bread you are making off of this church. I could get you to do what I want for absolutely nothing in return, but you would hate my control and scheme to take me down, but I'm offering you a partnership that will be mutually beneficial for us both."

Shapphire was stunned at his knowledge of her business. That was something she had kept from Rosé, so he was getting his information from another source, a source with some type of power and access. She filed that away in her mind to check on. She was also surprised at how articulate he was. He sounded educated, and that she didn't expect.

"What business are you in?" she asked, already having an idea.

"I'm into import, export, amongst other things," Yero said, smirking at her.

Just as I thought, she thought smugly.

She wasn't disgusted or turned off by what he was saying. In fact, she was very intrigued.

"What exactly do you want from me?" she asked, warming up to the idea of a 'partnership'.

"You are the most influential, well-connected woman in this city, and your reach extends all over this country, but I'm only concerned with this city and state for the time being. I want you to work your magic. You have a knack for getting affluent and powerful people to do what you want. We all know it rarely is easy to separate people from their money, but you are very successful at doing just that. Your little black book is what I want access to. I know that you own keys to plenty of closets. The threat of exposure has a way of keeping people in line and doing what you want," Yero said seriously.

Shapphire caught the subliminal shot at her, but she respected his meticulous ruthlessness.

"So you want me to pave the way for you to move your product?" she asked, already plotting on which strings she could pull.

Yero nodded in agreement before she even finished her question.

"I basically want diplomatic immunity for me and mine in North Carolina. I want the powers that be to turn a blind eye to my activities."

"What if the people I approach don't want to play ball with us?" she asked seriously.

She didn't realize she said 'us'.

"Everyone has a closet of skeletons, Pastor Stone. All we have to do is acquire the keys, and we control the bodies," he said with a smirk. "I'm not leaving anything to chance; either they get down on their own free will, or they will get down because of my will. One way or the other, they will get with the program. If you have any problems, we'll handle it. Trust me, I will rarely have to show my face because I don't need the attention. A little mystique will go a long way. Our relationship will work perfectly because I'm the owner of the franchise, and you're my star player. It's your job to recruit the rest of the team. You're the face of the franchise, Pastor Stone. My Luca, so to speak," he said seriously.

"So if I agree to do this, what will happen with these?" she asked, indicating the pictures.

"The agreement is already made because it was never a choice for you but to answer; once we establish a level of trust I feel comfortable with, I will give you the negatives," Yero said seriously.

Shapphire doubted that he would give her all of the negatives, but she really didn't mind because she understood the method to his madness. She reached across her desk to shake his hand.

"Well, I guess we have a deal . . ." she said, smirking at him . . . "Partner."

***

"Where the fuck this nigga at?" Junior mumbled to himself as he supervised the block.

For the past three days, Tyga had been missing in action, and he had a sneaky suspicion that he was laid up with that red dread bitch that popped up on the block over a week ago. To him, she was suspect, but he wasn't really worried because he knew that Tyga could take care of himself, and he didn't mind playing big dog on the block for a few days. He was starting to see that he had a knack for it. He was about to call out to one of the workers when he heard a sound that confused him at first. It sounded like a million bees buzzing, but he soon realized it was motorcycle engines. Perplexed, he looked up the block just as what seemed like a thousand bikes and Spyders turned onto the strip. At first, he thought it was a parade or something, but then he noticed the passengers riding on the motorcycles were facing the rear tire and dressed in all black. What was about to happen clicked in his mind, but before he could sound the alarm, it was too late. The guns were drawn.

"Drive-by!" he yelled as he dived behind a parked car.

His words were lost as gunshots erupted like the heavens had opened up and Zeus was aiming thunderbolts at the block. The sound was deafening. He cringed every time he heard one of his people scream in agony. He was so shook up it took him a few minutes to remember that he had a gun on his waist. He pulled it out and gripped it tightly, but the gunfire was so rapid that he was scared to stand up and let off a couple of shots on his own. He cowered behind the car hoping he didn't get hit and killed. His ears were ringing so loudly that it was a few minutes before he realized that the gunfire had stopped. He stood up and had to fight the contents of his stomach back down when his eyes took in the carnage around him, but he felt his eyes well up with tears when he looked and saw Wallace lying face down in a pool of blood. He turned away and wiped his eyes. He knew in his heart that Tyga was dead somewhere because he knew that no one would have tried like they did today if he was still breathing. He was about to disappear because he heard the police sirens in the distance, but a voice belonging to someone he thought was dead stopped him in his tracks.

"Drop the gun, Junior."

He spun around slowly and saw Wallace standing there, healthy as he was before the shooting started, with a gun pointed at his chest. He dropped the gun he was holding and started copping pleas.

"Damn, lil' bro, I thought you were dead. I seen all that blood around your body and thought you were gone," Junior said, studying the blood stains on Wallace's shirt. "Where the fuck you get some fake blood? Whatever, we need to get going before the jakes get here," he added, hoping he could get out of the situation with his life.

It was obvious that Wallace was a part of what went down today, so if he could talk his way out of his current predicament, then the lil nigga would die, but he had to get out with his life first.

"Yero sends his regards," Wallace said with a smirk before lighting his ass up with hollow points.

Wallace looked up when the sound of a motorcycle reached his ears.

"Come now, bwoy, before de pigs get here and mem have to hold court in de streets. Mem not doing any time in de white man's jail," Aza said seriously.

Wallace jumped onto the back and held on for dear life as they burned rubber, getting away from the scene. They disappeared in the opposite direction just as the police turned onto the block.

Chapter 8

Eileen Jackson was the youngest district attorney in the history of Durham County. She came out of nowhere to win the election after her opponents started dealing with scandals they couldn't recover from. She had her supporters and detractors, but her pros greatly outweighed the cons. She was a beautiful woman, and her opponents used that against her. They tried to paint her as an airhead blonde who only shopped and gossiped, but she battled the old guard who perpetuated those stereotypes. The older men who didn't think that women belonged in the political arena were hypocrites. They tried to use her looks against her, but every time they were alone with her, they tried to get her into bed. Also, the fact that she was a Democrat pissed people off more than it should, but she just laughed at their childishness and kept beating them at their own game. Her supporters, which were mostly women, loved her because she gave them hope. She was an advocate for the stay-at-home moms, the professional women, and for all the women who battled machismo of the world every day of their lives as they tried to better themselves. She was charming. She was blunt and direct. She made people want to vote for her. They wanted her to win. She loved her underdog status and played it up every chance she got. She was a winner, and the cameras loved her. She was destined for great things. It was written in the stars.

"Ms. Jackson, your four o'clock is here, a Ms. Stone," her secretary said over the intercom on her desk.

"Send her on in, Janny," Eileen said with a smile on her face.

She stood up and walked around her desk. Shapphire was one of her best friends and had played a pivotal role in her becoming the youngest district attorney in Durham County history. Some of the scandals her opponents were dealing with at the time were a little suspect to her, but she didn't question her good fortune because their scandals were the reason she won. She cleared her mind as her office door opened and in walked Pastor Shapphire Stone. *Looks can truly be deceiving*, she thought as she opened her arms to embrace her friend.

"Shapphire, so nice of you to drop by," she said as she stepped back to look at her. "You're looking good," she added with a twinkle in her eye.

Just like everybody else, she had heard about Shapphire's shady dealings, but nothing could be proven, and she was known to be ruthless to her enemies, so people tended to leave well enough alone. Eileen walked back around her desk and sat down.

"You're looking fabulous yourself, Eileen," Shapphire said with a smile as she took a seat in front of her desk. "It seems as if power and success agree with you," she added slyly.

"Yes, it does," Eileen said with a smirk. "What brings you down to the slums, pastor?" she asked intently.

She knew that Shapphire rarely did anything without reason.

"I've come to see if you're content with just being a district attorney or do you feel as if your talents are being wasted putting criminals in prison?" Shapphire said seriously.

She had plans to carry out, and Eileen was an important cog in the machine.

"What do you mean?" Eileen asked seriously.

She sat up a little straighter in her chair with an interested look on her face. She had a feeling she knew what Shapphire meant, but she didn't want to assume anything.

"Do you want to spend the rest of your life as a district attorney, or are your aspirations higher?" Shapphire asked, looking around her office and rolling her eyes.

Her message was clear: *you can do so much better*.

"You're only thirty-four, Eileen," she added slyly.

"Of course, I aspire for a much higher office, but I also know that I will have to put in the work to make it," Eileen said, giving the most diplomatic answer she could.

She refused to feed into what Shapphire was saying until she had more to go off of.

Shapphire listened to her answer and decided to cut the chase.

"Being the youngest District Attorney in the history of Durham County sounds great, but . . ." she said, leaning forward in her seat. "Being the youngest governor in the history of North Carolina sounds so much better," she finished with a flourish.

"Governor!" Eileen shouted, shocked at what she was hearing.

She realized how loud she was and calmed down.

"You can't be serious," she said in a stage whisper, not ready to believe.

"I couldn't be more serious, Eileen," Shapphire said with an intent look on her face. "You know I don't play with stuff like this," she added seriously.

"What about Micheals and Beaufort?" Eileen asked, referring to the two front-runners in the race.

She had a sneaky suspicion of what Shapphire would say, but she wanted to hear her say it.

"Eileen, if you agree to run, you will win. No questions asked," Shapphire said seriously.

She refused to say more until she committed.

"How will I win is the question?" Eileen asked as she looked into Shapphire's eyes.

"The same way you won your current position," Shapphire said as she returned her stare.

Eileen was quiet for a few minutes, thinking about her life. The question she kept coming back to was, did she want to be governor of North Carolina? The answer was a resounding yes, but did she want it this way? Her answer surprised her—she wanted it anyway she could get it.

"Will any of this fall back on me in the future?" she asked quietly.

Her reputation must remain pristine.

"Has it so far?" Shapphire asked, subtlety letting her know that it could, but it won't as long as she cooperated.

Eileen was quiet for a few more minutes before she came to a decision. Shapphire saw the answer in her eyes before she even opened her mouth.

"You know we only have eight months until the election, right?" Eileen asked, wondering if they could hand her the victory in such short time.

"Well, I guess we have a lot of work to do . . ." Shapphire said with a smile . . . "Governor."

***

Yero had North Carolina on fire. Durham was his homebase, but he was letting it be known that the Tar Heel State was his to do with as he pleased. The triangle— Durham, Raleigh, and Chapel Hill—were first to fall to his expansion. Niggas had two options: cop from him and eat like a fat cat, or get replaced with your homeboy who was about his money and hoped the authorities found your body before it decomposed. Some cities were about their money, and at his prices, who wouldn't be? But some bucked on some pride shit and had to be taught a lesson. His team was ruthless when it came to putting down demonstrations.

Niggas were really bitch-made when it came to it. Real violence to them was shooting into a crowd during a drive-by, but they folded up like lawn chairs when kick doors started popping off and whole families disappeared. His rule was: *if you could read and write, you could snitch to the police*, so family trees were disappearing like they never existed. God said ashes to ashes and dust to dust. One way or the other, you would turn into it if you bucked against Yero. He slowly took control of the major cities—Greensboro, Winston-Salem, Fayetteville, Wilmington, Greenville, and Charlotte—then sent teams into the smaller towns to consolidate his money-making capabilities. He networked with real hittas in these cities because his plans wouldn't work without them. No one was taking over a city without help from the locals, so he made sure to incorporate who he needed to in order to make it work. He ran shit like a CEO of a major corporation. He delegated to his team and stayed behind the scenes. Niggas knew his name, but only a few knew his face, and that's how he liked it. He had P.R. and Casper in control of the 919, Jah in charge of the 336. Jay-O in charge of the 252. Hollywood in charge of the 910, and Towny held down the 704. They all had lieutenants who reported to them and made sure that all the money was correct. The niggas on his team were gorillas, but the women on the squad brought it all together. Suai, Aza, and Light were cunning and deadly, but add his sister Dynasty to the mix, and they became cyanide to the dumb-ass niggas who were weak enough to trust a big booty and a smile. His pressure was being felt in high and low places.

***

Fat Mack looked out over the crowd of his team and wondered if they were feeling him. That nigga Yero was moving weight in Charlotte, and he wasn't from the city. Niggas didn't even know what this nigga looked like, but niggas from the boulevard to Hidden Valley were moving his product. Fat Mack was tired of it, especially when his product was collecting dust due to the prices Yero was giving the hood, so he called the meeting to put an end to his reign.

"We can't continue to let this outta town nigga disrespect our city like this. He a bullshitting nigga fa real. We the Queen City, dog, and we got our own shit. This the QC, and you betta know it," he ranted as he walked back and forth in front of them.

"He got the best prices around, though," a voice shouted from the crowd.

Fat Mack whipped around, trying to locate the source of that voice, because that wasn't the message he was trying to get across.

"It's not about that. It's about repping our city and supporting our city. Fuck that nigga fa real!" he yelled.

"So you want niggas to stop fucking with this nigga, right?" Rock Steady asked as he stood up.

Fat Mack looked at his second-in-command and wondered what he was doing. They had discussed the meeting beforehand, and Rock Steady knew what he was trying to do.

"Yeah," he answered reluctantly.

"And who do you want niggas to cop dope from?" Rock Steady asked as he made his way up front.

Fat Mack couldn't believe this nigga was questioning him, but he forced himself to calm down and answer him.

"Cop dope from you, right?" Rock Steady asked before Fat Mack could open his mouth. "If you want that to happen, you gonna have to lower your prices and get better dope, but niggas know you're not gonna do it, 'cause you would've smartened up and tried to compete with Yero, but you haven't," he added seriously.

He had a look of disgust on his face that anyone in the crowd could read.

Fat Mack was fuming. He couldn't believe how Rock Steady was trying him, and in front of the crew.

"So what is you saying?" he asked quietly, with murder in his eyes.

He was letting him know it was gonna be problems after the meeting was over.

"I'm letting you know that it's over for you, Fat Boy," Rock Steady said, pulling a pistol out of his waist and putting holes in his face.

He turned to address the rest of the crew with a stern look on his face.

"Who else don't want to fuck with Yero and his team?" he asked seriously.

No one said a word. It was so quiet you could hear a mouse piss on cotton.

"Well, clean this shit up, then," he said before stepping outside.

He pulled his cellphone out of his pocket and dialed a number.

"Tell Y.O. that shit in Charlotte has been handled," he told whoever was on the other end before hanging up.

***

"What the fuck is happening in my city?" Police Chief Dayton screamed at the group of officers gathered in front of him. "Last time I checked, the war was over in Iraq. So why is it a warzone in my fucking streets?" He stopped pacing and glared at his officers.

Every department was present—robbery, homicide, narcotic division, and vice squad. The city of Durham was going through an unprecedented wave of violence, and it was all because of one man.

"Who the fuck is this bastard Y.O.?" he asked rhetorically because no one knew who he was. "Detectives, you are in the streets every day and are supposed to have this shit under control. Somebody needs to tell me something, and tell me something now!" he yelled at his detectives.

The vein in the middle of his forehead looked like it was about to burst, so they knew he was ready to explode. The mayor was putting pressure on him to get results, so he was breathing fire on his people. Every detective in the squad room was silent with their heads down, avoiding the chief's gaze.

"Since y'all think we're in church with all this quiet shit; we're going to do it like this. Detective Davis, tell me, who the fuck Y.O. is?" he asked with feigned calmness.

Detective Jerome Davis shrugged and smirked at the chief.

"They say he is the cause of all this drama in the streets, but he is smarter than most of his ilk, and he seems to be careful. Never arrested or in trouble at all. No one seems to know what he looks like or if he's even the one in charge. Y.O. seems to be an enigma. He's a ghost. No record. No traffic tickets, citations, nothing. Like I said, this guy, whoever he is, is smarter than most and very, very careful. More than likely he's going to have to slip up for us to catch him, or someone close to him will have to snitch on him, and so far neither of the two has happened as of yet," he reported nonchalantly. He knew for a fact that Yero was smarter than the average hustler. It wasn't even close.

"You should work on your tone, detective, because you sound as if you admire this clown," Police Chief Dayton sneered amid the chuckles from the other detectives in the room.

Detective Davis smirked and shrugged again.

Police Chief Dayton was incensed, and he let it be known.

"This shit stops today, now . . ." he screamed as he smacked the table with the palm of his hand, making some detectives jump a little in their seats. "Get subpoenas and search warrants. Do whatever you need to do to stop this violence, or heads will roll. I want to know who this Y.O. is

A.S.A.P., like yesterday. This meeting is over. Detective Davis, get your ass in my office now!" he ordered before he stomped into his office and sat down behind his desk.

He was a big man, 6'3" and 260 lbs. So he made the desk in front of him seem small. His white skin was flushed and blotchy because of his anger. He tried to take deep, calming breaths like his doctor instructed him to do when he was angry, but when Detective Davis walked into his office and closed the door behind him, he let loose.

"What the fuck is your problem?" he screamed at the man with the perpetual smirk on his face.

"Before you continue with your reprimand, I have a message and a gift for you," Detective Davis said with a full smile on his face as he pulled a manila envelope from inside his suit jacket and tossed it onto the desk.

Police Chief Dayton continued to glare at the detective, but it was obvious that the look wasn't having the usual effect, so he redirected his gaze to the manila envelope lying in front of him. Even though his stomach was in knots, he picked it up and flipped it around in his hands as he looked for clues as to what it could contain. When he looked back up at Detective Davis, he found him glaring at him with a scowl on his face. Nervously, he tore open the envelope and shook the contents onto his desk. He picked up what looked like pictures and flipped them over. When his eyes landed on the images, he cried out a little. He was vividly captured sucking a man off as the man stood there with a whip in his hand and a black leather mask on his face. He had on a diaper and a bonnet on his head. He flipped through the stack of pictures and cringed as he witnessed his most degrading acts caught on camera. It was humiliating. There were shots of him getting penetrated by different men, of him getting pissed on, and getting humiliated in the most disgusting way possible. To a career lawman like himself, the pictures were TNT. He looked up at Detective Davis with a defeated look on his face.

"What does he want?" he asked quietly.

Detective Davis shook his head at the pitiful sight before him. His respect for Yero rose another notch as he witnessed him defeat another powerful foe without laying a single finger on him. He was building an impenetrable fortress around himself by controlling the secrets of the city's elite. His power to break the will of a person who stood in his way was unsurpassed by any other. You had to respect his military.

"Yero Owens told me to tell you that if he knew you were a female, he would've made you his bitch a long time ago. You are no longer your own man. You will remain as Police Chief, but as of today, you are effectively working for the new mayor of Durham. You will protect his interests at all costs. You are basically a puppet. If we get so much as a whisper of insubordination, we will destroy you. If you try to pull a bitch move and eat your gun, we will make sure you're remembered for being the biggest closeted homosexual in uniform. Have a nice day, you faggot-ass mu'fucka," he spat before walking out, slamming the door behind him.

Police Chief Dayton looked at the pictures in his hands, thinking about his life, his career, his family. It seemed as if the only two options left for him were to eat his gun or become a slave to a drug lord. He was already warned that his reputation will be destroyed if he took option one. He didn't want his children to deal with that fallout, so that left him no choice. He got up, locked his door, and closed his blinds. He then walked over to his wall safe, opened it, and pulled out one of his precious toys. Back at his desk, he picked the pictures back up and felt himself start to harden. He was too much of a coward to kill himself, and he loved the idea of being under someone's control.

I'm somebody's bitch, he thought giddily as he popped his pacifier into his mouth and massaged himself.

Chapter 9

"This Y.O. is doing numbers and making his presence felt up in North Carolina," Precious said admirably as she fed another stack of bills to the money counter. "Tangie really came through this time. Papi is ecstatic with our progress in the Tar Heel State. The way Y.O. and his team dirt napping niggas, we shouldn't have any problems moving into Virginia," she added as she rubber-banded another stack of bills before tossing it into the duffel bag lying at her feet.

"That nigga got me fantasizing about his fine ass, and I've never sweated a man before, but his gangsta gets me wet every time I think about it," Tiphany said, fanning herself with a stack of money as she looked at the newspaper article she had gotten framed hanging on their wall.

Precious followed her gaze and smirked when she saw what she was looking at.

"I can't believe you had that blown up and framed," she chuckled and shook her head at her sister's craziness.

"The shit he did to Grey was on some Godfather shit, legendary. He burned **La Muerte Antes La Deshonra** (*Death before Dishonor*) into his chest, P. Then he strung that bitch nigga up like a scarecrow. That shit fucked the pigs up when they hit the scene," Tiphany said, feeling her panties get moist.

Gangstas turned her on like nothing else in the world.

"That bitch Henderson had to throw our names in that shit, like he always does when it's a murder in this city," Precious said with disgust.

"I don't know why you just don't let me bury his ass in the country somewhere," Tiphany said seriously.

Precious was shaking her head *no* before Tiphany even finished talking.

"Too much risk for us. Everyone knows he's far from objective when it comes to his accusations. The more he rants and raves in front of the media, the more unstable he appears. People in high places know how he feels about us. Every time he steps out of pocket, our lawyers are filing complaints with the Atlanta Police Department. He'll kill himself, Loca, trust me. It's Chess, baby girl, not Checkers," she said, dropping knowledge.

"Hmph, mark my words, P, we are going to have to bag that nigga before it's all said and done," Tiphany said seriously as she rolled up a blunt of za.

She wanted to say more, but she let it go because she trusted her sister like no other. They sat quietly and smoked as they continued to count up their money.

***

Butta was sitting in his 2024 Chevy Tahoe smoking a blunt and talking to one of his jump-offs on the phone when he saw a lot of police cars pull into the parking lot of the luxury condos he was at. He was sitting in the alley up under Loca's condo waiting on her to drop the bags of money down to him, so he wasn't seen by the pigs as they got out of their cars, but he didn't want to bet on that luck lasting long. He slid down in his seat until only his eyes were visible above the dashboard. He kept his eyes on the police as he dialed up the twins because when he saw Captain Henderson, he knew without a doubt who he was there for.

***

Tiphany snatched her phone off of the table when it started ringing and looked at the screen. When she saw who it was, she answered.

"What's up, baby?" she asked.

She had a lot of love for her team of young boys because they held her down, and they loved her back. She treated them like family, and the favor was returned.

"Fuck!" she shouted as she listened to Butta's warning. "Good look, the bags are on the way," she said, hanging up before she started stuffing all the money in the duffel bags.

"What's up?" Precious asked in a panic as she copied her sister.

"Captain Henderson and his goons are about to knock on our door. We need to get this money to Butta because you know he's going to confiscate it, and we don't have time to go through the process of getting our shit back," Tiphany said as she carried a duffel bag to the balcony.

She opened the sliding door and looked over the railing for Butta. When she saw that he was ready, she dropped the duffel bag down to him.

"That nigga stay fucking with us," Precious said as she copied her sister's maneuver.

Tiphany didn't respond as she made another trip. It took them three trips apiece before they got all of the bags out of the condo. Precious grabbed the air freshener and tried to get the weed smell under control. A few seconds after emptying the whole can, there was a knock at their front door. She was about to answer the door, but Tiphany stopped her with a wicked smile on her face.

"Let him sweat for a minute," she said seriously.

When it sounded like the police were on the verge of kicking the door in, they answered.

"Who is it?" Precious asked sweetly. She was fighting not to laugh out loud.

"It's the Atlanta Police Department, and we have a search warrant for this residence."

They both recognized the voice of their arch-nemesis, Captain Henderson.

"I thought they fired your pussy ass," Tiphany said sarcastically when Precious opened the door.

Captain Henderson looked at the two women he couldn't stand the most in the world and said through clenched teeth, "We have a search warrant for these premises."

He held up the document for them to see. Precious tried to take the document from his hand, but he snatched it back just out of her reach.

"If I don't read the search warrant, Captain, you will not be coming in here. Follow protocol or follow the bread crumbs back to your car," she said seriously.

Captain Henderson was seething, but he knew that he had to follow the rules or risk his investigation, so he handed her the document.

"You're searching for drugs and weapons?" Tiphany questioned incredulously as she read the warrant over her sister's shoulder. "You already know we're both registered to carry, and you big dumb ass are not going to find any drugs in here," she added, looking at him with disgust on her face.

Captain Henderson took a step forward and raised his hand as if to strike her, but one of his officers grabbed him.

"Nigga, you not crazy," Tiphany said with a scowl marring her beautiful face.

"You would strike a woman, wouldn't you, pussy boy?" Precious asked sarcastically. She looked amused, but the murder in her eyes told a different story.

"Search this property, and tear it up until we find what we are looking for," Captain Henderson told his officers through clenched teeth.

"Before I let you officers search, let me just warn you that we do have a high-tech security system recording your every move. So if you do anything you're not supposed to do, you will lose your job right along with your unstable Captain,"

Precious said seriously as she locked eyes with each and every officer standing in their doorway.

When she was sure that her message was received loud and clear, she stepped aside and let them in. She turned back to Captain Henderson, who was still standing in the hallway, and smiled.

"You're not going to plant anything this time?" she asked sweetly.

Captain Henderson took a deep breath and brushed past her without responding. Precious turned and watched him disappear to the bedroom where some of his officers were before turning to her sister with a smirk gracing her lips.

"This shit is too easy, Loca," she said with a chuckle.

"Mark my words, P, we're gonna have to dead that nigga, P. I'm telling you," Tiphany whispered to her sister seriously as she watched the officers searching the apartment.

Precious didn't respond, but she was starting to realize that maybe she was right.

***

Gutta was keeping a close eye on his rearview mirror as he drove the back roads to his home in Garner. Yero and his team had Raleigh in a vice grip. If you weren't selling for them, you weren't selling for nobody, and if you bucked, you ended up missing. Niggas didn't really have shit bad to say about Y.O. because his prices were sweet, but a few niggas did have a problem with a Durham nigga running weight in Raleigh. The ones complaining were usually the broke niggas standing on the sidelines with their hands out, but niggas about their paper were getting money and keeping their beef, if they had any, to themselves. He was one of the niggas who chose not to fuck with Yero.

He didn't have a problem with him, but he wasn't a follower. When Yero made his presence known, he was doing his own thing with his own team in Kentwood, so he wasn't paying too much attention to him until P.R. and Casper got on some guerrilla warfare type of shit. They were telling niggas straight up that if you weren't moving their product, you weren't moving shit, but they were fair with the prices as long as your money was right. Niggas thought they were just talking until people started dying. When shit got hot, the bitch came up out of a lot of niggas, and they started flipping sides. His whole team left him to work for P.R. and Casper, but he refused to fold. His connect's prices weren't that much higher than Y.O.'s, so he continued to do him. After two attempts on his life, he moved him and his girl to a house out in Garner, right outside of Raleigh. He was sneaking into the city every other night to make plays to some of his most loyal clientele. He had been doing that for a couple of weeks, and the more and more he went unnoticed, the more confidence he gained. He had even lowered his prices a little and started moving weight again, stealing some of his old customers back in the process. He thought he was being slick. He thought that P.R. and Casper weren't watching their territory like they were supposed to, but he thought wrong. His every move was being clocked, and his time was about up.

Gutta wasn't stupid, though, and that's why his eyes kept straying to the rearview mirror to make sure he wasn't being followed home. Only two people knew where he rested his head, and his girl Taboo was waiting on him to get back to her. When he pulled onto his street, he started feeling apprehensive all of a sudden. He hated Garner, and he hated how his house was so isolated. Every time he came home from a recent trip to Raleigh, he missed his city more than ever. He was always nostalgic, but his wifey Taboo made the sacrifices he was making for them worth it. He had met her a couple of months before he left Raleigh for Garner. He usually wasn't so quick to wife a chick up, but she was so real, so sexy, and so gangsta he had to keep her around. He pulled into his driveway, parked, and got out. Standing there looking at his dark yard, his feeling of apprehension increased. He pulled his gun out of his waist and kept it ready until he got to his front door. He was about to put his key in the lock when the door was opened by his wifey. Taboo was standing there wearing a red sheer negligee with six-inch red leather Marc Jacobs fuck-me pumps adorning her feet and a smile ghosting around her lips. Gutta slid his gun back into his waist and scooped her up in his arms.

"Damn, girl, you got my dick hard as hell," he said, putting his nose into her neck as he breathed in her scent.

He was palming her ass as he grounded his dick on her panty-less pussy. He was ready to fuck.

"Boy, put me down," Taboo said, laughing as she wiggled out of his arms even though the friction his jeans were causing against her clit was feeling good. "You have to eat first. I cooked chicken Alfredo with cheesy garlic bread, your favorite meal, and you're going to eat before you get your dick wet," she said as she grabbed him by his hand and led him into the kitchen.

"Damn, girl, I don't know what I would do without you," Gutta said as he sat down at the table as she fixed his plate. He took his gun and set it in front of him. She poured him a glass of wine and set it next to his plate.

"Damn, this shit smells good," Gutta said as he dug in.

He was about to take a sip of his wine, but stopped when he saw that she was watching him eat instead of fixing herself a plate.

"You not gonna eat, baby?" he asked before taking a sip of wine.

"Not right now, G. I'm just enjoying watching you eat, baby," she said, smiling at him.

Gutta shrugged and took another sip of his wine before he resumed eating. He grabbed a piece of garlic bread and took a bite, but before he could swallow it, felt like his throat had closed up on him. He started choking because he couldn't get enough air into his lungs. He tried to reach for his wine glass but only succeeded in knocking it over. He looked to Taboo for some help only to find her sitting up on the counter top with her negligee bunched around her waist, playing with her pussy. The smile on her face told him what it was before her next words left her mouth and confirmed it.

"Yero sends his regards," she said, breathing hard as she brought herself to an orgasm.

Gutta couldn't believe it. He tried to reach for his pistol, but his strength was gone, and he toppled out of his seat. He took his last breath watching Taboo, his supposedly wifey, come all over her fingers.

Taboo sucked her juices off of her fingers, then went to work. She grabbed the Clorox and wiped down the whole kitchen. Earlier that day she had sanitized the whole house to make sure her DNA was nowhere to be found. She had packed up all of the clothes and jewelry Gutta had brought her, then she cleaned out his stash and his jewels. All of that was sitting in the car Gutta had also brought her. She changed out of the lingerie she had on into jeans, a hoodie, and some sneakers. She took the Clorox and poured it all over his body to speed up the decomposition. She poured some into his mouth, also to mask the poison for as long as possible. Satisfied that all the traces of her existence had been erased from the house, she left Garner, never to return again unless she had to catch another body.

Chapter 10
(Six Months Later)

"Why in the fuck did we have to leave New York?" Niko asked his mother angrily.

"Niko!" Taji shouted at her brother.

She couldn't believe he was disrespecting their mother like that. She knew that if their father was still alive, he wouldn't stand for it. Stari agreed with her sister. She was shocked at Niko's mouth, also, but she was too distraught over her father's death to comment on it. Guardian, the baby of the group, wanted to know the answers to his brother's questions, also, so he kept quiet and waited to see how their mother would react. Niko knew that he was being disrespectful, but with his father dead, he was the man of the house now, and he wanted to know why they were running from New York.

Consuela stared into the defiant face of her oldest son and knew that he was trying to be the man his father prepared him to be, but he wasn't ready, and it was because of her that the burden was now resting squarely upon his shoulders. She stared at him, standing there, looking so much like his father that it hurt her heart sometimes to look him in the face and wondered what she could tell him to quell the pain and rage in his heart. She decided on the truth.

"The Japanese killed your father," she finally said.

Her stress made her revert to her mother tongue, Spanish, because she found some solace in the little remembrance of home.

"But why, madre?" Stari asked, infuriated that somebody would violate her family like that.

"All will be revealed in due time," Consuela said in a tone that brooked no argument from her kids.

She locked eyes with her oldest son and dared him to continue questioning her.

Niko scoffed when he saw the look on his mother's face, letting her know that he was far from finished, but he knew that he wouldn't get anything more out of her until she was ready to tell him. They all knew when she talked to them in her native tongue she was stressed, so he dropped his questions for now, but he would find out what he needed to know sooner or later. Sooner rather than later.

"Since we have to be in this slow ass city, I'ma go find something to get into. Guardian, let's ride," he said as he left the kitchen.

Guardian was younger than his brother by a little over a year, and he followed his lead more often than not, so he got up from his seat, kissed his mother on the cheek, and followed behind his brother. Consuela watched her two sons walk out of the kitchen with a heavy heart. She knew the move to North Carolina was necessary, but how could she tell her children that the move was more for her benefit than theirs. She felt the tears well up in her eyes, got up from her seat, and hurried to her room. She knew her children would hate her if they ever found that she was the reason their father was dead. Taji and Stari looked at each other when they were the only two left in the kitchen. They had seen the tears in their mother's eyes, and wondered exactly what was happening to their family.

***

"Girl, how in the hell did you get Hollywood to buy you this BMW?" Ya Ya asked as they cruised the streets of the

Bull City looking young, fly, and flashy in the new 2022 M3 droptop Coupé.

"My mama always told me that pussy runs the world, and with this cat in between my legs, I definitely run Hollywood's," Beza said with a chuckle as she pulled to a stop at a red light.

With the top down and the sun out, they had everyone's attention. You couldn't tell them they weren't the baddest bitches in the city.

"Bitches like us belong in shit like this," Ya Ya said, laughing as she gave Beza a high five.

"Shit, it's not doing us any good because these niggas in this city scared to holla at us," Beza said sarcastically.

"I know, girl. Yero and his niggas really bringing the bitch out of niggas," Ya Ya said, shaking her head sadly.

"Fuck these niggas anyway. That nigga Y.O. can get it anytime and anyway he wants it," Beza said seriously as thoughts of Yero had her panties wet.

"What about Hollywood?" Ya Ya asked with a smirk on her face.

"What about him?" Beza asked incredulously. "He doesn't compare to Y.O. Period," she added seriously.

"That Jamaican bitch Suai popped up on the scene and accomplished what none of us could: capture Yero's attention," Ya Ya said, looking at Beza's expression.

She knew Beza and Suai didn't get along, or to be more blunt, couldn't stand each other.

"Fuck that dread-head bitch," Beza spat as she pulled off when the light turned green. "You hungry?" she asked when she felt her stomach grumble a little.

"Hell yeah. Let's go to Giovanni's," Ya Ya said, feeling like some Italian.

"Sounds good to me," Beza said as she maneuvered through traffic. "We're only five minutes away," she added.

She ran into another red light outside of the restaurant.

"Damn, look at that Trackhawk," Ya Ya said, pointing to the parking lot of the restaurant. "That whip belong to an out-of-towner," she added adamantly.

She knew every baller in the city, and what they liked to stunt in, but she didn't recognize this Jeep, and whoever was driving it was definitely saucy. Beza looked over at the SUV Ya Ya was referring to and had to admit that it was nice. It had a vanilla cream paint job with cherry-colored leather interior, and the color scheme meshed perfectly. She was impressed, but she wouldn't show it like Ya Ya was. She turned on her turn signal before pulling into the parking lot.

"That nigga sitting in the passenger seat is a cutie pie, too," Ya Ya said, never taking her eyes off of the Jeep.

"I don't do passengers, baby girl," Beza said sarcastically as she got out of the car, ready to eat.

"Well, I'm going over to see who he is," Ya Ya said, getting out of the car.

She started walking over, but stopped when she looked back and saw that Beza wasn't following her.

"Bitch, come on and stop fronting like you're not curious, too," she added, rolling her eyes before walking off again.

Beza rolled her eyes back, but Ya Ya didn't see it because she was already strutting towards the Jeep. She sighed and followed behind her best friend because, truth be told, she did want to find out who the driver was.

***

Guardian was sitting in the Trackhawk listening to Moneybagg Yo on Apple Music waiting on his brother to bring their food out of the restaurant when he spotted the droptop M3 pull into the parking lot. He was a car enthusiast, so he recognized the BMW. He saw two females inside and figured they were out pushing their man's car with one of their friends. His interest was piqued, though, when they got out of the car, and he saw their bodies. The one thing he loved about the south so far were the women. They had bodies unlike any other group of women in the world: Cornbread-fed and built to last. On top of all that, they were gorgeous and knew how to carry themselves. The mamis in New Yitty would always be number one in his eyes, but the south was closing in on the top spot fast. He noticed them checking him and the Jeep out, but he played it cool. He knew they would walk over and be nosy before they got out of the car. No matter where you were, up top in New York or down south in North Carolina, curiosity always killed the cat.

***

"Excuse me, what is your name and whose car is this?" Ya Ya asked bluntly when they were standing outside the driver's side door.

Beza sighed and rolled her eyes at her friend's blunt and brash demeanor. She could be so ghetto sometimes.

Guardian smiled when he heard her questions because they were exactly what he expected her to ask. He looked up and studied them like they were studying him. Like he noticed before, their bodies were phenomenal, but what surprised him the most was that their looks matched. They were both gorgeous. It wasn't a far stretch to say that they could grace the covers of a few magazines.

Beza couldn't front; the boy was a cutie pie, but he was a youngin'. He looked to be eighteen or nineteen, but with his looks, his age didn't really matter. She also knew he was checking them out, but she didn't mind because she knew they were on point. She was the product of her black mother and Mexican father. She had an exotic look that captivated men and women. She had brown hair with blonde highlights and dark brown, cat eyes. Ya Ya was white and black with long, curly black hair that touched the middle of her back. She had green eyes that hypnotized people. What really

100

made her stand out was her tattoos. She had over fifty percent of her upper body covered with tattoos, and she had no plans to stop anytime soon. She gave off the aura that she didn't give a fuck, and men were attracted to that. To keep it short and sweet, they were beautiful, and they knew it.

"Are you going to answer my questions?" Ya Ya asked sassily with a hand on her hip.

Guardian smiled at her aggressiveness. It reminded him of back home.

"Which one you want me to answer first?" he asked sarcastically.

Ya Ya had the grace to blush.

"My name is Guardian, but people call me G, and this is my brother's truck," he answered truthfully.

He never felt the need to cap like most niggas did.

"And where's your brother?" Beza asked, ready to meet him.

She wasn't expecting anything to come of it, though, because men in Durham were just too scared of Y.O. and his team to holla at them.

"He's standing right behind you," Guardian said with a smirk.

He was really surprised that they didn't hit him with the usual quips that most women used when they found out his name—'*Can you guard me or I'm an angel looking for a Guardian,*' or some crazy shit like that. He never gave those corny types the time of day.

Beza and Ya Ya both turned around to find a man with long locks standing there, staring at them with bags of food in his hands and curiosity in his eyes.

Oh my God, this nigga is sexy, and he looks familiar, Beza thought as her eyes took him in.

"Who you got with you, G?" Niko asked as he handed him the bags of food.

He never took his eyes off of the females, though. He wasn't like most men who instinctively trusted a big butt and a smile. He knew that women could be just as dangerous as men.

Guardian was already eating, so he had to swallow the food before answering.

"The one with the blonde highlights — name is, and the mixed shorty name is — damn, bro, I don't even know their names because these two pretty but rude ladies never bothered to tell me their names. They were asking all the questions, though," he teased with a smirk.

Beza and Ya Ya both felt themselves blushing because he was telling the truth.

"My name is Ya Ya, and this is my best friend Beza."

"And what is your name?" Beza asked.

She was having a hard time keeping her eyes off of him, and she could tell that he was feeling the same way.

"My name is Niko," he answered as he looked into her eyes.

Both women were beautiful, but it was something about Beza that drew him in like a moth to a flame.

"Where are your boyfriends?" he asked seriously.

He knew that women who looked like them had either boyfriends or husbands.

"Who said we have boyfriends?" Ya Ya asked playfully.

"Either this city full of lames or . . ." Guardian paused with a sly smile on his face . . . "You two are doing each other." He laughed at the look of disgust on their faces.

Niko cracked a small smile.

"You wish, nigga," Beza said, rolling her eyes at him.

She couldn't believe how sexy Niko was, and the more she looked at him, the more he reminded her of somebody she knew, but she couldn't connect the dots. You could tell that him and Guardian were brothers because of their dimples and cocoa brown skin, but that's where the similarities ended. Guardian had dark, dark brown eyes and had a low-cut Caesar with waves. Niko had locks that hung to his waist with light brown eyes that seemed to look through you. Both of them looked good to her, but Niko had an aura that she was attached to.

"Would it matter if we had boyfriends?" she asked, locking eyes with him.

Niko looked at her for a few seconds as the lessons of his father coursed through his mind.

"To us it matters," he said seriously. "Our father taught us to never touch another man's property. Women can make a man act out of character. Women have been known to start wars and cause division between the closest of brothers. We are taught not to invite problems where problems need not to exist. So, to answer your question again, yes, it would matter if you had men in your lives because we don't look for problems. We just handle them if they come our way." He had to stop talking because the death of their father was still too fresh in his mind, and talking about the lessons he had taught them brought all of that pain to the forefront.

Beza heard the pain in his voice and wondered what had caused it. She wanted to ask, but felt like it wasn't her place to.

"So y'all not scared of Y.O. like the rest of these niggas around here?" Ya Ya asked curiously.

Most men showed the bitch in them when they found out that their boyfriends were on Yero's team.

"First of all, we don't know any Y.O., and secondly, we're not scared of no man. Last time I checked, all men bleed," Niko said seriously as he leaned back against the Jeep.

He never heard of this nigga she was referring to like he was Captain America, but he filed the name away because he needed to know the players in this city.

"Give me your phone, Beza," he demanded.

I know this nigga not demanding shit, Beza thought indignantly, but she found herself handing him her phone like she couldn't resist. Niko quickly typed a number into Beza's phone.

"Guardian, give me *that* phone," Niko told his brother, his eyes never leaving hers.

Guardian didn't pause in his eating as he took a Caviar "Tyrannophone" iPhone out of his pocket and handed it to him. Niko handed it to Beza.

"What am I supposed to do with this phone?" she asked with a confused look. *This nigga tripping*, she thought wryly.

"It's obvious you're in search of something new, or you wouldn't be holding this conversation with me. So I'm giving you an alternative path to the one you're walking on now. All you have to do is, once you're ready, call the number I just added to your contacts," Niko said seriously.

Beza looked down at the device in her hand. It wasn't like any iPhone she'd ever seen; the back was encased in hardened titanium and 24K gold, featuring a 3D design that felt heavy and dangerous in her palm. It felt more like a weapon than a piece of tech.

"Now, type your number into that phone," he added, referring to the Caviar "Tyrannophone" he'd taken from Guardian and handed to her. *What better way to make your presence felt than to take a nigga's bitch*, he thought.

Beza was about to respond to him until Ya Ya grabbed her arm to get her attention.

"You know Hollywood doesn't play," she whispered in Spanish.

Whenever they wanted to discuss something in private, they used Spanish.

"I know that, but what's wrong with having a backup plan?" Beza asked with a smirk on her face.

Niko and Guardian smiled at each other because they didn't know that they understood the language.

"You don't even know if these dudes are built for this shit. What the fuck is wrong with you!" Ya Ya said sternly as she looked at Beza like she was crazy.

They both knew how Yero and his team gave it up, but it was obvious that Beza was experiencing temporary amnesia because she was violating in a major way right now.

"Girl, bye. I need a boss in my life, not a worker," Beza said seriously.

Ya Ya wanted to argue with her, but the look on Beza's face let her know she was gonna do what she wanted to do, regardless, so she rolled her eyes and let it go, inputting her number into the phone Niko had given her.

"What do you expect from me?" Beza asked Niko in English, handing his phone back to him after saving her number in his contacts.

She really wasn't expecting too much. Right now it was all fun and games for her, even though he had her intrigued.

"Me, I'm not expecting nothing from you, ma, not right now at least. You're not happy with your man, so I'm giving you an option, but let me tell you something real. Don't call the phone if you're not ready. I don't play games with what belongs to me. When you step into my world, you will know your position. Life is like a chessboard, and even though the queen is one of the most powerful pieces on the board, she's only as powerful as the king allows her to be," Niko said, handing Beza her phone back and pocketing the iPhone she'd returned to him. "Love and loyalty, trust and respect is a must. I don't know how it's done in the south, but me and mine are always first. Don't call the phone unless you're ready to give what I'm offering in return," he added before sliding into the driver's seat and closing the door.

Beza couldn't lie to herself. She was feeling him a lot, but she was in a situation. She knew a lot of niggas who could talk a good game, but most of them were fronters. He was a better talker than any she had heard before, but she wasn't about to jump out there on a maybe.

"We'll see," she said noncommittally.

"Yeah, I guess we will," Niko said as he started the Jeep.

The engine was so loud it drew the attention of everyone in earshot. He put the Trackhawk in reverse and started to pull out when another car pulled to a stop right behind his whip, blocking him in. He looked into the rearview mirror and knew the niggas in the other car were trouble. He glanced at Beza and Ya Ya, and the looks on their faces only confirmed his suspicions.

"Oh my God," Ya Ya said when she saw who was inside of the car.

Her mouth was dry, and her heart was beating fast. She was nothing short of terrified. Niko put the Jeep back in park and got out. He left it running in case they had to move quickly. He glanced over at Guardian and saw that he had his pistols in his lap. He focused his attention back on the niggas who were mean-mugging him, ready for whatever. He guessed his introduction to the city of Medicine would come sooner rather than later.

Chapter 11

"Man, I'm tired of doing this lil' nigga shit," Towny complained as he puffed on a blunt of exotic. "This not even our area code to be working," he added sullenly as he passed the blunt to Jay-O, who was driving the car they were riding in.

"Nigga stop complaining," Jay-O joked as he took a long pull on the blunt, holding the smoke in his lungs for a few seconds to get the full effect before exhaling it into the air. "We're getting paid to pick up money, and do something we was doing for free anyway—put pressure on niggas. We the kings in this city, and the bitches know it. So stop fucking complaining because you're starting to sound like one of them bitches we left back at the house," he added, taking another pull of the blunt before passing it to Jah, who was sitting in the back seat lost in his own thoughts. "Tell this nigga to shut the fuck up, Jah," he said as he pulled to a stop at the red light.

He glanced back at Jah and waited for him to say something. He always kept it real, raw, and uncut.

"Yeah, Towny, you sounding real sissified right now. You act like you want to go against Y.O. or some shit. Pipe down with the bullshit because I'm eating lovely and nobody going to fuck my ends up," Jah said seriously.

He knew shit sewed up right now, and for the foreseeable future, that was a fact of life.

"Man, that nigga don't respect us. He be treating us like pussy-ass do-boys," Towny said seriously.

"Yo, shut the fuck up," Jah said seriously. "Let that shit go. You're getting too comfortable with that mouth," he added angrily as he stared a hole in the back of his head.

Jay-O stared at the look on Jah's face and knew that his homeboy was crazy. They all grew up together and were close-knit, almost like brothers, but Jah was off his rocker. He was an action-type nigga. He didn't do a lot of talking like most men did. He shot first and then asked questions, if he asked questions at all. Truth be told, he was a little scared of him.

"Yo, Jah, ain't that your bitch Ya Ya over there with Beza rapping with some niggas?" Towny asked, leaning forward in his seat to get a better look.

Jah leaned in between the two front seats to get a look at what Towny was pointing at. He clenched his jaw when he saw his girl in some nigga's face.

"Pull in there," he said quietly.

Jay-O whipped into the parking lot of the restaurant. He saw that the niggas looked like they were about to leave and pulled his car up behind theirs to block them.

Don't run now, bitch-ass niggas, he thought sardonically.

He saw the fear on Beza and Ya Ya's face and smiled at how powerful their fear made him feel. Before anyone could say a word, Jah had hopped out of the back seat and smacked Ya Ya so hard she fell to the ground holding a busted lip.

"What the fuck is wrong with you, bitch?" she screamed in Spanish as she sucked the blood from her lip.

She usually wouldn't have talked to him like that in public, but he had put his hands on her in front of people and embarrassed her, so fuck him. She knew that she would pay for it later, but right in that moment, she didn't give a fuck.

Jah started to reach down and snatch her ass up, but stopped when one of the niggas opened their mouth and spoke to him. He looked up with an incredulous look on his face and said, "Nigga, you better mind your fucking business before it gets ugly out here." His face was so tight it looked like it was carved from granite.

Niko smirked at the nigga. He wasn't fazed at all with the tough guy act he was putting on. Shit didn't impress him.

"You heard what I said, son. Don't put your hands on a woman in my presence. If that's your girl, then wait till you get her home," he said seriously.

His New York accent grew more pronounced the angrier he got.

Jah didn't tolerate disrespect from nobody, and he definitely wasn't about to let a New York nigga try his gangsta. He started to reach for his pistol on his waist, but stopped when the nigga in the passenger seat of the Jeep stood up with two Glock 21's in his hands.

"I wouldn't do that if I was you, my nigga," Guardian said as he waved the guns in his hands around like air-traffic controller batons. "Now I suggest you hop back into that hooptie and get missing. My brother is a little more lenient than I am, so don't try me, or I'll make sure you and ya man's be eating through straws indefinitely," he added seriously.

Jah had murder in his eyes at having a New Yorker pointing guns at him, but there was nothing he could do right now. They had won this battle, but he would definitely start the war. Jay-O couldn't believe what was happening. He wasn't used to having guns pointed at him, and he was a little shook up. He stared at the two *Up North* niggas and could not find even a little bit of fear. He knew word would spread that they got bitched out by two out-of-towners if they didn't try to save face.

"Beza, you better tell these niggas who the fuck they dealing with," he said with false bravado.

Beza was frozen with shock. She couldn't believe what was transpiring right in front of her. She should have gotten his number and kept it moving, but she didn't listen to Ya Ya like she should've. Now shit was about to hit the fan.

"Nigga, we don't give a fuck who you are, son," Niko said seriously.

He had sized the three niggas up instantly. The driver was pussy and would only get violent if he had the advantage. The passenger was a bitch, too, but he would follow his peoples' lead on anything. The nigga who had smacked shorty was the gorilla of the group. He was built for war, but he was too emotional and would act without thinking; that's why the domestic violence happened. Alone, none of them were a threat to him and his people, but together they could be a problem; not a serious one, but a problem, nonetheless.

"I think you would be better served if you found out who you were trying to flex on," Niko added with a smirk on his face.

Jah wanted so bad to pull his gun out and pop both of them, but he let sleeping dogs lie, for now. He looked down at Ya Ya one last time to let her know she had it coming, then he hopped back into the whip with Jay-O and Towny. Before they pulled out, he made the gun symbol with his fingers and pointed it at them, letting them know it was far from over. Jay-O burnt rubber as he hit a U-turn and sped out of the parking lot.

When they disappeared into traffic, Beza rushed over and helped Ya Ya up off the ground. Ya Ya shot her a look that said it all. Beza didn't say anything because she knew she had fucked up.

"You a'ight, ma?" Guardian asked Ya Ya after the situation calmed down a little.

He was feeling her style and didn't like a coward putting his hands on her.

"Yeah, I'm good, G," she said, smiling at him self-consciously.

She was frowning on the inside, though, because she knew a busted lip was the least she would endure at Jah's hands when she got home. Niko hopped back into the Jeep, but before he pulled off, he looked over at Beza.

"When you are ready, ma, call the phone, but know this: children play, boys fight, but men kill. I don't play games, and I don't fight over women because it's too plentiful out here. The rest is self-explanatory, B.S. Make sure you're ready to cut all ties to your old world if and when you call," he said before backing out of the parking space and leaving the restaurant.

"Girl, what are you going to do about that nigga?" Ya Ya asked as she checked the damage to her lip in her compact mirror.

"The same thing we been doing before we met them New York niggas. We owe our loyalty to our men right now, not them. So we're going to come up with a good lie in case someone asks us about them," Beza said as they walked back towards the car.

Their appetites had deserted them the moment Jay-O, Jah, and Towny had pulled up. She knew it was going to be some shit, not for her because Hollywood was soft when it came to her. She knew that Jah put his hands on Ya Ya whenever she had done something he didn't like, and the look on his face when he looked at her before he left scared her.

"You want to stay with me for a few days until Jah calms down?" she asked, concern evident in her voice and on her face.

Ya Ya sighed and thought about it. It sounded like a good idea, a wonderful idea, but she knew Jah and the way he got embarrassed today; she knew he wouldn't calm down anytime soon.

"Nah, girl, I'm going to go home and get this shit over with," she said, resigned to her fate.

"You need to leave that bitch-ass nigga, chica," Beza said softly.

She felt sorry for her girl, who was more sister than friend.

"I just might do that," Ya Ya said, looking in the direction where the Trackhawk disappeared into traffic.

She turned back to Beza with a smirk on her face and a twinkle in her green eyes.

"If you're not going to do anything about Niko, why do you still have that phone of yours in your hand and haven't called him yet?" she asked slyly.

"Oh, this . . ." Beza said smiling mischievously as she held up her phone. "Calling him is just gonna to be my backup plan." She laughed as they got into the car.

They pulled off not knowing that a firestorm was about to hit the city, and they were the gasoline that started it all.

***

Yero was riding around in one of his hoopties checking on his traps. In other cities, he had a mystique surrounding him because they didn't know anything about him—how he looked, how he moved, or how he thought. Some made him out to be Goliath with superpowers, and he let them think what they wanted, because people were terrified of the unknown, but in his city, Bull City, he let his presence be felt. When most niggas started making money, they faded to the background and started shining on the men that helped make them rich. They were the ones who hit the clubs and bought out the bar every night, the ones riding around in expensive cars that cost more than people's houses and had no legitimate income coming in. The ones that bred jealousy, envy, and hate among the niggas who could make or break them by belittling them, stunting on them, and fucking their bitches. The ones who used the street code to rise to the top, then disregarded everything the concrete jungle taught them once they were there. The Feds were full of them men because they forgot the number one rule about being on top—never forget to balance fear with respect, because fear without balance becomes hate, and hate unchecked creates informants. Once Yero knew he would be in the streets, he studied its history, the history of the men that conquered the concrete jungles then were swallowed up by them. He studied the triumphs and failures, the highs and lows. He learned the lessons their mistakes were willing to teach him. He poured over court records and newspaper articles. He utilized the internet, and he learned. That's why he still threw on the hoodie and Timbs and mingled in the trenches. He made sure not to isolate his home base because he knew what it was like to be at the bottom. Niggas were going to hate regardless of what you did because they were just bitches, but he didn't add gas to the fire. He never got a clear picture. He never felt invincible either, but he felt like that gave him an edge, helped him stay on his toes because he knew anybody could be touched if the circumstances were right. He was turning onto Alston Avenue when his phone started to ring. He saw it was his sister and answered.

"Talk to me."

"Talk to me," Dynasty said, imitating him. "Nigga, miss me with that boss, Michael Corleone shit," she added, laughing.

Yero smiled and chuckled a little bit. His sister was his heart, his only remaining family, and they shared a bond that could withstand anything.

"What's up, Dy?" he asked.

"You remember them D.C. niggas I gave those T-shirts to?" she asked, getting straight to the point.

Yero remembered exactly who she was referring to. He had been against the move, but he relented because he trusted his sister and let her do her own thing.

"Big bra, I'm telling you these niggas some real thoroughbreds, and they dick game is sick, too," he imitated her to a tee. She always kept it raw and uncut with him on anything, even niggas she was sexing.

"Okay. Okay, you got that, brother dear," she said, laughing at him, but quickly turned serious again. "But them niggas testing me like I'm soft because I'm a bitch. These niggas not answering my calls, and a few of my people up there said they are balling out of control," she added angrily.

She hated when people underestimated her because she was a woman. She made examples out of people who tried her.

Yero remained silent because he knew she had her mind made up about whatever she called him about. They were completely different in demeanor, but he trusted her completely. He was more behind the scenes, and she was a shoot first, ask questions later type. He decided to test her.

"Let that shit go, Dy. I told you not to fuck with them niggas anyway," he said seriously.

He waited for her to explode because he knew she didn't like how he moved sometimes, but she respected his judgement.

This nigga done lost his mind, Dynasty thought angrily. "Big bra, respectfully, I'm not letting this go," she said seriously. "Them niggas are going to feel me in the worst way. You know I hate when mu'fuckas try me. So miss me with that diplomacy shit," she added, hoping he didn't force her to disobey him by going against his word, but she had her mind made up.

Yero smiled because she was so predictable.

"Do you, Dy, but get in and get out. Leave no traces of their bloodline. You set the example. You set it right," he said seriously.

"Big bra, you will read about them niggas. I promise," she said before hanging up.

Yero's phone rang again before he could blink. He saw that it was P.R. and answered.

"Talk to me." He pulled to a stop at a red light.

"We got a problem, dog," Puerto Rico said seriously.

"What's the problem?" Yero asked as his eyes locked onto a cream colored Trackhawk that had stopped at the light on the other side of the street.

The Jeep screamed money, money he didn't recognize, and it had him curious.

"Some New York niggas pulled pistols on Jay-O, Jah, and Towny earlier today," P.R. said angrily. "Jay-O said these niggas were trying to holler at Beza and Ya Ya, and pulled out on them for no reason," he added heatedly.

"You believe that?" Yero asked skeptically as he focused on the occupants inside of the Jeep across from him.

P.R. paused for a few seconds as he thought about it. No, he didn't believe it, but the point was that some out-of-town niggas tried members of their team.

"Nah, bra. I don't believe it went down like that, but the fact remains that some out-of-towners tried our niggas, and we need to handle it," he said seriously.

Yero didn't think it was a coincidence that as soon as he sees a Trackhawk that he didn't recognize, he was getting a report about some outta-towners moving out of pocket in his city. He and the driver of the Jeep had locked eyes, and it seemed as if neither one of them wanted to look away first.

"Them niggas riding in a cream-colored Jeep?" he asked P.R.

"Yeah, yeah, that's what Jah said," P.R. answered. "How you know? They already called you?" he asked.

"Nah, they didn't call me, but them niggas we talking about are sitting at the light across from me," Yero said, getting a vibe from the driver, and he couldn't understand why.

He wasn't feeling any aggression, malice, or envy coming from him. In fact, the nigga was looking at him like he knew him from somewhere, but he knew for a fact he had never seen these niggas before.

"Word up!" Puerto Rico grew excited. "Bra, follow them and find out where they are laying up so we can show them how we get down in Bull City," he added, ready to put in work.

"There's no need to follow them because their actions are telling me they will be around for a minute, and if that's the case, they will make their presence known. When they do, we'll handle it. Stay out of it, and tell Jah I said stand down. Get focused and get money. The city is ours, but we don't need the attention," Yero said seriously.

Puerto Rico didn't like it, but he respected it. Yero was his big brother, and he had never led him wrong before, so he would do what he asked.

"A'ight, dog, we'll play it your way," he said, switching his thought pattern. "Look, I need to shoot to Raleigh for a minute. It's some niggas ducking Casper for our money, so I'll get back at you later. One," he added.

"One," Yero said before hanging up his phone.

He finally broke the stare with the driver of the Jeep as he pulled off at the green light. If the niggas were somebody to know, they would see them again, but until then, he had important shit to worry about.

***

"Another bammer stunting in a hooptie," Guardian smirked when the car opposite them at the light pulled off. "These niggas down south are hilarious, bro," he added, chuckling.

Niko was silent for a few seconds as he replayed the last couple of minutes over in his mind. When he locked eyes with the driver of the hooptie, he felt something he couldn't explain. It was like he caught déjà vu, but he knew he had never seen the nigga before. Most men couldn't look him in the eyes, but that nigga was almost arrogant in the way he refused to break eye contact with him. He didn't know who the nigga was, but he was sure he was somebody and would find out exactly who when he made his move.

"Don't let appearances fool you, G. Some niggas know how to move in the jungle. A pussy is a pussy, and a gorilla is a gorilla, no matter what type of mask he's wearing. Sooner or later their true nature will come out," he said quietly as he pulled off.

He looked in the rearview at the hooptie until it disappeared. He couldn't help but feel like he had been dismissed. It was a feeling he didn't like at all.

Chapter 12

Ichino Tanaka stared at his reflection in the mirror and smiled. His black Armani suit with grey pinstripes draped over his 6'2" frame like it was made just for him, and it was. The money he paid his personal tailor was indeed well deserved. His motto was, "You had to look like money to make money." His everyday attire was custom made, from his pocket squares to the gold buckles on his imported Italian leather loafers. He studied his features and hated his heritage. He was half Japanese and black. His father, Hideki Tanaka, was a billionaire industrialist in Tokyo, Japan. Tanaka Industries grossed billions yearly, so his father was a very important person in his homeland. Also undisclosed to the general public was that his father was one of the leaders of the infamous Japanese Yakuza, one of the most feared gangs not only in Japan, but in the world. His mother was a whore his father used to dally with whenever he ventured into the States but was killed when she tried to blackmail him with exposure for having a half-breed son with a black woman. His father knew a half-breed son would be shunned in his circles, but he wanted his first-born son after having nothing but daughters. So he had Ichino reared in New York City, and when he was old enough, put him in charge of all Japanese interests despite protests from the elders in the community. Early on, he showed an acumen for making money just like his father. Despite his ethnicity, he was raised to feel superior to other races, but he used them to make money. He didn't consider himself a racist, but he felt like Japanese were far more superior and advanced, more efficient. Growing up, he was beat up and picked on relentlessly by his Japanese counterparts because of his mixed heritage, so he had learned to protect himself, and that he did with brutal proficiency. Eventually, he earned respect for being ruthless. The older he got, the more ruthless he became until fear was the foremost emotion people experienced whenever they laid eyes on him or heard his name. He loved money and women, and he knew how to acquire both. Despite the way the elders felt, he became a player in the world of sex, drugs, and murder. He sold cocaine and heroin to the blacks in New York and the Tri-State Area. He sold women to many wealthy clients overseas. He sold weapons to the insurgents and guerrillas in Third World countries. He had his hands in many pies, and it gave him access to many illicit things. He looked at the blacks with a mixture of disappointment and disgust because he saw vast potential they held as a people, but they were content to be drug dealers, and petty ones at that. With unity, they could be powerful, but he knew the chances of that happening were slim to none. They were still harping on what happened to them four hundred years ago. The Italians he dealt with could become a threat to him, but they were delusional. They wanted to be the American white man so bad it was hilarious. They thought that they could dress up in designer labels and be respectable, but in all actuality, they were just expensively dressed peasants. They thought that being called Dons and Godfathers—*'we're better than you'* titles—gave them respect, but it just proved they were living in a fantasy world. Most European countries had no control of their lives. Their addictions controlled them. Sex and drugs were all one needed for that control. Africans and their Third World countries were slaves to poverty. People used poverty as an excuse when it really was a choice. People chose to be poor. It was easier to sit on your ass than to get up and make your situation look better, so he only dealt with other races on a 'what can you do for me' basis. If you couldn't contribute to his endeavors, produce currency for his coffers, then you weren't on his radar. The one thing he did love about other races was their women, especially black and Latina women. He would occasionally fuck a white woman, but only if she was extraordinarily beautiful.

The body of a black woman is what drew him in. Lips, breasts, small waist, thick thighs, and a perfectly round ass got him every time. He loved the different hues they came in, from the light skin that seemed to be kissed by the sun to the dark milk chocolate that felt like satin. He found them beautiful, but Latinas were his passion because with them you were getting the best of both worlds. They had the submissiveness and freakiness of white women along with the bodies of black women. They were sensuous, erotic, but what he liked best was their willingness to submit to his every demand. They were loyal to their families to the bitter end, and loyalty was a trait he could definitely admire in a woman. He had a tendency to seduce the wives, girlfriends, mothers, sisters, or daughters of his rivals and business partners. He knew that if anything was to get him killed, it would be pussy. To him, every woman had a price tag; some prices were just higher than others.

In the reflection of the mirror, he saw one of his men enter the room and stand quietly at attention, waiting for him to acknowledge him. He saw a brief look of disgust flash across the man's features. It happened so fast he could've imagined it, but he knew he didn't. The full-blooded Japanese under his command hated serving a 'Hafu', a half-breed, as he was called behind his back, but they feared him, and that was all that mattered. Fuck respect; fear was a stronger motivation. He made the man wait a few more minutes before finally turning around and acknowledging him.

"What is it?" he asked seriously.

"We've found her," the man said, hiding his disgust for Ichino Tanaka.

Ichino brightened at that.

"Where?" he asked, not revealing his excitement at this revelation.

"In North Carolina," the man said flatly.

"Keep her under surveillance until further notice," Ichino said, dismissing the man. "Oh . . ." he stopped the man before he could leave the room. "And the next time I see a look of disgust cross your face when looking at me, that will be the last time you wear a face, understand?" He gave the man a look that almost loosened his bowels.

"Yes . . . yes sir," the man stammered as he backed out of the room.

Ichino smiled when he was alone again. Power was intoxicating, and the hard-on showing through his Armani slacks proved it. He pulled out his cell phone and prepared to make a trip to North Carolina. He had business to take care of.

* * *

Born Legends had Philly going crazy. Junkies and fiends were coming from all over for that stamp. Born Legends was the new brand of heroin that had the city on fire. It was also the name of a crew of young hittas, jackboys turned hustlers, who were making an unprecedented mark on the streets of Philadelphia. Mellz and Bolo were the masterminds behind Born Legends. Growing up poor made them hunger for the cars, clothes, jewels, and women that the hustlers sported every day in West Philly. They tried to hustle, starting off with work they had took from some hustlers, standing on corners trying to catch sales, but they quickly grew tired of the nickel and diming because profits weren't worth the risks. They quickly graduated to the art of robbing. They recruited three more of their homeboys and formed *Born Legends*. They terrorized the streets of Philly from Mt. Airy to Germantown to West Oak Lane and everywhere in between. They didn't discriminate either; if you were getting

121

money, stunting, or capping, they got you, but they still weren't living like they wanted to live. They still aspired to be the biggest niggas on their block. That all changed with a phone call Bolo received from his mother.

"Baby, your aunt Mara just left here," she said around the Newport he knew she had in her mouth.

"Was Towny with her?" he asked, wondering why she didn't call him.

He rocked with his cousin from down south.

"She came by herself. Her country ass up here to shine on me, to brag about how Towny taking care of her, paying all her bills and what not. She was even driving a brand new Tahoe. Hmph," she said enviously.

Bolo was wondering what his cousin was into down south when his mother interrupted his thoughts.

"Give your cousin a call and find out what he got going on down south. Y'all always been close, so hit him up," she said before hanging up on him.

Simply put, the call changed his life. It seemed as if Towny was the man down in North Carolina, or at least that's what he told him. He was down south doing numbers like an accountant during tax time. Bolo told Towny to meet up with him in Virginia so they could talk business. Towny showed up and blessed him. He gave Bolo a half a kilo of heroin that was eighty percent pure. When Bolo tried to put some money in his hand for the work, Towny surprised him.

"Naw, cuzzo, that's on me. Get money. Shit, it's not my work anyway."

That statement confused Bolo, but he didn't question his good fortune. He got back to Philly and put his whip game down on the half a key. He called up his team and became the embodiment of their name—Born Legends!

"Yo, we need to pick this money up," Mellz said as he sparked a freshly rolled blunt.

"I'm already on it," Bolo said as he watched the activity on the block.

"What's up with that country bammer cousin of yours?" Mellz asked, blowing a cloud of smoke into the air. "That nigga sweet, kid, and we need some more work. He not even charging us for the shit. Whoever he tricking out of their money down there is a certified sucka," he added with a chuckle as he held the blunt out for Bolo to take.

Bolo didn't say shit as he took the blunt from Mellz and took a deep pull. He was feeling kind of tight because Mellz was disrespecting his family when he was the reason they were doing numbers, but he kept his peace because he was really wondering the same things. Towny was giving them premium work for free. Every time he tried to pay him, he said something to the effect—"That shit ain't mine, bra, or don't worry about it." He tried to question Towny, but he just brushed him off. He left it alone, but it stayed on his mind.

"He's supposed to get at me this week," he assured Mellz.

Mellz was about to say something slick, but his phone started playing Marvin Gaye's 'Sexual Healing' ringtone.

He snatched the phone out of his pocket and walked off a few feet before he answered.

"What's up, baby? Please tell me you're in Philly?" He could already feel his dick getting hard at the thought of receiving a world class blow job.

"You know I am, baby," Skittles said with a giggle. "I want to see you," he added seductively.

Mellz grabbed his dick through his pants and moaned.

"Where are you, Ski?" he asked excitedly.

"I'm at the Four Seasons downtown," Skittles said. "Room 1057," he added, making sucking noises with his mouth.

"I'm on my way," Mellz said, calculating how long it would take him to get there in his head. "Answer the door in those boy shorts I like," he added, ready to go.

"Hurry, baby," Skittles giggled before hanging up.

Mellz put his phone back in his pocket and hurried back over to Bolo who had a big smile on his face matching his own.

"She must suck a mean dick with that smile on your face," Bolo said, smirking at Mellz.

He was happy his friend had a freak to get to.

"Dog, you don't know the half," Mellz said slyly. "Look, Wood is on 46th and Parrish. Bomb is over in Richland Allen Projects, and Twenty Mill is over in the Black Bottom. Tell them to meet you at the stash spot on Walton Ave so y'all can count up the money, and I'll meet y'all later on. Get at your peoples down south, too," he added before opening his car door and getting into his brand new money green Dodge Charger 392.

"Get at me when you finish with that bitch," Bolo said dapping his man up.

"No doubt," Mellz said before pulling off.

Bolo watched his car disappear off of the block and decided to call up one of his hoes so he could get his dick wet before heading to the stash house.

Chapter 13

"What's up, fam?" Bless asked, dapping Ceaz up.

"Ready to make it rain," Ceaz said, flashing a couple of bands for the strip club they were regulars at. "Before we go, Joe, let me put a bug in your ear." Ceaz grew serious.

"If it's about that bitch we beat out of that money, forget about it," Bless said seriously.

"Family, why shit on her when she's the connect?" Ceaz asked, confused at his actions.

"Man, that bitch thought she had a couple of suckas, but we flipped the script on that hoe. Fam, fuck her," Bless said seriously.

"You think she's just gonna let that go?" Ceaz asked skeptically.

"Bro, we run the Gardens," Bless said, looking at Ceaz like he had two heads. "A bitch or nigga not stupid enough to try us. Now let's go before we miss Strawberry's set at the club," he added, leaving the room, effectively ending the conversation.

Ceaz decided to let it go, but he didn't feel good about the moves Bless was making. He just hoped it didn't come back to bite them in the ass.

***

Potomac Gardens was one of the realest projects, if not the realest project, in Washington, D.C. It was called Little Iraq because it went down like the Middle East during wartime. Murder, robbery, rape, and home invasions were regular occurrences. Broad daylight or nightfall, it didn't matter; it went down. If you had any bitch in you at all, it would be exposed once you entered the Gardens. Regular residents had to prove themselves every day because the young wolves were always on the prowl for a come up; so strangers that had no business being in the Gardens definitely became food. If you weren't built for violence, then you didn't step foot inside of the Gardens. A direct contributor to D.C.'s murder rate, the Gardens were the playground of choice for the thugs, killers, and hoodrats.

Kandy was a longtime resident of the Gardens. She was a baddie with a body that could stop traffic, but she was ran through. All the dope boys knew what Kandy tasted like, so no one took her serious. She harbored resentment because of that, and it festered. She no longer enjoyed the company of men, but she kept it to herself because she needed to feel useful. She needed to make money, and if Bless and Ceaz knew she no longer fancied dick, they might not use her anymore. She was the conductor of the hood grapevine. There wasn't too much that went on in the Gardens that she didn't know about. She was the Wendy Williams of the projects, and that was how she remained useful to the guys. She was sitting at her window in her apartment in the Gardens watching the comings and goings of everything around her. Bless and Ceaz paid her to report anything out of the ordinary happening in the Gardens. She loved it because she was nosey by nature. Shady niggas always did their dirt in the open, thinking that no one was watching, but she was always watching, and she happily let Bless and Ceaz know what she saw every time she caught a sheisty nigga doing grimey shit. When that same nigga turned up missing, she didn't blink an eye. As long as she got paid, she didn't give a damn because it was all a part of the game. She was about to go to the bathroom when an unfamiliar vehicle pulling into the Gardens stopped her. She watched as the car parked a couple of blocks down from her apartment. She knew that the car didn't belong to anyone who stayed in the projects because she knew what everyone in the Gardens drove. She had to pee badly, but she held it a little longer to see who got out of the car. When she saw three women get out, she tried to make out their features, but with the dusk settling in, it was hard. She thought she recognized one of the women, but she wasn't sure. She was bouncing from leg to leg now because she had to pee so bad, but yet she held it to see who they were going to visit. The three of them split up and headed in different directions. The driver was headed towards Ceaz's mother's apartment, and the other two headed towards Bless' mother's apartment. Kandy didn't believe in coincidences. The women were giving her a weird feeling in the pit of her stomach, so she grabbed her phone and started dialing the police, but stopped when Bless' warning invaded her thoughts— *"Never call the police. Call us and we'll handle it."*

She hung up before the phone started ringing and dialed Bless' cell phone. After getting the voicemail on his phone and leaving a message, she hung up. She looked for the women, but didn't see them. Unable to hold her bladder any longer, she raced to the bathroom to relieve herself. She hoped nothing bad happened on her watch because she knew Bless would blame her, and she didn't want to feel his wrath.

***

"Look, this is what we're going to do," Dynasty said to Aza and Light as she scoped out the activity going around them in the Gardens. "We're sending these niggas messages. Kill everybody inside of the apartments. Niggas want to play with my money; we'll play with their bloodlines," she added, scowling at the D.C. niggas moving around the projects.

She wanted to kill everything repping Chocolate City, but she had revenge to exact, and that was more important. She had been forever soured against the DMV.

"Let de blood flow," Aza said, ready to put in work.

"Stick to the plan," Dynasty said before getting out of the car.

Aza and Light followed her out of the car.

"No witnesses," she warned before walking off towards Ceaz's mother's crib.

Aza and Light walked over to Bless' mother's apartment. When they were standing on her stoop, they surreptitiously pulled out their pistols and held them by their sides, out of sight from whoever might answer the door. Light knocked and waited. Aza kept one eye on their surroundings because she was gonna dead whoever looked at them too long.

Ms. Griffin was on her last cigarette, and her nagging grandchildren were getting on her last nerve. Bless was supposed to pick his sons up, but he was missing in action as usual, and he wasn't answering his phone. Her head was pounding, and his sons were upstairs jumping on the bed. She was about to get up, march upstairs, and whoop their little asses when a knock at the door stopped her.

"Y'all better hope this is ya sorry ass daddy or a ride for ya, because if it's not, I'm going to beat that ass when I get upstairs. Jumping on my damn bed," she shouted as she walked over to the front door.

She snatched it open without bothering to see who was standing on her stoop first. When she saw the two women with locks, she assumed that her son sent them to pick up his sons.

"I'm so glad you are here to pick these hardheaded kids up," she said as she walked away from the door, leaving it open for them to enter. "BJ and Tez, pack yo' shit," she yelled upstairs.

Aza and Light looked at each other with quizzical looks on their faces and shrugged. They walked into the apartment and closed the door behind them. Light raised her gun. Ms. Griffin turned around ready to question them about her son's whereabouts, but when she opened her mouth, she swallowed a bullet. With a look of shock on her face, she crumbled to the ground dead.

Aza and Light stepped over her body and slowly made their way upstairs. They didn't want any surprises. The first room they encountered contained the two little boys they assumed were Bless' sons. One was lying across a twin bed, and the other one was sitting in front of a TV playing a video game. The little boy lying across the bed looked up when they filled the doorway.

"BJ, two women are standing in the doorway," Tez said to his older brother. "Who are they?" he asked, looking at the two women curiously.

"Probably two bitches dad sent to get us," BJ said, never taking his eyes off of the video game.

Aza and Light looked at each other with amused expressions on their faces.

"How old are ye bwoys?" Aza asked politely.

"I'm ten and my brother is twelve," Tez said proudly.

He didn't know that he had just signed their death certificates. Aza raised her gun and made his face look like a tic-tac-toe board. She quickly turned and did his brother the same way. The silencer attached to the end of her pistol made the shot sound like someone was coughing. After making sure no one else was in the apartment, they disappeared as quickly as they appeared.

***

Ms. Hawks was getting ready for Bible study when she heard someone knocking on her front door. With her Bible in her hand, she went to answer it.

"Who is it?" she asked politely as she peeped through the window on the door.

She didn't recognize the young woman standing on her stoop, but in the Gardens, that didn't really matter.

"I was sent by Ceaz, your son."

Ms. Hawks rolled her eyes as she opened the door, wondering what foolishness her son was trying to pull now. She didn't agree with his lifestyle and refused to accept any benefits that came from his drug dealing.

"If you're here to drop off some money from my son, then you are wasting your time," she said, leaving the door as she continued to get ready for Bible study. "I've told that boy that I don't want none of that devil money," she added.

She frowned as she thought about the things her son was doing to their community. She couldn't control his actions, but she loved him and would continue to pray that God delivered him back to his grace.

Dynasty walked into the apartment and closed the door behind her. She already knew from Ceaz that his mother was by herself most of the time unless she was with her church friends. Pillow talk was a woman's secret weapon.

"No, ma'am, Ceaz didn't send any money, but I do have a message for you," she said, pulling out her gun with the silencer attached.

Ms. Hawks heard something sinister in her voice that made her turn around. When she saw the gun, she knew her son's sins had come home to roost. She immediately started praying.

"As I walk through the valley of the shadow of death . . ."

Dynasty was respectful and allowed her to finish.

"Do what you came to do," Ms. Hawks said, holding her Bible against her chest like a shield. "I'm at peace with God," she added before taking a deep breath to calm her nerves.

"When I send your son to wherever I'm about to send you, tell him I said that pussy runs the world," Dynasty said, pulling the trigger.

The shots were so soft Ms. Hawks didn't even realize she was hit until she felt the burning sensation in her chest. She looked down and saw three holes in her blouse, bleeding profusely. The last thing she saw before she crumbled to the ground and died was the three holes forming a perfect triangle through her Bible.

Dynasty searched the apartment just to make sure it was empty. Her bloodlust was far from sated. When she found the apartment void of any more living, she disappeared out of the back door and into the darkness.

***

Kandy was back at her window in time to see the two women leave Ms. Griffin's apartment, get back into their car, and leave the Gardens, but she saw no sign of the third woman. She picked up her phone and again tried to get in contact with the guys, but again she got voicemail. She didn't bother to leave a message because it was full from the numerous calls she had been sending to Bless and Ceaz. Again, she contemplated calling the authorities, but before she could make a decision, she heard a knock at her door. She jumped because her nerves were raw at this point, and she wasn't expecting any company. The knock, for some reason, had her a little afraid. It was a feeling she couldn't explain, but it was there. She walked to the door and looked out of the peephole. Her heart stopped when she recognized the woman standing there calmly. Now that she could see her features clearly, she knew the woman from seeing her with Bless and Ceaz. The woman was looking directly at the peephole with a smirk on her face, like she knew she was being studied, and her next words confirmed that she did.

"Open the door, Kandy," Dynasty said seriously.

Kandy didn't know what to do, but the gun that suddenly appeared in the woman's hand quickly made the decision for her. She opened the door and wondered if she would live to see sunrise.

"You still have that strap-on dildo?" Dynasty asked, smiling at the fear in her eyes.

Kandy nodded *yes*, too afraid to not answer. She wondered how she knew about that. Dynasty stepped into the apartment, forcing Kandy in the living room, and closed the door. She had major work to put in with only a little time to do it.

Chapter 14

"I've never seen anything like this," Precious said, looking out the windshield at the rain falling while the sun was shining bright.

"Down here in the South, they say it means the devil is beating his wife," Tiphany said grimly.

They had been stuck in traffic on Peachtree for the last thirty minutes, and she didn't like the feeling of being boxed in. The fact that it was raining while the sun was out felt ominous to her. Her head was on a swivel as she took in everything around them. Precious looked over at her twin and recognized the murder in her eyes. She tensed because she knew something was wrong, but she didn't know what it was.

"What's wrong, Loca?" she asked seriously.

"Don't react suddenly, but I think we're about to be hit," Tiphany said in Spanish as her mind whirled with plans to survive.

She was in her lioness mode. Kill or be killed.

"By who?" Precious asked seriously, as she easily fell into their native tongue.

She knew that when Loca spoke in Spanish, someone was about to die.

"I don't know, but I've never seen so many men dressed in all black on Peachtree. One or two, and I wouldn't have paid it any attention, but I've seen at least five of them since we've been stuck in traffic. It's obvious to me that they're not civilians," Tiphany said as she casually pressed a sequence of buttons on the car radio to open a secret compartment in the console between the front seats.

She eased two .40-cal Berettas into her lap as her eyes continued to scan their surroundings. She closed her eyes briefly and took a deep breath to calm her nerves. When the shooting started, she wouldn't have time to think, only react.

"What are you thinking?" Precious asked, wondering what mindset her sister was in.

Whatever it was, she was with it. She reached into the secret compartment and eased her Glock 21 into her lap. Tiphany didn't respond as she watched the men in black get into position. She now saw at least ten of them strategically positioned along the street. She sensed it was about to go down any second now.

"Open the sunroof, and get us out of this fucking traffic. Do not stop moving," Tiphany instructed as she memorized the positions of the men because once the shooting started, she couldn't afford to waste a shot.

Precious hated when Loca got on her *Mission Impossible* shit, but she knew better than to try to talk her out of it. She looked in the rearview to check how close the car behind her was as she put the car in reverse. She kept her foot on the brake and waited for it to pop off. Almost instantly, the men in black simultaneously pulled assault rifles and an assortment of other artillery from under their trench coats and let loose, but they all received a surprise that wasn't in their briefing packets. The Mercedes the twins were riding in was bulletproof.

Tiphany smirked at the looks of surprise on the assassins' faces when their bullets ricocheted off of their car, but she didn't waste time enjoying the slight edge the armored car gave them. She took advantage of it as she popped out of the sunroof with two .40s in her hands and sent angels of death to bless niggas.

"You pussies thought it was going to be easy, but I'ma Alvarez. Think again," she screamed in Spanish as she made every shot count.

When things started getting hot, she ducked back into the car and screamed at her sister.

"Move, bitch."

Precious took her foot off the brakes and mashed down on the gas pedal, ramming the abandoned car behind her. The damage to their car was the least of her worries. She was focused on keeping them alive. When the shooting started, a lot of people abandoned their cars immediately as the assassins weren't discriminating with their bullets. She turned the wheel to the right, mashed the gas, and hit one of the gunmen before he could reload his rifle. She made it to the sidewalk and maneuvered the Mercedes until she was able to drive. She didn't give a fuck who or what she hit as long as she and her sister were safe.

"The motherfuckers are swarming like ants to cake crumbs," she screamed as she hit a pedestrian who was trying to get to safety.

The bullets striking their car sounded like a thousand bees attacking. Tiphany popped back out of the sunroof after reloading two fresh clips into her guns and dropped two more assassins. It seemed as if every time she deaded one, two more took his place. She had a feeling they were not getting out of this alive, but it wasn't going to be easy to kill her or her sister. She had to make sure no shots were wasted because she was on her last two clips. She ducked back into the car and looked over at her sister with a wild look in her eyes.

"Where the fuck are the police when you need them?" she screamed in Spanish as she watched the chaos going on around them. "We should hear them by now," she added angrily.

She popped back out of the sunroof and dropped a shooter trying to sneak up on her blindside.

"This is a setup," Precious shouted angrily as she tried to get them to safety.

Downtown Atlanta looked like a warzone with bodies littered all over. She just hoped they didn't end up like them.

"Somebody with deep pockets trying to get us out of the way," she added as her mind whirled with possible suspects.

A bullet hitting the driver's side window reminded her to get her mind back on the now. The spider-webbing cracks in the window let her know that their time was running out.

Before Tiphany could blink, one of the assassins dived onto the roof of the car and stuck a pistol through the sunroof, aiming to finish them, and collect bounties on their heads. Loca didn't think; she just reacted. She grabbed the arm of the shooter and snatched him further into the car to throw him off balance and give him less room to get off a clear shot. The assassin let off a shot, hitting her in the shoulder. Loca screamed as she twisted his wrist, dislocating it, and made him drop the gun.

Everything was happening so fast that Precious was stunned for a few seconds, but when she heard the gunshot and her twin scream in pain, she reacted instinctively. She lifted the Glock from her lap and pumped shots into the assassin's body until he stopped moving. She slammed down on the brakes and pushed his body back out of the sunroof before turning to her sister who was moaning in pain as she held onto her bleeding shoulder. She almost cried when she saw how much pain her twin was in, but she kept it together as she tore her blouse to use for a tourniquet.

"Shit, shit, shit," Tiphany kept screaming in pain as Precious tied up her wound.

"Hold on . . . Hold on. I hear sirens," Precious said desperately.

She looked up and noticed that the men in black had disappeared as quietly as they appeared, but the carnage they left behind spoke volumes. They were lucky to be alive, but they were, and whoever was behind the hit would die a slow and painful death. She suddenly heard what sounded like a million-man march and looked in the rearview. When she saw their nemesis, Captain Henderson, leading the charge on what had to be at least a hundred officers in riot gear, she groaned. She didn't have the energy to deal with his bullshit right then.

"What's wrong?" Tiphany asked in a low voice with pain.

Before Precious could answer, Captain Henderson made his presence known.

"Precious and Tiphany Alvarez, put your hands in the air where I can see them. I repeat: Put your hands in the air where I can see them," he said through the bullhorn he was carrying.

"Pinche puto," Tiphany whispered harshly when she heard his voice.

"I'm not going to repeat myself, twins, put your hands where I can see them, or use of force will be the next step," Captain Henderson prayed that they wanted to go out in a blaze of glory because he was itching to put bullets into each of them.

Precious put both of her arms out of the sunroof because she knew Captain Henderson was capable of anything. They had embarrassed him enough to be sure of that.

"Put your hands up, Loca. Don't give this pig a reason," she whispered urgently.

She could see the anxiousness in Captain Henderson's face through the rearview mirror, and she didn't trust him to follow protocol. Tiphany raised her hand and flipped the police the bird.

"Tiphany Alvarez, you have five seconds to raise your hands. Five . . . Four . . . Three . . ."

"She can't raise her other arm because she's been shot in her shoulder," Precious screamed at the officers.

She wanted to make sure she was heard because Henderson's proclivity to color outside the lines was well documented. She glanced at her sister and saw a smirk on her face.

"Cut the shit, Loca," she gritted.

"He is a bitch," Tiphany said seriously, but she calmed down for her twin.

"Go," Captain Henderson said to the officers under his command. "And don't fuck up my crime scene, people, or I will be one pissed-off Captain," he added as he watched Forensics crawling all over the place.

He felt a deep sense of satisfaction because there was no way the infamous Alvarez twins would wiggle their way out of this one.

Precious had her door snatched open, and she was dragged out of the car. The officers slammed her onto her stomach and handcuffed her. She had every right to belligerently curse the officers out, but she kept her calm.

"I can't wait until my lawyer gets here. I'm sure someone out here is filming this, and when my lawyer gets ahold of the footage, I'm gonna have all of your jobs." She looked over and saw that her sister was getting medical assistance before they snatched her up and marched her to one of the awaiting cruisers.

Captain Henderson told the officers to hold up for a second. He walked over with a huge smile on his face and gloated.

"Looks like you bit off more than you could chew this time, Alvarez." He loved seeing her in handcuffs.

"I wonder why the police response was so long?" Precious asked sarcastically. "It seems as if someone wanted us to die, but it didn't work, did it? I guarantee we'll be back in the streets in 72 hours or less." She smiled when his face hardened into a mask of fury.

Captain Henderson wanted to smack the smug look off her face, but he calmed himself because no matter what she or her lawyers said, he had them dead to rights.

"Get this bitch out of my face," he barked before spinning on his heels and marching over to where the EMTs were still working on Tiphany Alvarez's shoulder.

He told them to give him a few seconds with her before they loaded her onto the ambulance.

"It's over for you, bitch," he whispered when they were alone.

Tiphany opened her eyes to find Captain Henderson glaring at her. She was groggy from the sedative the paramedics gave her, but she did what she did best, antagonize him.

"Fuck you, bitch-ass nigga. I'ma Alvarez, we hard to kill," she whispered groggily.

"I'll be front and center when the state of Georgia sticks that needle in your arm," he said before he grabbed her injured shoulder and squeezed until she passed out.

He stood up and waved the paramedics back over.

"Hurry, I think she passed out." He walked away with a huge smile on his face.

It was like a huge weight had been lifted off of his shoulders with the culmination of the biggest arrest of his career. He could now see the rites of passage to retirement on the horizon. If he dropped dead right then, he would die a happy man.

***

"Repeat the shit you just said again," Bless told Kandy.

He was pacing back and forth in her apartment and had been doing so for the last hour. He had so much rage inside of him at the moment, he thought he would incinerate from the heat of it. He had just found out that his mother and two sons had been found murdered in her apartment, and he was ready to body something. *How could this happen?*

He questioned himself silently as he thought about the ultimate violation paid to him and Ceaz. Somebody was gonna bleed and die slow for it.

Kandy snapped out of her daydream when he told her to repeat what she knew for what seemed like the thousandth time. She was trying to reminisce about the night Dynasty sexed her like no one ever had before. Her strap-on dildo had been put to good use last night, and when Dynasty had crept out of her apartment that morning before the sun rose, she took Kandy's loyalties with her. She was really starting to get aggravated because Bless kept asking, no, telling her to repeat her story, the story Dynasty gave her. So when she got fly at the mouth, she should've expected the consequences that came with it.

"Damn, Bless, how many times do you want me to tell you the same story?" she asked seriously.

Smack!

Kandy couldn't believe Bless had put his hands on her. Everything that Dynasty had told her last night was running through her mind as she held her bleeding lip and her nostrils flared. Bless drew back to strike her again, but Ceaz stepped in and stopped him.

"Fam, chill the fuck out," he said, staring at Bless seriously. "I understand how you are feeling, but you going crazy on the wrong one," he added before turning to Kandy, who was still glaring at Bless. "Kandy, he didn't mean to do that, but understand our losses. My moms, his moms, and his two sons . . ." He choked up, but he fought through it. "Just run it by us one more time, please." He looked at her with all of the pain he was feeling displayed in his gaze.

Kandy softened at the look in his eyes. She could empathize with him, and he almost had her wanting to tell him the truth . . . Almost.

"I was at the window was at the window watching everything like I normally do when a car I didn't recognize pulled in to the Gardens . . ."

"And niggas didn't think to stop that bitch?" Bless fumed as he continued to pace.

Death was what the lookouts from that shift was gonna get when he dealt with whoever murdered his family.

"The car parked a block away from my apartment. Three women got out. Two went to Ms. Griffin's crib, and the driver went to Ms. Hawks' crib. I couldn't see their features because it was already dark, but the driver reminded me of a female I've seen with you both. They were all let into the apartment, so I didn't think anything was wrong, but something didn't seem right to me, so I kept calling y'all over and over again, but neither of you answered. I left voicemails until I couldn't leave anymore. I wanted to call the police, but you said to never do that. So I watched and waited. About thirty minutes later, they left just as quietly as they came. I dozed off and didn't wake up until you beat on my door this morning. That's it again." Kandy folded her arms across her chest and showed her weariness and impatience.

Ceaz digested what she said and could only come up with one person who had a reason to try them on that level. To make matters worse, the reasons for the tragedies were because of them. He looked at Bless and saw that he had reached the same conclusions.

"Joe, that bitch and her whole family will die. That's word on my dead seeds," Bless promised before stalking out of the apartment.

With the sound of the door being slammed shut echoing in their ears, Ceaz and Kandy looked at each other for what seemed like an eternity, but was only a few seconds. Ceaz broke eye contact and took a deep breath.

"Look, Kandy, don't be mad at Bless. This shit is unbelievable. To lose your whole family . . ." He couldn't even finish until he calmed down. "Look, we got you, Kandy. Just rest easy and keep doing what you do for us. My word, we're gonna take care of you." He kissed her on the cheek and left the apartment.

Kandy's heart was heavy for Ceaz, but it didn't stop her from picking up her phone and checking in with Dynasty.

Chapter 15

Niko walked into the kitchen of their house to find his brother sitting at the breakfast nook, eating a sub.

"What's up, G?" he asked as he sat down beside him and snatched the other half of his sub and took a bite.

"Waiting on you to decide what we're going to do down here," Guardian said seriously.

He was ready to make moves and show the South how New York got down.

"I've done some research, and this nigga Y.O. had shit on lock," Niko said seriously. "Him and his team have their fingers in all sorts of pies, but he's not really messing with that Fentanyl. So that we can carve out our piece of the pie with that." Niko started eating again as he waited on his brother's response.

Guardian was quiet for a few minutes as he thought about what Niko just dropped on him.

"So he don't have a stamp on the streets?" he asked curiously.

"Yeah, it's one for the heroin, but nothing for that Fent. We can get it fresh off the boat and crush the game." Niko was sure they could mark out some territory in the city and get money because no matter where him and his family were, they were going to eat. "This is a heroin city, and we bringing something new to the table," he added seriously.

Guardian saw the seriousness in his brother's face and couldn't agree with him more, but he knew there could be repercussions behind a move like that also. He was ready to dive out of the frying pan and into the fire, but he knew that they had to move accordingly.

"If we put this on the streets, it's going to cause some problems because he will feel it in his pockets. Our product will be stronger than heroin, more addictive than heroin, and he will feel the loss of our profits. Fentanyl will bring that murder, money, mayhem to any set. So we're gonna need a team because I'm not trusting these country niggas with my life or my money because, as we've seen, they are emotional."

He knew what they were about to do was dangerous, but they had to play the hand fate had dealt them, and if they were going to play, then they would play to win. Niko had already reached those same conclusions and was about to let Guardian know they were on the same accord when their sisters walked into the kitchen, being their usual loud and boisterous selves.

"What's up with our two fine, sexy-ass brothers?" Taji asked loudly when she spotted them sitting at the breakfast nook.

"What's good, G and Niko?" Stari asked, rolling her eyes at their loud sister.

Niko and Guardian looked at each other and smirked. They had both seen this act a hundred times before and knew what was coming next. Even though their sisters were older than them, their father made it clear as they were growing up that men were the providers, planners, and protectors of the family, always and forever.

"What do you want?" Niko asked, smirking at them.

Taji and Stari looked at each other and started laughing.

"Were we that obvious?" Stari asked with a chuckle.

"Y'all both been doing this shit to Pops for years. So it's nothing new," Niko said with a smile. "What is it?" He asked curiously.

"We want to go out and party," Taji said with a whine.

"Yeah, we want to go to the club," Stari said, pleading with her brothers. "We've been cooped up in this house since we been down here. We feel like hostages," she added with a frown.

"Stari, you still in contact with that lil' nigga Chi Chi from Baisley Park Projects?" Niko asked, seeing a solution to his recent dilemma.

"Why?" she asked suspiciously as she eyed her brother, wondering how he even knew about her dealings with him.

"We about to make some moves down here, and we need some New York niggas on the team. We not trusting these country-ass niggas," he said seriously.

"Shit, I've heard some good things about these country boys," Taji said in an exaggerated country twang. "Cornbread and pussy is what they love to eat," she added, laughing and giving her sister a high five.

Guardian shook his head at their silliness. He loved them to death, but he had to keep an eye on them.

"Yeah, I still be hitting Chi Chi up," Stari said, glad she now had a reason to bring her little yea yea to NC. "So you want me to get him and his people down here?" she asked, already dialing his number.

"Tell him money is in the air, and if him and his niggas are trying to breathe, get down here as soon as possible," Niko said.

"So we can go to the club?" Taji asked as Stari tried to get in contact with Chi Chi.

"Yeah, you can go. Me and G need to show our faces, so we'll take you this Friday." Niko could tell she didn't like the idea of them going to the club with them.

They didn't like going anywhere with them because they scared most guys away. Taji didn't want to go with them because they cock-blocking, scaring niggas away, and she knew Stari didn't want to go with them either, but they would take what they could get right then.

Stari hung up her phone and looked at her brother.

"He didn't answer, but I left him a message, letting him know to call back ASAP."

"A'ight, let's talk about how we gonna get this money," Niko said seriously.

They all gathered around and discussed how they were going to eat, regardless of who or what had shit on smash.

Consuela was about to enter the kitchen for something to eat but stopped short when she heard her kids talking. She didn't want to deal with any questions from her children about their father. Ever since Niko had confronted her about leaving New York, she had been dealing with the guilt that refused to stop eating at her heart for being the reason why their father was dead. So, like a coward, she stood outside of the kitchen door and listened to her kids plotting on a way to get into the drug game. She sighed and shook her head. She was steadily losing control of her kids and, to make matters worse, she was losing control of herself. Ever since Manny's death, their anchor in a storm, life itself had been spiraling out of control, and she felt like there was nothing she could do to stop it. She turned and was about to head back to her bedroom when the doorbell rang.

"I got it," she yelled to her kids as she padded to the front door.

She looked out of the peephole and saw a young man in a FedEx delivery uniform holding a package.

Who ordered something? Probably one of the girls, she thought as she opened the door. "How may I help you?" she asked after she opened the door.

"I'm looking for a Ms. Consuela Perez," he said, consulting his clipboard.

"That's me," she said, perplexed as she accepted the clipboard. *Who would be sending me something because I didn't order anything,* she questioned herself as she signed the clipboard.

"Here you go, ma'am," he said, handing her the nicely wrapped package.

"Thank you," Consuela said before closing the door.

She looked at the package with trepidation for a few seconds before tearing it open. When she saw the contents inside, her heart started beating a hundred miles per hour.

Inside lay a crepe silk gold evening gown by Alexander McQueen. On top of that was a gold heart-shaped locket that she thought lost to her forever. As she rubbed the material of the dress between her fingers, the night she wore it, along with the locket, came rushing back.

"Baby, this is for our family," Manny said as he zipped her up. "All he wants is to prove . . ." He let that go as he shook his head for the hundredth time that day. He questioned whether he was doing the right thing, and for the hundredth and one time, he told himself he didn't have a choice. "All he wants is to have dinner with you and I'll be clear," he added as he silently tried to convince himself of that fact.

Consuela looked at her husband's face—the face she fell in love with at such a young age—in the mirror as he attached a gold heart-shaped locket around her neck and felt the love she had in her heart for him ease her worries like a balm.

"You know I'll do anything for you, Manny," she told him with all the love in her being, and that statement couldn't be more true.

Manny smiled and kissed the back of her neck softly before leaving the room. He didn't want her to see the anguish in his eyes at what he was being forced to do.

***

Consuela felt her eyes well up as that memory replayed in her mind because she knew that was the beginning of the end for her marriage. She picked the locket up and looked at it as it spun on the end of its chain. She wondered if she regretted anything she had done up to that point. She realized that she didn't feel regret as much as resigned sadness. The choices she had made were the reason her children were safe, the reason they were in North Carolina, and the main reason they were fatherless. The past she was trying to run from had caught up to her in the form of an Alexander McQueen and a locket her husband had bought her for another man. She picked up the ivory envelope and removed the letter it contained. When she saw the familiar script on the paper, the tears she had been fighting to hold back flowed down her cheeks. She was feeling an emotion she didn't expect to feel as she read his words—excitement. As much as she tried to deny her feelings, she couldn't any longer. She had been summoned and she would answer. With that decision came a feeling of drifting in an ocean with no land in sight. It was a feeling she was all too familiar with, a feeling she was addicted to. Ichiro Tanaka was back to claim her as his, and she was powerless to stop him. Did she even want to?

***

Baisley Park Projects was one of the roughest in Queens, New York. Niggas went hard for their project. Murder was a pastime, and money was a religion. Violators got the business, period. No if, and, or buts about it. If you weren't from Baisley, you couldn't eat in Baisley, but obviously some bitches forgot the rules and that had Chi Chi vexed. Niggas from *Forty Downs Projects* were using the apartments of some females who stayed in Baisley to hustle out of, and he wasn't feeling that shit at all. A lame named Troop ran a clique from Forty Projects called *Forty Thieves*, and they were making noise all through Queens with their ruthless ways of getting money and dealing with violations, but Chi Chi didn't give a fuck about how much noise they were making anywhere else in Queens. He wasn't about to let them eat in Baisley if Baisley wasn't eating.

148

"Anybody have any questions about what they are supposed to do?" Chi Chi asked as he looked around at his niggas crowded around him.

"Son, these niggas hit up Pops for getting money in his own building," Show Off said angrily. "So they have to feel it," he added, ready to put in work.

"You sure these disguises are going to work?" Eat 'Em Up asked as he plucked at the dirty rags they were all wearing.

"Son, they will never see us coming," Chi Chi said seriously. "We're dressed like homeless people looking to get high. The element of surprise is ours. So use it to your advantage," he added as he locked eyes with everyone in his clique.

Chi Chi ran an up-and-coming clique of hustlers and shooters out of Baisley Park called the *Ghetto Gunners*. He, Show Off, Pops, Khaos, Black Face, Eat 'Em Up, and Red Star all grew up together, and they repped their projects like it was a badge of honor. They were seeing money fast and steady until them *Forty* niggas violated and moved in on their turf. Now it was time to rectify the situation.

"In and out. Don't waste time playing around with these clowns . . . ," Chi Chi said seriously. "Dead 'em and get missing."

"Let's move," Khaos said before crossing the street towards the projects.

They all moved with limps, hunched over to play the part of derelicts. Anyone watching would've seen a group of homeless men shuffling into the projects.

Chi Chi and Red Star entered building one, ready to put in work. They were headed for the elevators when they were stopped by a nigga they recognized as being a part of *Forty Thieves*. Chi Chi's heart started beating fast as he reached into his coat and gripped his pistol, thinking they had been recognized. He spotted the walkie-talkie on the lookout's hip as soon as he turned around and was about to blow the nigga's wig back, but relaxed when the dude opened his mouth.

"What y'all two stinkin' mu'fuckas want?" The look on his face was one of utter disgust.

"We trying to cop something to smoke, my man," Chi Chi said, resisting his urge to shoot this nigga in his face.

"Let me see some money, bum-ass niggas," the dude said seriously.

He wasn't about to send no begging ass niggas up to the top.

Chi Chi showed him sixty dollars and held onto his patience. The nigga was really getting under his skin, but he kept his eyes on the prize.

"Oh, them checks must've came today, B," the dude said, laughing. "Go up to the eighth floor. Somebody will meet you," he added as he used the walkie-talkie to alert the top floor.

Chi Chi and Red Star hopped onto the elevator and pressed the eighth floor.

"I hate them niggas," Red Star spat once they were on their way up to the top floor.

"Chill, son. We're about to get right," Chi Chi said, eager to bust his gun.

The doors to the elevator opened up, and they stepped off to find a man standing there, waiting on them.

"Which one of you got the money?" he asked them with an attitude.

"I do," Chi Chi said, wondering where he was going with his question.

"Well, you're the only one going in," he said seriously. "I'm not letting both of you stinkin' mufukas in there and getting my ass chewed out," he added, wrinkling his nose up as their stench assaulted his nose.

"Man, this nigga might try to shit me out of my stuff," Red Star argued, pointing at Chi Chi.

He needed to be inside of the apartment too.

"I don't give a fuck. Only one of you is going inside," the man said seriously.

He crossed his arms across his chest and scowled at them.

Red Star was about to argue further, but Chi Chi stopped him.

"I'ma go in and handle business. Just make sure you ready to go when I finish. Leave this bitch smoking," he said, giving Red Star a look, hoping he caught the hidden meaning in his message.

"A'ight, man, but hurry up, 'cause I'll slice his ass up," Red Star responded, letting Chi Chi know he was on point.

"I'm ready," Chi Chi told the man when everything was settled.

The man looked at them curiously, but whatever it was he was thinking, he let it go as he turned and used a special knock to let the people inside know it was him. The door opened up to show one of the biggest niggas Chi Chi and Red Star had ever seen standing there. He looked like John Coffey from the *Green Mile*, only he carried two revolvers in shoulder holsters.

"This stinking mu'fucka trying to cop," the man told the Green Mile look-alike as he pointed at Chi Chi.

The big man stared at Chi Chi for a few seconds before stepping aside and letting him in. Chi Chi walked into the apartment with his exaggerated limp and took in the scene in front of him. Sitting at a table in the kitchen was the traitorous bitch Kenya, who was letting the *Forty* niggas use her apartment to hustle out of, playing cards with another female and two niggas he assumed correctly was *Forty Thieves*. He really didn't give a fuck who they were because everybody inside the apartment would die.

"Give me your money," the big man ordered in a voice that sounded like thunder.

He took the money, walked over to one of the men playing cards, and handed it to him.

"Kenya, go grab three from the back so we can get this stinking looking mu'fucka up outta here," the man said, causing the room to explode in laughter.

"I got you, baby," she said before getting up and sashaying to one of the back bedrooms.

"Yo, son, my man, you look like you need a bath," the comedian joked, causing more laughter.

Chi Chi smirked in acknowledgement of his lame-ass joke as he made note of where everyone was standing or sitting. He knew who his first victim would be—The Green Mile was standing against the wall with his tree-trunk arms crossed over his chest, with his hands resting close to the butts of his pistols. He looked up when he heard Kenya re-enter the room and saw that she was looking at him a little too closely. All at the same time, recognition lit up her eyes, and she started screaming. He pulled his pistol, a 9mm Beretta, and started the massacre. His first three slugs caught Green Mile in the chest, taking him out of the fight immediately. One of the men sitting at the table tried to reach for a gun lying near but caught a slug to the face. The comedian tried to use the other female as a shield, hoping to appeal to his mercy, but he didn't know mercy was a foreign word in Baisley. Chi Chi pumped a slug into the female's face, and when she slumped in the nigga's arms, pumped two hot ones in his face. He looked over at Kenya, who was whimpering, started begging when she saw that his attention locked onto her.

"Please, Chi Chi, please don't kill me," she cried out.

"I told you about fucking with them *Forty* niggas, so it's no understanding with me," Chi Chi said before he silenced her forever.

He walked to the front door and opened it. He stepped out to find Red Star pulling the lookout's tongue through the slit in his throat. He chuckled at Red Star's crazy ass. He loved his razor and never left home without it.

"Let's go, dog," he told him as he checked the hallway to make sure no one was trying to be a concerned citizen.

He would murder whoever got nosy. He wasn't taking any chances. They made it back to the elevator without encountering anybody. Chi Chi kept his gun inside his front jacket pocket as the elevator made it back down to the ground floor. When the door opened, he spotted the nigga they had first encountered when they walked into the building trying to talk to some chickenhead.

"Hey," he started to say when he spotted them, but stopped when he noticed they weren't walking with the limps and hunchbacks they were rocking earlier.

At the same time, his walkie-talkie exploded with news of what was going on in Baisley Park Projects. *Forty Thieves* niggas were dying, and when he locked eyes with Chi Chi, he knew he was soon to join them. He tried to reach for his pistol, but Chi Chi was already moving.

Chi Chi didn't bother to bring his pistol out of his coat but raised his pocket and emptied the rest of the clip in the nigga and the bitch he was talking to. He killed her just for giving the clown the time of day. Before he and Red Star exited the building, their limps and hunchbacks were back in effect. They kept their faces down to the ground so they couldn't be easily identified as they made their way across the street and into Baisley Pond Park. They heard the sirens in the distance getting closer, so they hurried to their backpacks they had stashed in the park earlier. They shipped out of their disguises and put on the clothes and shoes they had inside of the bookbags. Red Star dressed in a red Amiri sweatsuit with a pair of Uptowns on his feet. Chi Chi dressed in a black Dior tracksuit with a pair of construction Timbs. He took the dirty turban off his head and shook his locks free. It felt good to let his hair hit the air after being wrapped up for so long. They stuffed their disguises into the bookbags and slung them over their shoulders. Now they looked just like any other student walking the streets, except their auras let people know to mind their business. They blended into the crowd that was gathering in front of the building they had just left ten minutes earlier. Chi Chi wanted to hear what people were saying. If anyone had identified them or not. If people were trying to snitch, and there was no better place to get the information than the project grapevine.

"Girl, they say it's dead bodies strewn all over the eighth floor," an older lady said to her friend.

"Hmph, it's a damn shame people are not even safe in their own apartments," her friend said, shaking her head sadly.

"Damn, somebody lit them niggas up," a Baisley hoodrat said, excited by the violence.

"Fuck them niggas, yo, straight up," a lame said vehemently.

He was glad them *Forty* niggas had caught it because one of them was sexing his baby moms, and he been too pussy to do anything about it.

"Who did it?" an old wino asked curiously.

He knew the number to Crime Stoppers by heart.

"The only people I seen were two bums leaving the building earlier," a female said, standing on her tiptoes to get a better view of the bodies being rolled out on stretchers.

Chi Chi had heard enough. He tapped Red Star on the shoulder, and they headed towards their rendezvous spot. He pulled his phone out of his pocket and checked on his people.

"Show Off, you good?"

"I was grazed by one of them clowns, but I'm good. I'm at Minnie's spot on Hillside Ave."

"Black Face, you good?"

"Me and Khaos are lounging around at Tiffany's spot."

"Eat 'Em Up," he called the last of his team.

"I'm in Cambria Heights at Tasha's spot, waiting on you and Star. Oh, and just to let you know, Tasha is pissed about something."

"We on the way," Chi Chi said before hanging up.

He was satisfied now that his team was secure. They would meet later to figure out their next move because he knew Troop would retaliate, and they needed to be ready.

Chapter 16

Eileen Jackson was floating on clouds. It had been a week since she had been elected Governor of North Carolina, and it was still hard for her to believe it. Everything Shapphire had promised her would happen had happened. Candidates who had a chance to win the election suddenly found themselves withdrawing from the race because of scandals they couldn't recover from. When she threw her name into the race, the move was met with a lot of skepticism because she was a general unknown. Political insiders dismissed her as a long shot, and some gave her no chance at all. They figured that her campaign would be underfunded and understaffed, but Shapphire worked her magic again. She had made sure that her campaign was financially able to do anything she wanted to do, and she had enough staff to run a department store. When the contributions to her coffers from known and unknown supporters became public knowledge, the whispers started up. She was hearing rumors that she was using inappropriate funds, but before those rumors could gain traction, the two front runners for the Governor's Mansion, John Micheals and William Beaufort, were lit with two of the biggest scandals in the North Carolina political arena since the exposure of John Edwards' mistress and love child. John Micheals was fighting to stay indictment-free after his proclivity for underage girls was exposed via pictures delivered to the Raleigh News and Observer newspaper. William Beaufort obviously had an affinity for gay clubs. New reporters were staked out in front of one such club and caught him leaving with a drag queen. It made for an interesting segment on the nightly news, so she was suddenly the most unlikely front runner. With Shapphire Stone pulling strings and calling in favors and the enigmatic Yero Owens filling her coffers with unlimited funds, she won in a landslide. The public adored her even as her contemporaries tried to tear her down by calling her inexperienced and a novice, but it didn't stop women and minorities from voting for her. When it was all said and done, she was the new Governor of North Carolina. The intercom on her desk buzzed, snapping her out of her reverie. She walked over and hit the button to respond.

"Yes, Janny."

"Ms. Stone is here to see you," her secretary responded back.

"Send her in, please," Eileen said with a smile on her face.

She walked around her desk and awaited her friend. When her office door opened and Shapphire walked in, she opened her arms and enveloped her in a hug.

"Thank you," she whispered in her ear.

"No thanks is needed, Eileen. I just delivered what I promised," Shapphire said, returning the hug. "Yero send his regards," she added as she stepped out of the embrace.

"Speaking of which . . . ," Eileen said with a sly look on her face as she leaned against the desk and folded her arms across her chest . . . "When will I meet my mysterious benefactor?" she asked seriously.

"He doesn't think it's prudent to be seen with you. He wishes to remain in the background and let us do his bidding," Shapphire said airily.

She was watching Eileen's face as she talked, and she saw exactly what she thought she would see—defiance.

"Do his bidding?" Eileen asked skeptically.

She didn't like the sound of that. She wasn't anyone's puppet.

"Yes, his bidding. You are on his team whether you want to be or not, Eileen. Without his money and my connections, you wouldn't be in the position you're currently in," Shapphire said seriously.

Eileen was silent for a few minutes as she digested what she had just been told. Her face remained expressionless as she came to her decision.

"I don't know what type of hold he had on you, but I refuse to be anyone's puppet, Shapphire. I appreciate everything he's done for me so far, but I will not have strings attached to me during my tenure as Governor."

Shapphire wasn't surprised at anything coming out of her mouth. In fact, she expected it. She stood up, ready to go now that her fact-finding mission was complete.

"I'll have Yero call you. It seems as if you two have a few things to discuss," she said, locking eyes with Eileen.

Eileen held the stare with Shapphire, knowing she was a formidable opponent, but at that moment, that fact wasn't enough to sway her decision, so she smirked and said, "You have him do that."

Shapphire didn't bother to respond as she spun on her heels and left the office. Before she made it to her car, she had her cell phone to her ear, updating Yero on the situation. After giving her report, she hung up and put the phone back into her purse. Before getting into her car, she looked up to where she knew Eileen was standing at her window, looking down at her. She smirked and nodded before sliding into her brand new Mercedes-Benz AMG S 600. She pulled off without a second thought to Eileen and her insubordination. She would fall in line. Everyone did whether they wanted to or not.

Eileen watched Shapphire's car until she could no longer see it. She turned away from the window with the picture of Shapphire's smirk stuck in her mind. It struck her as sinister, almost as if she was sending a message. Whatever it was, Eileen wasn't taking any chances. She picked up the phone on her desk and grabbed her Rolodex. People in high places owed her some favors, so she decided to call them in. She had a feeling she was going to need them.

***

"What the fuck you mean, Joe?" Bless screamed at Ceaz. "You telling me you're not going to your own mother's funeral, my mother, and sons' funerals. You're going to miss that?" He looked at Ceaz as if he was looking at a stranger.

"Joe, I'm telling you to stop sleeping on this bitch because she is far from soft," Ceaz said, trying to reason with him.

He had a feeling Dynasty was still lurking somewhere, waiting to pop off.

"I told you from the jump not to switch up on that bitch and beat her for her money," he added, letting it be known who was at fault.

"Fuck all of that, nigga. The only thing I want to know is, are you going to the funerals?" Bless asked, staring at his best friend in the eyes.

Ceaz was quiet for a few minutes as he locked gazes with Bless. He already knew that he wasn't going to the funerals because his gut told him not to go, and he trusted his instincts, but he knew his decision not to go to the funerals would sever their relationship forever. He shook his head *no*, unable to say it aloud. Bless looked at him and smirked. He shook his head but wasn't surprised at all. Ceaz had never been built for violence. He loved to get money, and he loved to bust his gun; that's why they made a good team, but best friend or not, he couldn't fuck with a nigga who whined about going to his own mother's funeral. Any man that turned his back on his family was a coward, point-blank, period.

"Joe, you acting like a cold pussy. If you don't show up to the funerals, don't you or this bitch show your faces back in the Gardens," he said seriously.

He bumped into Ceaz as he made his way out of the apartment.

Ceaz wasn't moved by anything Bless said because he didn't care. He wanted to live, and he felt like Dynasty was still waiting to get at them. He never planned on going back to the Gardens anyway. When he heard the front door slam, he turned to Kandy, who was staring at him apprehensively, and asked, "You want to take a trip?"

"Where we going?" she asked, wanting to also get out of D.C.

"I don't know, but money isn't an ointment for the scars I'm carrying. It's better than a Band-Aid, though," Ceaz said, chuckling as he bent down to pick up two duffel bags full of cash lying at his feet. "Let's just ride," he said seriously.

"Let's ride then," Kandy said, grabbing a few necessities before leading the way out of the apartment.

Ceaz knew Kandy was a jump-off, and he didn't know what kind of life he could have with her, or if he would keep her around long enough to find out, but watching her ass jump as he followed her out of the apartment reminded him that her pussy was good enough to take his mind off of his problems for a little while.

***

Jah looked over at Ya Ya's sleeping form and smirked. Ever since he had caught her with them niggas at that restaurant, he had her ass on lockdown. He wouldn't even allow her to go outside because the disrespect he felt that day had him ready to murder somebody. The more he thought about that day, the more he wanted to beat her ass again, but he controlled his anger and let her sleep. He slipped out of bed and headed to the bathroom. After relieving himself, he followed his nose to the kitchen. Even though it was past noon, Marie—Ya Ya's mother—was cooking breakfast. He stood in the doorway and watched her as she moved around the kitchen. He felt his dick get hard as her ass bounced around in the robe she was wearing. Ya Ya was built like a brickhouse, but she inherited it from her mother. In his opinion the original was always better. He walked upon her until his dick was pressed into the crack of her ass. He smiled when she jumped.

"Boy, you scared me," she said after she looked over her shoulder and saw that it was him. "You almost made me burn this French toast. You hungry?" she asked, trying to ignore his hard dick pressed against her ass.

"Yeah, I'm hungry but not for food," he said before kissing her on the neck.

He reached around and slipped his fingers inside of her panty-less pussy.

"We can't do this, Jah," Marie whispered as she swallowed her moan. "Ya Ya is in the back bedroom. She might hear us," she added as that familiar guilt she felt for fucking her daughter's boyfriend washed over her.

"She's sleep and it doesn't matter because both of you belong to me." Jah said arrogantly as he lifted her robe up to her waist revealing one of God's greatest creations—a big juicy ass.

He pulled his dick out and slid into her wet, tight pussy.

"Damn, this pussy good," he grunted as he pounded her out, causing her ass cheeks to smack against his thighs.

Marie tried to bite her lip to keep from screaming out, but it was impossible to hold back when she was getting dicked down so good. She kept looking over her shoulder as she continued to enjoy the dick to make sure her daughter didn't walk in on them. Even though she didn't want to hurt her daughter, the fact that she was in the back bedroom while she was fucking Jah added to the excitement and had her pussy cumming like never before.

Jah saw that she was making an effort to be quiet, but he wanted Ya Ya to hear her and cut the stove off before they set a fire. Then he grabbed a stick of butter sitting on the counter and rub it around her asshole. He pulled out of her pussy and slid into her tight asshole. He smirked when she screamed out.

"Whose body is this?" he asked as he drilled her tight hole.

Marie knew what he was trying to do, and she wanted to fight it, but she couldn't. She was forty-five years old getting fucked by a young boy who was making her feel like she had never felt before in her life, and to be honest she didn't want to fight. She wanted to be fucked. She apologized in her mind to her daughter as she answered his question.

"This your body, papi," she moaned as she started fingering herself.

"Who do you belong to?" Jah asked as he went deep.

He was feeling like Scarface.

"This is yours Jah, all yours. Oh my God." Marie screamed as she exploded into another orgasm.

"Always remember that you're my bitch," Jah told her as he pulled out and came all over her ass.

He used her robe to wipe his dick off. He reached over her, grabbed a piece of French toast, a piece of sausage, wrapped it up like a pig in the blanket, and started eating it as he walked out of the kitchen with a limp in his walk like Magic Don Juan.

Marie's body was still shaking with the aftershocks of her last orgasm. Tears cascaded down her cheeks as she thought about what she had just done. She hated herself. She ran to the bathroom and slammed the door. As much as she hated hurting her daughter, she hated even more the fact that if Jah walked into the bathroom and wanted to fuck her again, she would do it without question.

Ya Ya had listened to Jah disrespect her in the most disgusting fashion. The hatred she felt for him was now shared by her mother. As far as she was concerned, she was now an orphan. Jah walked back into their room and once again she feigned sleep. She didn't want to give him the satisfaction of seeing her pain. When he dressed and left the room again, she breathed a sigh of relief. She knew she had to escape him, or she was going up for a murder charge.

***

Eileen was getting ready to leave her office for the day when her phone rang. She didn't recognize the number on her Caller I.D. but decided to answer anyway.

"Hello."

"May I speak with Ms. Jackson, please?"

"This is she. Who's calling?" she didn't recognize the voice.

"This is Yero," he said.

"And to what do I owe the pleasure?" she purred, not at all surprised to hear from him.

"Shapphire told me of your earlier conversation and suggested we get together," he said truthfully.

"Oh, is Shapphire giving orders now?" she asked slyly, fishing for information.

She wanted to decline his invitation, but her curiosity got the best of her. She had to meet him at least one time.

"We're partners . . . ," Yero answered, chuckling at her pathetic attempt to milk him for information.

"So are we going to meet?" he asked, like she really didn't have a choice.

Eileen didn't like his tone, but she found herself agreeing.

"When and where?" she asked, twisting the phone cord around her finger as she tried to imagine what he looked like. *Probably not my type*, she thought.

"Do you know Komoto's?" Yero asked.

"Yes," she answered, silently applauding his selection.

"Friday at eight," he said before hanging up.

Eileen frowned at the phone in her hand before hanging it up. Despite her misgivings, she was going to finally get a chance to meet the mysterious Yero Owens.

Chapter 17

Bless was starting to relax a little bit more and more as the funeral progressed because it was starting to look as if Dynasty wasn't going to show her face. During the last two days as he prepared for the funerals, he racked his brain trying to figure out how Dynasty would attack, and the funeral was the most obvious place to strike, so he prepared for that eventuality because, despite what Ceaz said, he didn't think she was weak—or at least, not anymore. The fact that she murdered their families proved that she was more dangerous than he gave her credit for, and he was on point because he wasn't about to run and hide like his ex-best friend. He wasn't scared of no bitch, period. The thought of Ceaz turning his back on him because he thought something was going to happen pissed him off, and that was unforgivable. To make matters worse, he had heard that Ceaz had left town with Kandy, the neighborhood thot. If he caught either one of them in D.C. again, it will be some slow singing and flower bringing going on. He refocused back on the events going on around him and relaxed even more when he saw it coming to a close. He had shooters strategically placed around the church waiting for that bitch to show her face so he could give her a closed casket like she did his family. He was a gangsta, and he now saw her as a gangstress, so he was on his shit. He looked back towards the front of the church and felt his resolve harden. The four closed caskets, especially the two little ones holding his sons, made his stomach boil and grit his teeth. The sight had him wishing she would show up so he could release the beast on her. The night before, he had visited the bodies of his mother, two sons, and Ceaz's mother—his godmother—to see them one last time because he knew that the caskets would be closed during the service. When he saw the damage done to his family, he cried like he hadn't since he was a little boy when his Nana died. He looked at the posters he had placed on top of each casket showing them as they were in life. He wanted to remember them as they were, not as they are now, but he knew that nothing could erase the images stuck in his head from seeing them last night. At that moment, he hated Ceaz more than Dynasty for making him go through this alone. When the preacher told everyone to bow their heads, he and his shooters kept theirs up, searching and seeking for something to destroy. When it was time to carry the caskets, he made sure he was a pallbearer on his mother's casket. Hers was the first one in line with his sons next, and his godmother pulled up the rear. He had shooters on his mother's casket with him, and when they walked out of the church, their instincts were locked in on any and everything around them. If it looked like it didn't belong, they would make it disappear. Bless was so focused on his surroundings that at first he missed *it*, but when it happened again, he told everybody to stop.

"What the fuck was that?" one of his shooters asked when it happened again, so he knew he wasn't tripping.

"Sit this mu'fucka down and get your guns out," Bless ordered.

There's no way, he thought as they sat the casket down on the ground.

"When I open this casket, if it's not the dead body of my mother, fill it up with hollow tips," he told his shooters.

Bless was torn; on one hand, he wanted to shoot the casket up without opening it, but what if his mother was trying to get out? He looked at the casket for a few seconds with trepidation before unlocking the top. Before he could lift it up, all hell broke loose around him. He looked up and saw two females with locks astride two Kawasaki street bikes shooting automatic weapons into the crowd milling around the church. They weren't discriminating with their shots, either. They were killing the old, the young, the healthy, and the infirm. With his heart about to beat out of his chest, he slowly lifted the top of the casket up. He breathed a sigh of relief when his eyes saw his mother's resting face. He was about to close the casket and rejoin the firefight when something caught his eye that made his heart skip a beat. Her hands were encased in a pair of black leather gloves. His eyes travelled back up to his mother's face and found her eyes open, staring at him with a smirk on her face. Before he could move or say anything, it was too late.

"Your bitch ass thought it was over," Dynasty said seriously.

She pulled the mini Uzi from beside her stomach and let off a three-shot burst into his face. Before anyone could react, she jumped out of the casket and killed two of the shooters trying to escape her wrath. She wanted to kill everybody who attended the funeral, but she saw Aza and Light waiting for her to come on. She let off another three rounds into another shooter before running over and jumping onto the back of the bike Aza was driving. Aza didn't waste time moving. She took off. The police were converging on the scene, and she didn't want to get into a high-speed chase. One of the police cruisers saw them trying to flee the scene and gave chase. Dynasty turned a little and emptied the clip into his windshield, causing him to sideswipe a parked car and flip over, blocking the street and stopping any further pursuit. They followed their planned escape route and made it to the Southview Terrace Projects, where they had a Ford minivan stashed. They gave their bikes to some teenagers and got missing. Before getting on the highway, they stopped at a gas station and changed clothes. They wrapped the guns up in their old clothes after pouring bleach over everything and disposed of it all in a dumpster. Dynasty took off the synthetic mask she was wearing and looked at it with pride before also dousing it in bleach and throwing it in the dumpster. All three of them had on eyeglasses, cardigan sweaters, long skirts, and flat-bottom shoes. The police wouldn't dare try to stop three school teachers on the way home from an education convention.

***

The Star Bar in Raleigh was jumping. It was Friday night, and the ballers, bad bitches, and fronting-ass niggas were out in full force. The Triangle was well represented. Raleigh, Durham, and Chapel Hill were in the house, but it was Durham and Raleigh who were making the most noise. Niggas were repping their cities, bottles were being popped, and women were choosing. New York was also in the building, and they were making their presence felt.

"See, this is why I didn't want to go to the club with Niko and G," Taji said with an attitude as she took a sip of her *Blue Motorcycle*. "They hating so hard that niggas scared to dance with us. Standing there with mean mugs, screw-facing every nigga who approach us like we not grown," she added, rolling her eyes in their direction.

"They act like they're our boyfriends instead of our brothers, younger brothers at that," Stari said as she flirted with some dude at the other end of the bar. "Besides, if these niggas letting some weak-ass mean mug stop them from getting a piece of this—" she smacked her juicy ass—"then I don't want they asses anyway. I need a real gangsta in my life," she added seriously.

"Well, I guess we're going to play the bar all night then," Taji said contemptuously as she eyed a couple of cuties eyeing her.

If her brothers disappeared, she would be able to get her groove on like she wanted to, but so far, it looked like the night would turn out to be a wash.

"Pipe down, baby girl, the night is still young," Stari said, rocking her hips to the song. "Let's dance together." She grabbed her sister's hand and dragged her to the dance floor. "Last time I check, my milkshake still brings all the boys to the yard," she added as she started grinding on Taji.

Taji looked at her brothers and laughed at the looks on their faces. *I might have some fun after all*, she thought as she grabbed Stari's face and kissed her, bringing whistles and catcalls from the crowd.

***

Consuela was glad that her children had decided to go out that night as she looked at herself in the full-length mirror, because she knew that if they saw her all dressed up and glowing, they would have questions that she couldn't, or wouldn't, answer. She couldn't remember the last time she had spent the day pampering herself in preparation for a date, but she had gotten her hair done, a manicure and pedicure, a wax, her eyebrows arched, and she even bought some new lingerie from Victoria's Secret. She was feeling beautiful, and it was finally time to stop deceiving herself. She looked at her reflection again and grabbed the locket that sat in the hollow of her throat. It had been over a year since her husband was killed, and she thought about the events that led to his demise. She only had one regret: leaving her kids fatherless, but she didn't regret loving another man. Manny rejected her love in the name of a dollar and forced her to love another. She chose to stop running and chose instead to live. She chose to be happy, and being with Ichiro Tanaka did that. She grabbed her gold clutch and her car keys before she left the house. Life was calling.

***

"Mem don't see why ye have ta go see dis woman," Suai said seriously as she drove the car.

She glanced over at Yero in the passenger seat and saw that he was smirking at her.

"What?" she asked, sucking her teeth as she rolled her eyes at him. She didn't have too many female mannerisms, but the ones she did have seemed to only surface when she was dealing with him.

"What did I tell you about that jealous shit?" he asked quietly. "I told you we all have positions to play in life. You should know this. You showed me you were ready to be my queen, so I gave you that, but the queen is only as strong as the king allows her to be. By you questioning me, you're not playing your position correctly. 'Dis woman,' as you call her, is the new Governor of North Carolina. I'm securing our position in life, Suai. Hustling is only a stepping stone for us. So stop the jealousy, 'cause it doesn't suit you at all. You have my loyalty, Suai. Just look at how these females acting now that you are in position. I don't play when it come to who I trust, especially with my other half because she is my reflection, and I am hers. So I'm telling you now to play your position or get out of the game," he said seriously.

He knew she was digesting what he had just said because they thought just alike. That's why she was in position and others weren't.

"Mem got ye, bwoy," she said quietly after she had processed his words. "Mem don't even act like dis, and mem gonna play mem position, but bwoy . . . ye mem drug," she added truthfully as she made a left turn into the private parking garage Yero used downtown.

She showed the attendant their paid pass, and the arm bar was raised to allow them entrance. She followed the ramp to the top level as she thought of what Yero said. She knew that she was acting out of character, but when it came to him, she couldn't seem to help it. He was the only man besides her father who could make her deal with emotions. She glanced over at him, wanting him to say something, but she knew that he wouldn't until he had something to say.

Yero had noticed that the parking garage wasn't as bright as it usually was when he came through. He looked up and noticed that the majority of the light fixtures were busted out. His guard instantly went up, and he started paying closer attention to his surroundings. When they entered the third level, he was looking to his right and saw a group of men dressed in business suits stuffing a body inside the trunk of a car. Yero instantly knew he wasn't supposed to see what he was seeing. He was a witness to a crime unintentionally, but he knew that wouldn't matter to the people he just saw committing the crime. Problems could arise from this, but it couldn't be helped. He figured they were mafia-type white men cleaning up a problem until one of the men turned and looked directly at him. Even though the lighting was dim, he could tell that the man wasn't white but Asian. The man was sending a message with his eyes, and Yero got the message loud and clear, but he refused to break his stare off until they were out of sight.

"What were dem men doing, baby?" Suai asked after they were out of the way.

She saw him staring at the men on the third level, and the way his body tensed up, she knew they could be potential problems, so she wanted to know what was on his mind.

"Niggas were stuffing their trunk with dead weight, but it's not our business unless they make it our business," Yero had a bad feeling in the pit of his stomach, and that feeling had him checking the passenger side mirror to see if they were being pursued.

Suai stayed silent as she found a parking space on the fifth level to pull into. Before she could turn the engine off, Yero was out of the car and standing at the entrance ramp with gun in hand. The way he was standing made it known that he was expecting company. She pulled her gun and stood beside him, ready to kill and die with her king.

"We expecting trouble?" she asked seriously as she peered down the dark ramp.

"Better safe than sorry, Suai," he said quietly as he gripped his pistol tightly.

He took a deep breath and forced himself to calm down because he knew that one mistake could cost them their lives. He waited ten more minutes before he spoke again.

"Leave the car we rode in and take the Charger back with you." He didn't want to take any chances.

Suai wanted to ask him what was on his mind, but she held her tongue as their conversation from earlier marinated in her mind. She knew he wouldn't tell her anything wrong, and she knew he wouldn't keep anything from her, either. So she kissed him on the cheek and walked over to the coal-black Dodge Charger Daytona. After gaining his trust, he had given her the keys to the kingdom. She had keys to all of the cars and stash spots. Something she didn't take for granted. She adjusted the driver's seat, sat her pistol in her lap, and pulled out. She slowed to a stop beside Yero and hit the button to let the window down.

"Be safe, baby," she said quietly as she peered up at him.

She was still amazed at how strong their connection was. It was like they were made for each other.

"I'll be home later on tonight," he said as he bent down and lightly kissed her on the lips. He was amazed at how fast she had worked her way into his heart, but every test he threw at her, she passed with flying colors. "Keep your eyes and ears open. Watch everything around you." He stood up and tapped on the roof of the car.

Suai rolled her window back up and pulled off. Yero watched her taillights until they disappeared down the exit ramp. He looked at his watch and knew that he was going to be late, but that couldn't be helped. He walked over to his cars and wondered which one he should pull out for the occasion. He had five luxury cars—a 2021 Mercedes-Benz S600 the color of champagne, a 2022 brandy-wine red Audi

R8, a 2020 silver Chevrolet Corvette Z06, a 2023 midnight blue Chevrolet Suburban 271, and the Dodge Charger that Suai pulled off in—but he wasn't like most hustlers with money. He didn't flash on niggas trying to stunt and shine because that made niggas hate and covet what he worked hard for. So he kept it low-key and rode around in his hooptie and left people speculating about how much money he was really making. He finally decided on the Audi. He hopped in and pulled out. When he reached the third level, it was empty of any Asians, so he put them out of his mind as he sped off toward his destination. He had moves to make.

***

Casper was sitting in his '96 cherry red bubble Caprice on 26-inch chrome Ashanti's, macking a sexy redbone in the parking lot of the *Star Bar* when he spotted TyJay, a hustler from Kentwood in Raleigh, who owed him and P.R. money for some work they had fronted him a couple of months ago. The nigga had been ducking them for the past month because he didn't want to pay them, but now he was at the club with an entourage like he was balling. Casper's eyes grew red as he watched the nigga shined up with jewelry he knew he bought with their money. He pushed the redbone from between his legs and grabbed his cell phone.

"What's wrong, baby?" the redbone asked when she noticed his change of attitude.

She planned on drinking off of him all night.

"Bitch, get your bird ass out of my face," he barked as he dialed P.R. up.

"Well, fuck you too then," she said before sucking her teeth and stomping off.

Casper didn't even look her way anymore as he waited for his partner to pick up the phone. His eyes were locked on his prey as he paid his way into the club. It was a reason he was called Casper; he turned niggas into ghosts.

"You'll never guess who at the club tonight . . ."

***

Puerto Rico was on his way to get some pussy when his phone rang. He was about to ignore it until he saw Casper's name across the screen.

"What's good, bra?" he asked when he picked up.

He reached over and cut the stereo down so he could hear.

"Who?" he asked curiously.

"That bitch nigga TyJay at the Star Bar stunting and iced up," Casper said angrily.

He was ready to get it popping.

"What!" P.R. yelled as he sat up in his seat. His high from that blunt of Runtz he had just smoked was gone. "Wait on me, and make sure that bitch-ass nigga stay there," he instructed Casper before hanging up.

He pulled a U-turn in the middle of the street, causing other drivers to swerve and blow their horns, but he didn't give a fuck because he was on a mission. His booty call would have to wait because he had some better pussy to fuck.

Chapter 18

Consuela pulled up to the valet parking at the Japanese restaurant *Komoto's* and waited behind a few cars in front of her. When it was her turn, a young man rushed over to help her out of her car and take the keys from her. She blushed as she gave him her hand and stepped out of the car because his eyes were roaming her body like he wanted to eat her up. The young man had to be her daughter's age, but she was pleased with his attention because it let her know she still had it even after giving birth to four kids. She was feeling so good that night, she decided to be a little daring. She squeezed his hand in hers, stepped close to his body, and whispered in his ear.

"Do you like older women?" She stepped back and lightly chuckled when she saw that he was blushing.

She also noticed that he was speechless and decided to save him.

"Don't worry, baby, you're too young for me, but you are cute, though," she said before disengaging their hands and sashaying into the sexy restaurant entrance.

She could feel the eyes of men—married and single— following her movements, and that made her switch her hips a little more as she approached the maître d'.

"Reservations for Tanaka," she told him.

She gave him a little smile when she noticed that he was having a hard time keeping his eyes above her neckline.

"Yes, madam. Mr. Tanaka called and said he would be a little late, but he said you are to make yourself comfortable and feel free to order without him," he said nervously.

"Follow me please, and I will lead you to your table," he added before turning to lead the way.

Consuela noticed that his whole demeanor changed the moment she uttered the Tanaka name. She had forgotten just how much fear and respect that name evoked, but one thing she didn't forget was how protected that name made her feel. She followed the maître d' as they wove their way between the dining patrons until they reached her table. After pulling out her seat and making sure she was comfortable, the maître d' asked her if she would like anything while she waited.

"Yes, a glass of Château Lafite or Château Margaux, please. The year doesn't matter," she told him as she looked around the restaurant to make sure she didn't see anyone she recognized because, until she told her children—if she ever did—secrecy was of the utmost importance. Even though the table was secluded, she was still nervous about being seen in public with Ichiro—hence the glass of wine she just ordered.

"Here you go, madam," the maître d' said as he placed the glass of wine in front of her.

"Do you need anything else?" he asked, anxious to please her.

"No. Thank you," she said as she looked up at him and flashed a brief smile that let him know that he was dismissed.

She waited until he had scurried away before she picked up her wine and took a sip. She sighed as the red wine slid down her throat and instantly calmed her nerves. The French knew how to make a wine that was like an erotic massage to the tongue. She took another sip as she settled in to await her destiny.

***

"Girl, I'm getting tired of dancing and kissing you," Taji said, smiling at her sister.

"These niggas down here scared to dance with us. I hate pussy, soft-ass niggas, word up," Stari said as she frowned and rolled her eyes at some niggas who were standing on the wall staring at them.

"That's why I didn't want to come with our brothers," Taji said, disgusted at the tactics Niko and Guardian were using.

They were standing at the edge of the dance floor with their arms crossed, mean-mugging any niggas who even acted like they were interested in touching them. She was more aggravated than mad because if these North Carolina niggas were too pussy to dance with them because of a screw face, then she didn't want them, but it did make for one whack night at the club. So she was having fun with her sister, making niggas' dick hard.

"I'm gonna go check them two niggas because they fucking up our flow. It's been months since I've had some dick, and I'm anxious to test some N.C. dick out," Stari said, laughing.

She started to walk over to her brothers and tell them about themselves, but a hand lightly grabbed her, so she turned around to curse him out, and she was about to let him have it until she saw he was a light-skinned cutie.

"You was ready to cuss my ass out if I was ugly," Puerto Rico said, laughing when he saw the look on her face. "My name P.R., ma," he added, introducing himself.

"You damn right I was about to bless you out, but you are a cutie, so I'll let you pass this time," Stari said playfully. "My name is Stari," she added, introducing herself.

"You are in the North—cock it back now, ma, not New York," P.R. said, smirking at her.

"No matter where I am, I'll always be New York through and through," she said as she danced with him.

She looked over her shoulder and saw her sister dancing with a tall, brown-skinned, rugged nigga with cornrows, and from what she could see, he was a cutie, too.

"Let me guess, that's your homeboy dancing with my sister?" she asked, nodding in their direction.

P.R. looked over his shoulder and saw Casper grinding with her sister. He smirked and turned back to her.

"Yeah, that's my nigga. We decided to show them two niggas—" he nodded at her brothers—"that they weren't scaring nobody. All that mean-mugging don't mean nothing. These other niggas might be scared, but me and my team don't scare easy. So we decided to see what's up with y'all. Are those your boyfriends?" he asked as he returned the stares he was getting from them.

Stari looked over her shoulder and laughed at how tight her brothers were looking.

"Those are our brothers. They just like to show us how pussy niggas are. They always say that if niggas scared of a facial expression, then we don't need them, but they be fucking up our flow," she said as she got up in his space to feel how big his dick was.

"Well, I guess tonight is your lucky night, because baby, I'm far from pussy," P.R. said, pulling her close so she could feel his soldier trying to salute her.

"Hold that thought," Stari said as her pussy got wet. "I have to use the bathroom," she added before walking over to grab her sister and heading to the bathroom.

Casper walked over to P.R.

"What's up with them niggas?" he asked, nodding at Niko and Guardian.

"Those are their brothers, but fuck them. Let's head to the bar and wait on this bitch nigga to come out of VIP. If he is not out of there in the next twenty minutes, we are going to leave him in there with holes in his face," P.R. said before walking towards the bar.

Casper shot a quick smirk at Niko and Guardian before following him.

***

"This some bullshit," Guardian said, laughing as he counted out five blue faces and slapped them into Niko's outstretched palm.

"You knew the bet was lost when they started dancing and kissing each other." Niko smirked as he pocketed his newly won money.

"It's cool because I'll get back another way, but I'm about to go snatch one of these niggas' girls," Guardian said, eyeing some southern domes who were sucking on their straws very suggestively.

"Be easy, duke," Niko warned his little brother.

He knew how Guardian was with women, and he knew niggas in the club were already feeling some type of way about them. They were strapped, but he wanted to avoid trouble so soon after that episode at the restaurant a week ago. Trouble in the air though; he could smell it.

"I got you, big brother," Guardian assured him before walking off.

Niko was about to head towards the bar when the phone in his pocket started vibrating. He answered because the only person who would call that phone was Beza.

"Took you long enough," he said over the music.

***

Beza entered the *Star Bar* night club looking like a million bucks. She had on a burgundy halter-top Prada dress with a pair of Prada-stamped crocodile-leather pumps of the same color adorning her feet. Her hair was bone-straight down her back. It was so long and lustrous, females swore under their breaths that it was fake, but it was all hers. Her accessories complemented her outfit perfectly. Her diamond B charm sat perfectly atop her cleavage. Every time the lights hit it, rainbows reflected off of the VVS's. Her platinum J12 Chromatic Chanel watch gave her wrist an understated elegance. She checked the time and noticed that it was still early. She was happy to be out because ever since Jay-O, Towny, and Jah had told Hollywood about seeing her with Niko, he had been acting real emotional, and she couldn't take it anymore. The fact that she couldn't get Niko off her mind wasn't helping matters, either. She didn't usually go out by herself, but Jah had Ya Ya on house arrest, and she had to get away from Hollywood if only for a couple of hours. She walked to the end of the bar and ordered an apple martini. When she had her drink, she found a table and sat down. She was lifting her glass to her lips when she saw him. Across the room, Niko stood shoulder-to-shoulder with his younger brother, watching the dance floor. She tried to see who or what he was staring at, but the dance floor was too crowded. She reached into her purse, grabbed her cell phone and scanned through the contacts until she found the number he'd typed in that day at the restaurant. She remembered him telling her not to call the phone until she was ready. Despite a lot of doubts she was having, she was ready to cut ties with Hollywood and start something new. She took a deep breath and dialed the number as she kept her eyes on him.

"Where are you?" Niko asked, looking around the club after hearing the music on her end.

"I'm over by the bar, waving my hand in the air."

"Stay there," he ordered after he spotted her.

He hung up and made his way through the crowd. The night was starting to look up.

***

"Girl, we got some cuties out there waiting on us," Taji said, happy that the night wasn't a bust.

She was reapplying her lip gloss in the mirror.

"Papi got a big dick too girl," Stari said, pulling out her cell phone to check her messages.

She looked up when four loud ass girls walked into the bathroom. She turned up her nose in disgust at their hairdos and outfits. Bitches were busted. She decided to try Chi Chi again while he was on her mind. If he didn't answer this time, she would just tell Niko to forget about him.

**

"Son, we need to find a way to make some ends," Blackface said as he passed the blunt.

"Yeah, kid. Ever since we popped them *Forty* niggas, we been laying low. The whole objective was to dead them niggas and get money in our projects like before, but we holed up like bitches," Show Off said seriously.

"Speak for yourself on the bitch part, son," Khaos said with a smirk.

Chi Chi was about to open his mouth to allay their concerns when Tasha walked into the living room and threw a ringing cell phone into his lap.

"That bitch been calling you for days, nigga," she said before stomping back into her bedroom and slamming the door.

Chi Chi saw it was Stari calling and answered. It had been months since he had seen or heard from her.

"What's up, stranger?" he asked with a chuckle.

"Listen, you acting like you don't miss me," Stari said, laughing. "What? That bitch Tasha ain't doing her job?" she asked saucily.

"Your choice, ma, not mine, but what's good down there in the country?" Chi Chi had a feeling this wasn't a social call.

"My brothers said it's money in the air down here, and if you and your niggas trying to breathe, then head down here like yesterday. He doesn't trust these country niggas. You in or not?" she asked seriously.

"We in. Give us a few days," he said seriously.

The opportunity was perfect.

"See you then. Call me when you're on the way down," she said before hanging up.

Chi Chi hung up and smiled at his team.

"Nigga, don't hold us in suspense," Eat 'Em Up said.

"Niko obviously got something popping down south, and he don't trust them country boys, so he wants us to come down and get some money with him," Chi Chi said as he laid it all on the table.

All decisions were made together.

"I'm wit' it," Show Off said, ready to travel.

"Me too," Blackface said.

He had never been down south, and he was ready to see what's up with them country, cornbread-fed women down there.

Chi Chi looked around at everybody as they agreed. He got to Khaos, who was still thinking about it.

"What's it going to be, son?" he asked curiously.

Khaos looked around at his niggas, his family, and cracked a rare smile.

"You know I don't like Niko, but I'm wit' it," he said sardonically.

Tasha walked back into the living room on the way to the kitchen.

"You tell that bitch to stop calling my house?" she asked over her shoulder as she grabbed a Snapple from the refrigerator.

"Take yo' mu'fuckin ass back into the back room. Keep testing me, Tasha, and I'm gonna tighten yo' ass up," Chi Chi warned seriously.

He was vexed she was walking around in front of his team with half her ass hanging out of the shorts she was wearing. Tasha sucked her teeth and rolled her eyes as she walked back towards her bedroom.

"No, you keep testing me," she said before slamming her door behind her again.

"I still love you, Tasha," Eat 'Em Up yelled out.

"Fuck you, Eat 'Em Up," she yelled through the door.

Chi Chi cracked a smile. Eat 'Em Up knew how to make people laugh at the right times.

"Look, go home and take care of your business. There's no telling how long we'll be down south, so handle whatever it is you need to handle. All of you niggas know where the door is, so see yourselves out," he said before getting up and entering the bedroom with Tasha.

***

Stari hung up the phone and turned to face the four females who wouldn't be quiet while she was on the phone.

"You bitches rude as fuck," she bassed on them with a scowl on her face.

"Who the fuck you talking to, bitch?" The biggest girl in the group bassed back as she took a step towards her.

"Let it go, Stari," Taji said, grabbing her arm.

She knew how her sister would react to a challenge.

"Fuck that," Stari said, snatching out of her grasp.

Before anyone could react, she spit the razor out of her mouth and sliced the girl across the face, giving her a buck-fifty.

"I'm talking to your big, ugly ass bitch," she yelled at the girl as she rolled on the ground, trying to stop the blood from leaking out of her face.

"Act stupid if you want," Taji screamed when her friends acted like they wanted to do something.

They backed off when they saw that she had a razor, too.

"Now pick that bitch up before I carve the rest of you bitches up," Stari said seriously.

She loved violence. They were silent as the girls picked their friend up and out of the bathroom.

"Why you do that?" Taji asked, already knowing the answer to her own question.

"Fuck them hoes . . . shouldn't have tried me when I was on the phone," Stari said seriously. "Haven't they heard of Southern hospitality?" she smirked as she fixed her makeup.

Taji shook her head and laughed as she fixed hers, also.

***

"Showtime, playboy," P.R. whispered to Casper when he spotted Ty-Jay leaving the V.I.P. area with his entourage.

He set his drink on the bar and started walking towards him. Casper followed suit. When they entered the crowded dance floor, they pulled their pistols out of their waists.

"Remember me, pussy," P.R. whispered when he was less than a foot from his target.

He raised his gun and squeezed off three kill shots. There was no way Ty-Jay heard what P.R. said over the music, but something told him to stop talking to the woman on his arm and look up. What he saw made him piss on himself, but before he could react, he was lifted off of his feet by the slugs P.R. put into his stomach. The female on his arm saw the blood leaking out of his mouth and screamed, setting off a chain reaction.

Casper saw one of Ty-Jay's shooters reach for his gun and put a hole in his face. He saw another one getting ready to swing on P.R., who was taking care of another problem, and took him down. His blood was pumping because he was in his element. P.R. reached and snatched the chain off of Ty-Jay's neck and ran his pockets.

"Please. Please," Ty-Jay weakly begged for his life.

"I told you if you play pussy, you will get fucked. Now suck on this dick," P.R. said before sticking the barrel of his gun into his mouth and pulling the trigger.

The club was in pandemonium. When the gunshots started firing, people started stampeding towards the door. P.R. and Casper blended in with the crowd and left the club.

***

Niko saw the two dudes who were dancing with his sisters creeping through the crowd with their pistols in their hands. He looked around and saw who they were gunning for. He automatically started searching for his siblings because he knew what was going down. When the shots rang out, the crowd started stampeding. He was the only person moving towards the shooting; everybody else was trying to get away. The only thing on his mind was finding his people.

***

Stari and Taji were leaving the bathroom when the shots rang out. They automatically locked in on the scene unfolding on the dance floor. They saw the two dudes they were dancing with earlier making a movie. They were raised by gangstas, but they were kept away from certain things, so they had never seen anything like that before. Before they could process anything, Guardian appeared out of nowhere and started ushering them towards the exit.

"Let's go now," he barked as his eyes roamed over the crowd for their brother.

He wasn't worried because he knew Niko could take care of himself. His main concern was getting his sisters to safety.

***

Niko felt someone grab his arm. He turned ready to swing on whoever it was, but stopped himself when he saw that it was Beza.

"I'm looking for my people," he told her.

"I just saw your brother leaving with two females," she said, ready to go.

Niko looked at her skeptically.

"Trust me, Niko. I saw them leave. Why would I lie about something so easily checkable?" she asked, hurt that he was doubting her, but she understood it.

"You can call them after we get out of here. I know you're strapped, so we need to go because the police are about to shut the roads down and not let anyone leave," she said, looking into his eyes.

Niko locked eyes with her for a few seconds and decided to trust her. If she was lying to him and something happened to his family, she would die, plain and simple. They followed the crowd out of the club and disappeared before the police locked the scene down.

Chapter 19

Yero pulled up to the valet at *Komoto's*, parked, and got out of the car. He tossed the parking attendant his keys and briskly walked into the restaurant. He strode up to the maître d' and let him know about his reservations.

"Ahh, yes, sir. Your dinner guest has been waiting on you," the maître said, giving him a knowing look. "Please follow me." He spun on his heel and started to walk off until Yero stopped him.

"I can find my own way," he said, brushing past the stunned maître without a second glance.

"Well, I be . . ." the maître mumbled under his breath as he watched Yero walk away from him.

He returned back to his post, properly humbled.

***

Eileen looked at her watch for what felt like the hundredth time and felt her face flush with anger. She picked up her glass of wine and took a sip. She would give him ten more minutes; then she was leaving.

***

Consuela was starting to grow agitated because Ichino had yet to show. She was on her second glass of wine, and she was starting to feel it, so she decided to put some food on her stomach to offset the wine. When she turned around to find the maître d', she froze. She couldn't believe her eyes.

***

Yero was making his way through the restaurant, weaving through the tables, avoiding eating patrons as he looked for his dinner date. He noticed an older Latina staring at him from her table at the back of the restaurant, but he paid her no attention because from the quick glance he spared her, he knew that he had never seen her before, and he was used to women giving him the eye, so he wasn't bothered by it too much. He was surprised, though, when he was about to pass her table: she reached out and grabbed the sleeve of his suit jacket.

"Do I know you?" he asked in Spanish.

He was surprised at how easily he slipped into the language, but for some reason, it felt right.

"Who is your father?" Consuela asked in the same language as she searched his face.

Yero looked puzzled. He hadn't thought about his father in years, and to be totally honest, he could care less about the nigga, but nonetheless, her question still caught him off guard.

"Why?" he asked, his voice laced with more suspicion than curiosity.

Consuela continued to stare at him with a mixture of anger and amazement etched onto her face. Her heart was telling her that she was wrong, that what she was thinking couldn't be possible, but her mind was screaming at her.

Right! Right! Right! You slimy bastard, she thought angrily. "You look familiar to me, that's all," she told him softly in Spanish after she got her emotions under control.

She couldn't allow her thoughts to become cloudy. She needed all of her wits about her if she was going to obtain the information she felt this young man could provide her.

Before Yero could tell her that he had never seen her before, they were interrupted.

187

"Dueña!" Consuela looked up when she heard the familiar pet name, and felt her heart skip a beat at the sight of Ichino strolling towards them.

He was the only person to ever call her that. At first, she hated being called a mistress because of what it implied, but the more she fell in love with him, the more she grew to love what he said was a term of endearment. She glanced up at the young man and saw him staring at her. She felt her face flush when she realized that he understood what the name meant, even if he didn't understand its origin.

"Who do you have with you, bella?" Ichino asked when he reached the table.

He was talking to Consuela, but his eyes never left Yero's, who found himself staring into the eyes of an Oriental mu'fucka for the second time that night.

"Just a friend of my sons," Consuela said with a nervous smile.

"Your sons make friends fast," Ichino said sardonically. "What did you say your sons friend's name was again?" he asked her.

"She never did say what my name was," Yero said, not liking the vibe he was getting from the man.

On the outside, he was all Armani and cool elegance, but Yero had learned to look deeper than the exterior, and he could see a snake on two legs. The man was smiling at him like their meeting was a coincidence, but he didn't believe in coincidences and wasn't about to start now.

"I see my dinner date waiting, so if you would excuse me," Yero said, walking away without further interaction.

Ichino took the disrespect in stride as he turned his attention back to Consuela.

"I've missed you, Dueña," he whispered as he leaned in to kiss her lightly on her lips. "Did you miss me?" he asked before he kissed her again, this time more deeply.

"Yes," Consuela answered and shuddered when he finally released her lips.

She felt herself growing wet from the intensity in his eyes as he looked at her. All it took was one kiss for him to have her ready to do anything he asked. It was that power that he had over her that made her run in the first place, but she was back in the deep end, and this time she didn't want to be saved.

"Oh God, yes."

***

Eileen looked up from the menu she was reading when she felt a presence standing over her. When she laid eyes on the man standing there waiting on her acknowledgement, her breath caught in her throat. He was one of the sexiest men she ever had the pleasure to meet personally. She let her eyes roam over his muscular frame brazenly as she admired him. His Brioni suit looked tailor-made to fit his body. The light-grey color paired well with the brandy-wine-red hand-stitched Ascot Chang shirt and Hermès tie of the same color. She couldn't see his shoes, but she didn't doubt that they went perfectly with his suit. She assumed that this was the infamous Yero Owens Shapphire had told her so much about, but she wasn't expecting the man standing in front of her patiently as she looked him over. His looks lived up to Shapphire's description, but she was expecting a flashy dope boy who liked to wear his wealth, and he wasn't like that at all. This man had money, but it was subtle. His Louis Moinet Magistralis watch and monogrammed gold cuff links attested to that.

***

Yero recognized Eileen from the many newspaper articles and television spots about her during her surprise run to the Governor's Mansion. He didn't do white women because they just weren't his flavor, but he had to admit that the media didn't do Ms. Jackson justice. She was beautiful, and even sitting down, he could tell that she had a body most women, of any race, would kill for. The look in her eyes as she checked him out let him know that she liked what she was seeing, but also that he would have to be the aggressor, a role he didn't mind playing.

"Do I pass inspection?" he asked teasingly with a smirk on his face.

Eileen chuckled when she realized how rude she was being. She stood up and held out her hand.

"Eileen Jackson."

Yero felt his dick give a little jump when he saw just how nice her ass was. The black cocktail dress she was wearing fit her body like a glove and amplified every curve. He grasped her hand and gave it a light rub as he returned the unnecessary introductions.

"Yero Owens. Nice to finally meet you." He held onto her hand as his thumb continued to trace little circles inside her palm.

"I see that it is," Eileen said, smiling as she glanced at his lap before extracting her hand from his grasp and sitting down. "Shall we order as we talk?" she asked as she picked the menu back up.

Yero smiled as he took the seat across from her.

"Let me order for us both," he said before taking the menu out of her hands as he summoned the maître d'. "We'll both have the baked red snapper with steamed egg custard, bamboo shoot, and lily bulb soup with sugared oranges and strawberries for dessert. Also, let us have a bottle of your best champagne to commence our celebration."

"Right away, sir," the maître said before hurrying away to fill their orders.

"What are we celebrating?" Eileen asked curiously as she looked into his eyes.

"The start of a beautiful relationship," Yero said sincerely.

***

"Why did you run from me, Dueña?" Ichino asked Consuela as he held her hands across the table.

"I had to get my kids out of New York," she said seriously. "And away from you," she added silently as the memories she had long tried to suppress resurfaced.

"All of this," he said calmly, referring to their situation, "is your doing, Dueña. I couldn't find Manny that night. You were the only person who knew where he was hiding. If you didn't want him to die, then why did you reveal his location to me?" Ichino knew he was being unduly harsh, but he needed to reassert his dominance over her again.

The time she had spent hiding from him had diminished some of his control, and anything other than complete submission from her was unacceptable. Consuela felt the tears well up in her eyes as she looked at him. They both knew why she revealed her husband's location to him. She felt the tears cascade down her cheeks as the memories from that night washed over her. . .

"Why do you have to go in hiding, Manny?" she asked hysterically as he packed his bags. "So you're just going to leave me and your kids to fend for ourselves?" she looked at him with accusations in her eyes.

"Please don't do this, Suela," Manny said as he stopped packing and hugged her. "I have to do this for the safety of you and the kids," he whispered into her ear as she cried on his shoulder.

He wished he could tell her more, but that information would only get her killed.

"What did you do, Manny?" she asked sadly as she looked up into his eyes, the eyes that never failed to make her feel safe, but now the look in them was breaking her heart.

"Just trust me, Suela," Manny said, feeling his own heart breaking at the look in her eyes.

Consuela looked into the eyes of the man she had given her all to, and wondered why he couldn't seem to do right.

"Does this have anything to do with your debt?" she asked quietly, trying to get some type of understanding.

Manny briefly closed his eyes as her question hit home. What he had asked her to do, and what she agreed to do, and what she had been doing for damn near twenty years made him wonder how she could still love him, but he didn't have time for regrets. What's done is done, and he had to move on. He opened his eyes and looked into hers. The only emotions he saw dwelling in their depths were love and sadness; that alone almost made him buckle, but he stood strong.

"I have to go," he said in a whisper.

When she didn't reply, he kissed her on the lips softly and turned his back to her. The hardest thing he ever had to do in his life was grab his bags and walk out of that house, and essentially out of her life. Consuela waited until she heard the front door close before she jumped on the bed and cried herself to sleep.

A few hours later, she was nudged awake. Thinking that Manny had come back to them, she sat up and opened her eyes only to find Ichino sitting beside her on the bed she shared with her husband. She looked at his hands and realized that he had woken her with the barrel of the gun. She looked up into his eyes and saw that they were devoid of life. She didn't see the usual desire that usually dwelled in his gaze when he looked at her. They were empty, and she was scared.

"Where is he?" he asked calmly.

He was angry, but wouldn't allow her to see it. He would give her a chance to tell him what he knew she knew, but if she refused his grace, then he would kill her and her children.

Consuela knew exactly who he was looking for, but her heart wouldn't allow her to betray him. Ichino sighed. He saw the stubbornness in her face and decided to cut to the chase.

"I will kill you and all your children one by one, but I will allow my men to have their way with your daughters and make you watch. I will make you watch each child die before I have my way with you, then kill you. So know this: I will find him no matter what. So make this easier for you and myself. Where is he?"

Consuela felt the coldness of his words and believed that he would do everything he said he would. She thought about her kids and her husband. Her children were innocent, and Manny had made his bed. Now he has to die in it. She told him everything she had to to get him out of her house. Nothing on earth could compete with the love a mother had for her kids. . .

Ichino calling her name repeatedly snapped Consuela out of her reverie. She looked at him for a few seconds as tears continued to run down her cheeks, then slid her chair back and bolted from the restaurant.

"Is everything all right, sir?" the maître asked with a worried expression on his face.

"Everything is perfect, just perfect," Ichino said with a smile to reassure the maître.

He stood up, pulled his billfold from his pocket and tossed three hundred-dollar bills onto the table. He followed the same path Consuela had taken out of the restaurant with a smile on his face. The hatred he had witnessed in her eyes was exactly what he wanted to see. He needed to control her.

Chapter 20

Kim was working the bar at the *Pretty Flower* as usual when five Jet Li-looking mu'fuckas entered the club with their faces all screwed up. The twins had put her up on game about who might've been responsible for the attempt on their lives, so she was on point and reacted before any of them noodle-eating pussies could say 'Kung Fu'. She stepped on the panic button under her feet to alert the team she had posted around the club as she grabbed the two .40-cal Berettas they kept strapped under the bar and came up firing as the egg roll contingent let loose. Shit got hectic quickly; the hit squad was shooting any and everything. They weren't discriminating. She hit one in his neck and took their count from five to four. It would've been down to three, but a patron stepped in front of the bullet and caught a dirt nap. She had to duck down behind the bar when they concentrated their shots her way. When she stood back up, she saw that Domingo, one of Loca's soldiers, had taken down another shooter with a shot to the face. She fired another shot and hit another shooter in the stomach, taking him out of the fight. A tall black stripper named Panther broke a champagne bottle over a shooter's head, knocking him unconscious. Another stripper named Snow White slit the throat of the last shooter with a box cutter, then she finished off the shooter Kim had wounded, and the shooter Panther had knocked out.

"Domingo, call Gregory and tell him we have some work for him. Tell him that it's five bodied, and get here. A'ight? Also, get someone to take the body of the customer that got killed and drop them off somewhere they won't be found quickly. Panther, organize the girls and start cleaning this shit up because someone probably called the pigs, so move it," Kim ordered before sending word to the twins to let them know what happened.

* * *

When Eileen and Yero reached her room, he pulled a small baggie of white powder out of the inside pocket of his suit jacket and held it up for her to see.

"Mind if I indulge?" he asked.

"What is that?" Eileen asked innocently.

She was eyeing the baggie like a cat eyeing a mouse.

"It's cocaine. It will make the sex so much better," he said, turning his back to her as he opened the little baggie and took a sniff up each nostril.

He wiped his nose and held his head back as he turned to face her. She didn't have to know that he had just snorted a BC powder.

"You want to try it out?" he asked, pulling another bag out of his pocket.

"Maybe this one time won't hurt anything," Eileen said, accepting the small baggie that he tossed her.

If she hadn't been so inebriated, she would've thought twice before indulging, but she wasn't in her right mind as she opened up the bag and took a big sniff. She held her head back so she could feel the full effect. Yero watched with a smirk on his face. He took his suit jacket off and draped it on the back of the chair in the room. He positioned it so that the buttons were facing him and Eileen. He grabbed the rest of the small baggies out of his suit jacket before he finished undressing. When he was naked, he opened another baggie and spread a line of white powder along his erect dick.

Eileen was feeling good. When she was going through law school, she had used cocaine plenty of nights to stay up when she was studying for exams. She had loved the way it

195

made her feel, but she forced herself to cut back after she passed the bar. She quit cold turkey when she became the youngest district attorney in the history of Durham County. She had been drug-free for over a year until tonight, and as she looked at Yero's naked body, she didn't regret indulging again. Her eyes locked in on his dick as he spread a line of cocaine along his beautiful length. She licked her lips hungrily.

Yero saw how she was looking at him and smiled. He had her right where he wanted her.

"Come get it," he demanded.

Eileen felt her pussy tingle at the bass in his voice. She slowly rose from the couch and started to walk towards him, but stopped when he told her to get naked and crawl on her hands and knees. She looked at him puzzled because she wasn't used to taking orders from men, but this turned her on, and she did as she was told.

"Leave the heels on," Yero demanded when she reached to take them off. "Now crawl."

Eileen got down on her hands and knees before crawling over to him. Her pussy was incredibly wet from his dominance. Yero felt his dick grow another inch as the beautiful white woman crawled towards him. It was a sight to see. When she reached him, Eileen grabbed the base of his dick and snorted up the line of cocaine into one nostril. Yero put another line on his dick and watched as she snorted it up the other nostril. She slid him into her mouth and started sucking him off.

Yero felt his dick growing numb and in turn getting harder as she sucked him off. He grabbed her blonde hair to stop her movement and started fucking her face like it was her pussy. He felt his orgasm exploding from his dick. He let her swallow a little before he pulled out and let the rest of his "kids" splatter around her mouth and chin. When he saw that she was about to complain, he stuck his dick back into her mouth. He tossed her the rest of the cocaine to head off any protest she might've had. With his hand still gripping her hair, he walked her over to the couch and bent her over. He made sure that she was facing the camera he had stashed in the button of his jacket before he started fucking her from the back, doggystyle.

Eileen was snorting bag after bag of cocaine as Yero fucked her anyway he wanted to. The cocaine mixed with the multiple orgasms she was having made her pass out from the pleasure of it all.

***

"Open wider and take this dick," Ichino demanded.

Consuela immediately did as she was told and opened her mouth wider to receive his dick. She was lying on her back on the bed in Ichino's suite with her dress bunched up around her waist, leaving her breasts and pantyless pussy bare as Ichino slid his dick in between her breasts and into her mouth. She was using her tongue to lap at the head of his dick every time he got close to her mouth. After running out of the restaurant crying, she tried to leave, but the valet had taken too long to retrieve her car, giving Ichino ample time to catch up to her. When the valet finally did pull up in her car, Ichino put her in the passenger seat before getting into the driver's seat and pulling off. As he drove her to his hotel, Consuela couldn't deny that she was powerless to resist him. She wondered why she didn't demand that he stop her car and let her out so she could go home, but she sat quietly as he drove her to his suite and proceeded to do whatever he wanted with her body.

"Why are you still regretting your decision to tell me where Manny was?" Ichino groaned as her hot tongue licked the head of his dick again. "He sold you to me, Dueña," he added as he forcibly grabbed her jaw, raised up on his knees, and started fucking her mouth. "You are mine. Remember," he shouted as he choked her with his dick.

Consuela opened her eyes and locked onto his angry expression. Every time his hips thrust into her mouth, his facial expression changed, giving his visage many masks as he reasserted his dominance. She looked into his dark brown eyes and felt her senses heightened. When he reached back with his free hand and started manipulating her clitoris, she climaxed instantly.

"Remember," he growled as he felt his own orgasm building. "Remember."

Consuela let her memories take her back to their first date almost twenty years ago. . .

"Did you enjoy yourself?" Ichino asked her as they rode in the back of his Mercedes limousine.

He was staring at her, wondering why she had an effect on him that none of the hundreds of women before her ever had on him. He figured it was because unlike the others, she really didn't want him. She was there strictly as a favor to her husband.

"I enjoyed myself," Consuela said quietly as she wondered how much longer their 'date' would last. She was ready to go home to her husband and kids.

Ichino felt himself harden at her innocent personality. He decided to end this farce because time was money, and he didn't have any time to waste. He wanted, no, he needed to own her innocence. He moved over to sit beside her and placed his hand on her upper thigh.

"Are you ready to move on to phase two of our date?" he asked, smiling congenially at her.

"What?" Consuela asked, recoiling from his touch. "I don't know what phase you are referring to, but I'm only doing a favor for my husband because of a debt he owes you," she added seriously.

Ichino laughed at her naiveté to cover the anger he was feeling at the look of disgust she shot him when he touched her.

Consuela frowned a little when he started laughing. She was growing more and more uncomfortable by the minute.

"Your husband may have tried to protect your delicate sensibilities, but I don't have time for the games. Manny owes me more than you know, and one simple date wouldn't even begin to put a dent into his debt. A date with me consists of carnal pleasure, of me having my way with you. If you feel you can't provide this, I'm sure your two young daughters can be put to work," he said coldly as he stared into her eyes.

Consuela couldn't believe what she had just heard. She went over everything her husband had told her about this man in her head and knew that he would do everything he just said he would do. She could also tell that he really wanted her, and that he would harm her family if he couldn't have her. She had a sneaky suspicion that he had given Manny just enough rope to hang himself to put him in a position to ask for what he wanted as payment. She felt a little piece of her heart chip off at what Manny had done to her and their family. She knew she would never be the same after this, but figured it was a small price to pay for love.

"How long will I have to do this?" she asked, looking him in the eyes with as much dignity as she had left.

"Until all debts are paid or until I get tired of you," he said bluntly.

He had no reason to give her false hope. Consuela nodded as he said this because she expected nothing less.

"I'll do it," she said quietly, resigned to her fate.

Ichino smiled and unzipped his slacks.

"Come put those pretty little lips to work," he instructed her after pulling out his dick.

Consuela wanted to cry, but she refused to let him see her tears. She kept her poker face as she put him into her mouth and did what she had to do. . .

Consuela was pulled out of her reverie when she felt Ichino ejaculating. She looked into his eyes and saw his demise, but she knew he desired his dominance over her more than he desired her. He pulled his dick out of her mouth and let some excess cum hit her chin and lips.

"You belong to me," Ichino said before getting up and strolling into the bathroom.

She watched his muscular backside until he disappeared from view. As she closed her eyes and tasted his seed on her lips, she could only agree that she did indeed belong to him.

***

Yero looked over at the sleeping form of Eileen and shook his head. It was so easy to make people lose control of themselves. He slid out of bed and got dressed. When he was finished, he wrote a little note thanking her for an unforgettable night. He laid it on the nightstand and left the room. He would make sure she never forgot that night.

Chapter 21

"Damn Skittles, you haven't come to see me this much ever," Mellz said suspiciously.

He thought Skittles wanted to hit him up for some paper.

"What can I say, baby. . ." Skittles said coyly. . . "You have me addicted," he added, feeding his ego.

"You need to stop playing and move yo' ass up here," Mellz said, stretching his arms above his head.

They had been up most of the night doing what it do when Skittles let him know he was in town. He dropped everything and rushed straight to his hotel room, where he had been all night. For the last couple of weeks, Skittles had been coming up to Philly to see him every few days, and he had gotten used to them falling asleep together.

"I've told you Melvin that as long as you are hustling, we can't be a couple. I don't do jailbirds, baby, and you're throwing bricks at the penitentiary right now. So you need to take your dirty money and clean it up because any man I'm with has to take care of me," Skittles said seriously.

"Oh, so a nigga has to be prepared for you, huh?" Mellz said, frowning at him. "I have to be papered up to have you?"

"What?" Skittles asked when he saw how Mellz was looking at him. "Don't act like you don't know a bitch is expensive," he added, rolling his eyes.

"Look, me and my team are in the process of making a big move. This is the last one for me, then we can go live anywhere you want 'cause I'll have long paper," Mellz said, getting excited about the move.

"You been talking about this move for a few weeks now," Skittles said, rolling his eyes and sucking his teeth in frustration.

"My man Bolo has a country-ass cousin down south named Towny, who been breaking us off with work for free. He be saying the work don't belong to him, so he doesn't give a fuck about giving it to us for free. Don't worry, with this move we'll be able to do what we want," Mellz said, getting up out of bed. "Let me hop in the shower before I get up with my niggas," he added before walking into the bathroom and closing the door behind him.

Skittles was amazed at how stupid some hustlers were. They couldn't keep their mouths shut. *No wonder they told on they mamas when the alphabet boys put the pressure on,* he thought as he grabbed his cell phone and started typing a text message to his people.

"Come take a shower with me," Mellz yelled through the closed door.

Skittles finished his text before getting out of the bed. *Might as well milk this nigga before shit hits the fan,* he thought sardonically as he walked into the bathroom to enjoy the dead man walking.

* * *

Consuela silently stuck her key into the lock and unlocked her front door. She pushed it open as quietly as she could, hoping that her children weren't up. She didn't want them to see her in her present state. Ichino didn't allow her to take a shower or wash up before sending her home, so she looked like she had been having sex for hours, which was exactly what she had been doing. She had tried to find a store where she could stop and clean up a little bit, but at that time of morning, nothing was open. So she was creeping into her own house like a thief in the night, hoping that her children didn't catch their mother looking like a street-walking whore. When she closed the front door behind her and locked it, she stood still, trying to see if she could hear her kids moving around. After being met with complete silence, she briefly wondered why her children weren't home before dashing to the bathroom inside of her bedroom. After locking the door, she stripped down and stared at her reflection in the full-length mirror hanging on the back of the door. Staring at the dried cum spots and bruises marring her body brought a sense of shame at her actions, but also a sense of exhilaration. She couldn't explain the conflicting emotions because it was like she was at war with herself. She just knew the most imperative thing was to keep her rendezvous with Ichino a secret. If her children ever found out she was still sleeping with the man who killed their father, she could imagine their reactions. Just thinking about Niko's reaction made her shudder. She put it out of her mind as she ran herself a bubble bath. She was playing a game where there could be no winners. She just hoped that when she lost, she didn't lose everything.

***

After switching cars at the parking garage, Yero made his way home. He had tried calling Suai multiple times after noticing it was four A.M., but she didn't answer, which had him a little suspicious because Suai knew to answer his calls unless she was physically unable to. When he pulled onto his block, something told him to keep driving. As he passed his spot, he didn't notice anything out of the ordinary, but he better than most knew that looks were deceiving. He didn't see the Charger Suai had driven home and figured it was in the garage. He drove over to the next block and parked. He pulled his gun out and played the backyards and shortcuts until he was standing at the back door. He silently unlocked the door and slipped inside. After closing the door quietly, he let his eyes adjust to the darkness. He held his pistol out in front of him as he checked the kitchen. As he made his way to the living room, he froze. In the middle of the floor, Suai was tied naked to a chair. She was trying to talk, but the gag in her mouth prevented her from doing so. He went against his first instinct and started to go to her, but stopped when he looked into her eyes. They were darting back and forth like she was trying to tell him something. She was bucking against her restraints so hard that she tipped the chair over. Yero finally caught on, but it was too late. They weren't alone. He tried to turn around, but he was hit in the back with a cattle prod and knocked unconscious. The men he had seen earlier in the parking garage appeared out of seemingly nowhere and tied him up amid Suai's efforts to get out of her restraints. They picked him up and tossed him over their shoulders like a sack of flour and left the house, leaving Suai on the floor crying and trying to get loose.

A few hours later, a cup of ice-cold water was thrown into Yero's face, waking him up. He opened his eyes and groaned as he quickly shut them again. He had a massive headache, and the blinding lights wherever he was being held weren't helping matters any. He slowly opened his eyes again and looked down at himself. He saw that he was confined to an office chair with duct tape and still wearing his suit from the night before. He looked around, trying to figure out where he was, and felt rage flow through his body as his eyes landed on the same oriental-looking mu'fuckas from the parking garage the night before. He kept his face expressionless until he could figure out how to play his cards. He was in a cavernous, empty warehouse located God knows where, surrounded by a group of Asian men holding automatic pistols. He surmised that he would die because he witnessed something he wasn't supposed to last night. It didn't matter to these foreign mu'fuckas that he was a gangsta and would never speak about what he had seen. If this was the end, then he would die like a man. He wouldn't beg for anything. He studied his executioners, trying to find any weaknesses he could exploit, but he found none. They stood there, staring at him stoically like they were staring at a newly discovered species. After a few minutes of this, Yero grew tired of the bullshit and barked.

"Kill me if that's what's going to happen. Fuck you waiting for?" he eyed each man, personally challenging them to put him out of his misery.

"Whether you live or die is entirely up to you."

The men in front of him parted, and Yero looked at the oriental man he ran into last night at *Komoto's*, walking towards them impeccably dressed in a navy blue, double-breasted suit with a smile on his face.

"Mr. Yero Owens, we meet again," he said when he was standing directly in front of him.

Yero looked up at him with a confused look on his face.

How in the hell this nigga know my name? he questioned himself. *I never told him my name last night at the restaurant.*

"Don't be surprised, Y.O.," Ichino said, correctly deciphering the look on his face. "I do my homework on the underground of any state I visit or do business in. It's good to know who the major players are, or in this case, the major player," he added seriously.

Yero had questions, but he kept his peace. He figured with the way this desperado was talking, he would learn more by listening.

"You're probably wondering why I had you kidnapped," Ichino said when he saw that Yero wasn't very talkative. "The reason is really two-fold," he added as he started pacing back and forth. "My associates claim you witnessed something you weren't supposed to, so they followed your lady friend, tied her up, then called me. When I was made aware of the situation, I told them to bring you to me, and leave your lady friend unharmed. Running into you at the restaurant was a pure coincidence. Yes. I could've easily spoken to you then, but I've never been one to do things conventionally, so here we are. Any questions?" he asked, stopping again directly in front of Yero.

Once again, Yero decided to remain quiet.

"You're in a little bind, Mr. Major Player," Ichino said, deciding to get down to the reason he was there. "The Alvarez Twins have run into a few problems down in Georgia."

Yero perked up a little when he brought up the Twins.

"And as a result, you have no supplier for how long do you think?" Ichino asked rhetorically. "You never know when it comes to the Twins because they are eccentric, but you, you need product and can't afford any major delays in getting product to your people. The reason you and your lady friend are still alive is because I recognize your potential. I can respect a man who makes it happen instead of waiting for it to be handed to him. So I'm offering a compromise. You agree to buy my product, continue to build your foundation, and we all work in harmony. We can all work together and leave the warehouse alive and healthy." He looked at Yero intently, waiting on his reply.

Yero caught the subliminal threat and felt his rage spike to another level at his hopeless situation.

"When I get a chance, I'm going to kill you, noodle-eating motherfucker," he spat in Spanish.

"Disrespect is disrespect no matter the language it's spoken in. Now do you agree to my terms?" Ichino replied in Spanish with a smirk on his face.

Yero was surprised when he heard the man speak Spanish so fluently. He silently berated himself because he underestimated another man, something he never did. He looked at the man with a little more respect and promised himself to never make that mistake again. He weighed everything he had been told in his mind, the pros and cons, and came to one conclusion—he really wasn't being given a choice in the matter. It was either accept the deal or die, plain and simple. He saw accepting the deal as an answer to many of his arising problems. He needed a connect while the Twins worked out whatever their problems were. He needed to find out who this Ichino character was, and most importantly, he needed time to put a plan together on how to deal with these oriental mu'fuckas because they violated in the worst way by touching his people.

Touch one of mine; I bury a hundred of yours, he thought angrily as he locked eyes with the man standing so arrogantly in front of him. "What's the price point on the work?" he asked, feigning resignation.

"Cocaine at twelve apiece, heroin at fifty apiece. Best prices around," Ichino said with a huge smile.

To the average hustler he was basically giving his product away, but to a master strategist his plan was brilliant. To him the money was inconsequential. It was about the territory and control. He was getting the product for damn near free anyway, so he was making a profit. This way he was in control while letting the other man think he was the winner.

Yero couldn't believe the numbers he was hearing. His prices were lower than the twins by a couple of stacks, but he kept the surprise off of his face. The prices really didn't matter to him though because his loyalty was to the twins, but his mother didn't raise a fool, so he accepted the deal.

"Good," Ichino said before walking out of the warehouse.

An hour later, Yero walked into his spot to find Suai still trying to get free from her restraints. He rushed over and picked her up off of the floor. When she saw him, tears started flowing down her face. He gently untied the gag and kissed her tears.

"Mem gon kill dem. Mem word on dat," she said hoarsely as Yero finished untying her.

Yero had to fight to control his anger as he untied her wrists and ankles. Those areas were chafed and raw from where the rope had rubbed against her skin as she tried to get free. He vowed to himself that everyone involved in this disrespect would die. He looked Suai in her eyes and repeated his vow aloud as he picked her up in his arms.

"I promise, luv, that everyone involved in this disrespect will die. As I bathe you, I'ma run down everything that went down. You're not going to believe this shit," he told her as he carried her to the bathroom.

Suai was content just to listen to his voice as she laid her head against his shoulder. When they kidnapped him, she thought she would die. She was feeling guilty because she was the reason he was in the situation in the first place. If she had been on point, she wouldn't have been caught slipping and naked to a chair. She didn't want him to feel like she was a hindrance to him, so she would make up for her mistake. She would become those sushi-eating, Karate Kid mu'fuckas' worst nightmare. Remember Hiroshima?

Chapter 22

"What the hell do you mean you're not going to charge them?" Captain Henderson shouted as he shot up out of his seat, knocking it over. "We're talking about two of the biggest drug-dealing murderers in Fulton County, and you're saying you can't charge them?" He couldn't believe what he was hearing.

He looked around at the people assembled in the room and saw that he was alone in his outrage.

"We don't have enough to charge them," Reggie Eduardo, District Attorney of Fulton County, said seriously.

"Peachtree was littered with dead bodies," Captain Henderson could feel his anger rising because he could see that their decision was already made.

"None of the bodies that were civilian were killed by the guns your people confiscated from the Alvarez Twins. They were trying to protect themselves from being ambushed by hired killers. None of the civilians were killed by either Precious or Tiphany Alvarez," Mrs. Basil, Chief Medical Examiner of Fulton County, said matter of fact.

"There must be some mistake," Captain Henderson growled as he looked her in the eyes.

"We haven't made any mistakes," she said coolly. "Have you?"

Captain Henderson narrowed his eyes and snorted in disbelief. He couldn't believe the Twins were going to beat him again.

"You might be a little too close to the situation, Captain," Reggie said sympathetically.

Captain Henderson looked at him and smiled cruelly. "That's where you're wrong, Reggie. I'm not close enough," he said before he spun on his heels and walked out of the office.

Mrs. Basil looked over at Reggie and said gravely, "He's a loose cannon."

Reggie wholeheartedly agreed with her as he picked up his phone to place a call to the mayor. Something had to be done about Captain Henderson before he potentially did something they would all regret.

***

Beza looked over at Niko, who was doing a set of push-ups on the floor, and wondered where he had been her whole life. Since the shooting at the club two nights before, they had been holed up in a room at the DoubleTree, getting to know each other. He was guarded with the information he gave her about himself and his family, but he gave her enough to want more. She told him about her mother and how it felt to grow up as an only child, but she was tired of talking. She wanted him to touch her. For two days, she had done everything in her womanly power to entice him into making love to her. She even went so far as to stand naked in front of him only to have him say, "Put your clothes back on, ma. Respect yourself."

Despite her frustrations at his steadfastness, she was falling in love with him. He wasn't making love to her physically, but he was sexing her mentally, spiritually, and emotionally, unlike any man she had ever dealt with before. As far as she was concerned, Hollywood was in her rearview. She was on her way to Niko Island.

"Do we really have to leave?" she pouted when he had finished his push-ups.

She didn't want to leave the little world they had created. The way he was standing there, looking good in his wife-beater, she never wanted to leave him, period.

Niko saw the way she was looking at him and smirked. He knew she wasn't used to the type of shit he was doing with her. He knew most men wouldn't have hesitated to accept the pussy she was throwing his way, and that's why he wouldn't touch her because she expected him to. When she stood in front of him naked, it took every ounce of his willpower he possessed not to bend her over and make her scream his name, but he stood tall and told her to get dressed. Despite the frustration and rejection he saw in her eyes, he held firm no matter how much she affected him and his heart. When he broke his reasons down for not touching her, she understood and moved a little closer to becoming his woman.

"Yeah, ma. I have shit to do with my fam. It's been two days, and I need to see them," he told her as he walked towards the bathroom. "Be ready to go when I come out the shower," he added over his shoulder before closing the bathroom door behind him.

Beza rolled her eyes, but she secretly loved his dominant ways.

Ten minutes later, they were on the freeway in Beza's car.

"When you get all of your stuff packed up, call me, and I'll come scoop you," Niko said after he got off the phone with his siblings.

"Why can't I just drive to wherever you are?" Beza asked, puzzled.

"Because you're going to leave that nigga his car," Niko said seriously.

"What!" Beza screeched, not sure she had heard him correctly.

She chanced a quick glance his way and saw the way he was looking and knew he was serious.

"Repeat that, please."

"You heard me, ma," he said, not moved by her theatrics.

"Why?" Beza dared ask. She loved her car and didn't want to give Hollywood shit back.

"This car cost a lot of money, so if you leave that nigga, he's going to come looking for it. I don't care how pussy he is. I don't play childish games, B. I will murder that nigga if he disrespects me and mine, word up. So leave this car with him. I got you," Niko said seriously.

Beza was quiet for a few seconds as she thought about everything he had just said to her, and she knew he was right, so she kept her peace for the rest of the ride until he told her to pull over at the BP gas station on Fayetteville Street.

"You need something from the store?" she asked as she pulled into the parking lot.

"Nah, this is where my family is meeting us," he said casually.

"So you don't trust me to know where you lay your head?" Beza asked angrily as she parked at a vacant gas pump.

"Pipe down, love," Niko was amused at her little attitude. "It's not about trust. My family doesn't know we're rocking yet. So I'm not going to put them in jeopardy by bringing you around until I talk to them first," he added, breaking his reasoning down to her.

"Well, I'm waiting until they get here," she said stubbornly as she rolled her eyes at him.

She turned her head to hide her smile from him.

"Yo, you're a trip, B," Niko said, laughing.

"Whatever, nigga," Beza said, laughing along with him.

For the next ten minutes, they finalized their plans until they heard loud music. They looked up and saw two Chevy Tahoes pulling into the parking lot. One was hunter green, and the other was midnight blue.

"That's the family right there," Niko said with a smirk gracing his lips.

"Can I get a kiss, please?" Beza asked quietly.

She wasn't going to ask, but she couldn't help herself.

Niko wanted to keep her fiending, but the look on her face had him wanting to kiss her too.

"Come here," he told her.

Beza leaned across the console and met his lips with hers. She felt her panties moisten as their tongues explored each other's mouth.

"Damn, you have me wet as hell," she said when their kisses ended.

Niko smirked like he knew the power of his kisses.

"Don't get the big head, boy," she said, chuckling when she saw his expression.

"Call me when you're ready," Niko said before opening the car door and getting out.

Beza wanted to call out for another kiss, but she bit her lip to stop herself. She would maintain until next time. When he hit the roof of her car lightly, she turned the key in the ignition and pulled off.

"Oh, we not good enough to meet your new friend?" Stari asked sarcastically as she got out of the hunter green truck, followed by Guardian, Chi Chi, Black Face, and Eat 'Em Up. She walked up to her brother and hugged him. It had been two days since she had seen him in the flesh, and she missed him.

"You will meet her soon enough," Niko said as he looked over her shoulder at Chi Chi.

"He's ashamed of us," Taji joked as she hopped out of the midnight blue truck, followed by Red Star, Khaos, and Show Off.

"What's good, lil' Chi Chi?" Niko asked as he ignored his sister.

"It's just Chi Chi now, duke, and money is what's good," he said, cutting straight to the chase.

"We down here to breathe some of this air we've heard so much about," he added seriously.

"You all ate yet?" Niko asked, looking at his watch.

"Nah, we just got in not too long ago," Chi Chi said, realizing how hungry he actually was.

"Let's go get some food and talk," Niko said before walking towards the hunter green Tahoe.

"Bet," Chi Chi said.

He grabbed Stari by her arm as she tried to walk past him.

"How you gonna act while I'm down here?" He leaned over and whispered in her ear.

His dick got hard just from looking at her ass in the black leggings she was wearing.

Stari looked at the print in his pants and smirked.

"I might fuck you just to spite your bitch Tasha, or I might get some head from you. Depends on how these country boys acting," she said before snatching out of his grasp and getting into the truck.

Chi Chi frowned and got into the truck behind her. He had forgot how much she could piss him off. One thing he knew for sure was that she wouldn't be fucking no country *niggas while he was around, or he would burn they ass up. They say while in Rome do as the Romans do. Well, he was in the South, so he would turn one of them niggas* into barbeque, straight up!

***

Eileen was sitting at her desk, reminiscing about her night with Yero when her secretary walked into her office, carrying today's mail.

"Thank you, Janny," she said, ready for her to leave so she could get back to her fantasies of Yero.

"No problem, boss lady," Janny said before leaving the office.

Eileen was about to get back to her erotic daydreams when a FedEx package caught her eye. She picked it up and looked at it. When she couldn't find a return address, she was about to throw it back in the pile of mail, but something told her to open it. She used the letter opener to slit open the package and shook the contents onto her desk. When she saw a USB drive and a note attached to it, she was confused. She picked the note up and grew even more confused because all it said was 'Enjoy'. With a sense of dread, she popped the USB drive into her laptop and waited as it downloaded the contents onto her hard drive. When it was done, she opened the file and gasped. On the screen, she was being shown in all of her glory. The night she spent with Yero was being played out on her computer screen in 4K. She groaned and took her eyeglasses off. She rubbed the bridge of her nose and shook her head in disbelief. She couldn't believe how she had been able to fall for one of the oldest political tricks in the book. What she was watching on the computer would ruin her career completely. She had just pulled the USB from her laptop when her secretary informed her over the intercom that Shapphire Stone was waiting to see her. She groaned again as she told her secretary to send her in. She expected to see Shapphire walk in with a satisfied smile on her face, but was surprised to see the somber expression she was wearing.

"I received his message," she said, barely containing her anger.

"You brought this on yourself, Eileen," Shapphire said, dismissing her anger. "I told you to play by the rules," she added, taking a seat.

"Does he have a hold on you like this?" Eileen asked.

She seriously wanted to know. Shapphire just sat there staring at her, refusing to answer. Eileen took her silence as a yes and felt a little better, knowing that she wasn't alone. She was upset, more at herself than anybody, but she had to congratulate Yero on his technique. He didn't threaten her or anything so thuggish, but he got the desired result, and he gave her enough rope to hang herself.

"What will be expected of me?" she asked, resigned to her fate.

"Just continue your daily routine. If and when he needs you, he'll contact you. You're his, Eileen, and you better understand that quickly," Shapphire said as she stood up. "You'll benefit just like we all will. Just do your job and don't make waves because you will drown." She turned and headed for the door.

Before she opened it, she turned and tossed something onto her desk. "Keep your nose clean," she told her before making her exit. When the door closed, Eileen fingered the small bag of cocaine Shapphire had tossed onto her desk before leaving. Knowing that she had just signed her life away, she put her head down and cried for the first time in a long time.

Chapter 23

Beza walked into the condominium she shared with Hollywood and was glad he wasn't home. She knew he would bitch about her being gone for two days, but she wasn't trying to hear shit he had to say. She went straight to their bedroom and headed to his stash. She grabbed a Gucci bookbag out of her closet and opened his safe. She breathed a sigh of relief when she saw that he hadn't cleaned out his money yet. She started stuffing rubber-band stacks of cash into her bookbag. She moved to her jewelry box and dumped everything on top of the money, then she pulled the rest of her Gucci luggage out of her closet and started packing her belongings. An hour later, she was done packing up all that she was going to take with her. After dragging the luggage to the front room, she hopped into the shower. When she was dressed in a brand-new Christian Dior jogging suit with Dior runners adorning her feet, she called Niko. When she got his voicemail, she hung up and tried again. She also sent him a text message letting him know that she was ready to go. Realizing that she was hungry, she fixed something to eat and rolled a blunt to smoke while she waited for Niko. As soon as she finished making herself a salad and rolling her blunt, Hollywood walked in. She could tell he was surprised to see her standing in their kitchen, but he tried to hide it when she looked at him and rolled her eyes. She had always been able to read him like a book, and she could tell that he didn't know how to react to her sudden reappearance after missing her for the past two days. She made up her mind to ignore him, so she grabbed her food, a glass of wine, and with her blunt in her mouth, walked right past him into the living room like he wasn't even standing there looking like a sick puppy. When she sat down to eat, Hollywood had the nerve to try and kiss her, but she moved out of the way and looked at him like he was crazy.

"Nigga, don't touch me," she said, sucking her teeth and rolling her eyes at him.

She started eating her salad like he really was invisible.

"Why you acting like this, Beza?" Hollywood asked, confused by her actions. "You the one that was gone for two days and now you're tripping," he added, genuinely confused.

Beza couldn't believe how soft this nigga was. She didn't know what she had ever seen in him besides his money.

"You want to know the truth about my actions?" she asked, ready to dead the whole issue.

A small voice in her head was telling her to not poke the bear, but she didn't listen. In her eyes, he was soft.

"Yeah, let me know what's up, baby," he pleaded as he sat down beside her on the couch and grabbed her hand. "Help me help us get better," he added, looking into her eyes.

Beza wanted to laugh at the puppy-dog look on his face, and she would've if she wasn't so disgusted. She snatched her hand out of his and frowned at him.

"You are too soft for me, Hollywood. All you do is whine and complain about shit you're supposed to be putting your foot down about. You have too many bitch tendencies for me. If I wanted to be with a female, I would've started fucking Ya Ya," she said, giving it to him raw and uncut. "You . . . are . . . soft . . . nigga. That's why I'm leaving yo' ass," she taunted with a smirk on her face.

She should've been paying attention to how her words were affecting him.

Smack!

"Bitch, you got me fucked up!" Hollywood yelled in outrage.

He couldn't believe the shit she had just said out of her mouth. He treated this bitch like a queen, and she thought he was soft.

Beza was holding her face, still in shock from him smacking her. He had never put his hands on her before, and he damn sure wasn't about to start now. She raised her hand and smacked the shit out of him.

"Nigga, don't you ever put yo' hands on me again!" she screamed.

Smack!

"Bitch, fuck you!" Hollywood screamed down at her.

His last backhand had knocked her to the ground.

"You think I'ma soft-ass nigga? Well, tell me if this ass-whooping is soft!" he yelled as he stood over her.

Beza looked up into his face and didn't recognize the man standing over her. She knew she had pushed him too far and believed him when he said he was going to beat her ass. She got up and tried to run for the front door, but Hollywood was on her before she could move an inch.

"Naw, bitch, don't run now," he said, punching her in the back of her head, knocking her back down to the floor. "Run that mouth now, bitch," he taunted as she groaned on the floor.

Beza rolled over on her back and tried to plead with him.

"I'm sorry, baby. I was just mad at you. I wasn't leaving for good. I was just going to my mother's house for a few days to scare you," she said all of this in a sincere tone, hoping to reach him.

Hollywood reached down and snatched her up off of the floor by her hair.

"Ahhh!" she screamed. Her scalp felt like it was on fire.

"Don't scream now, bitch," he said seriously.

He kissed her, forcing his tongue into her mouth. Beza couldn't believe this was happening to her. She wasn't about to let him rape her on top of the beating he was already giving her. She brought her knee up and hit him in his groin as hard as she could.

"Son of a bitch!" Hollywood shouted in pain as he fell to the floor, holding his family jewels. "Bitch, I'ma kill you. That's my word."

Beza grabbed her cell phone and ran to the front door. She opened it, ran out, and started screaming.

"Help me, help me! He's beating me! Please help me!"

She ran out to the parking lot, trying to call Niko.

"What's going on, Miss?" a man who lived in her building asked.

His face was tight with anger as he looked at the bruises marking her beautiful skin. More and more tenants were responding to her pleas for help, most of them men.

"My boyfriend is trying to stop me from leaving him," Beza said, growing more and more frustrated every time she reached Niko's voicemail.

She left a few messages before hanging up. She looked up and saw Hollywood staggering towards her with his pistol in his hand and a scowl on his face.

"He got a gun! Please help me!" she screamed.

She was really scared that he might shoot her. The men in the parking lot formed a protective ring around her. They stared Hollywood down and let him know that he would have to go through them if he wanted her.

"You need to leave, man," one of them said forcefully.

"The police are on the way!" a woman yelled down from her second-floor window.

Hollywood looked around at all of the people in the parking lot and knew there were too many witnesses for him to do 'wanted poster' shit to Beza, so falling back for the time being was his only option. Plus, he was dirty and had some warrants on top of that. He couldn't afford to get locked up right then, so he let her win the battle, but he would definitely win the war because he was going to bust her ass.

"You better get the fuck out of my shit, bitch," he said before limping over to his Range Rover.

Beza felt like she didn't breathe easy again until he had pulled out of the parking lot. She texted Niko again, practically begging him to come pick her up now.

"Will you be all right, ma'am?" one of her neighbors asked with concern.

"Yes, thank you so much. My family is on the way. So I'll be all right. Thank you all again," Beza said effusively as she made her way back to the condo. When she was safely inside, she engaged all of the locks before she continued to try and reach Niko. When she reached voicemail again, she wanted to cry, but she fought her tears back. She grabbed her Gucci bookbag and went to finish cleaning Hollywood out. He would regret ever putting his hands on her.

***

Dynasty was starting to get impatient. Yero had called a meeting with the team to discuss a few things at two that afternoon, but it was now four and the meeting hadn't even started yet. They all were present except Jah, and it was obvious to her that he was purposely disrespecting her brother. She looked up where Yero was sitting, all calm and collected, and shook her head. They were siblings, but they were wired different. He was philosophical and she was brutal. He kept giving niggas rope to hang themselves with, but she strung niggas up herself. She loved him to death, but she didn't understand his madness. She was about to say something about starting the meeting when Jah swaggered in like they were his subjects and were supposed to wait on him.

"My bad I'm late, but I was handling some B.I. and it slipped my mind," Jah said with a smirk on his face.

Dynasty couldn't believe the bullshit that had just come out of his mouth. She wanted to murder his ass for disrespecting them with a lie, but she would let her brother handle it.

"Don't worry about it," Yero said, ready to start the meeting.

Dynasty couldn't believe her ears, but she kept her peace.

"I called this meeting to touch bases. I wanted you all to update me on your activities. I don't care about your personal business, just what can and have affected me and mine," Yero said, looking around and meeting everyone's eyes.

"Me and Casper popped that nigga TyJay and some of his people at the Star Bar this past weekend," P.R. stated casually, like catching a body was an everyday occurrence.

"Y'all niggas the ones who got the club shut down," Jay-O said, laughing.

"Any place, any time, work can and will be put in," Casper said, making the gun sign with his fingers.

"Me, Aza, and Light took care of that D.C. problem," Dynasty said seriously.

She wasn't in the mood to laugh and joke.

"My spots on time," Jah said, referring to the areas in the 336 under his control.

"Mine too," Towny said, referring to his spots in the 704.

"Roger that," Jay-O said. He had the 252 area code doing numbers.

"Hollywood has a reason for not being here, but he's good. Anybody else has anything to say before I end this meeting?" Yero asked, looking around the room.

His eyes briefly met Towny's, but he kept it moving. He continued when his question was met with silence.

"I'm sad to say this, but we have a snake in our presence," he said coldly.

"Who?" Dynasty shouted, hopping out of her seat, ready to chop the snake's head off.

"Sit down, Dy," Yero said seriously.

Dynasty sat the fuck down. She knew when her brother got like this, it was serious. She started eyeing mu'fuckas, wondering who the snake was.

"I'm only going to ask one time for the person to stand up and keep it real about your actions." Yero looked at everybody, making them uncomfortable with the intensity of his stare.

Everybody was looking at each other, wondering who it was. No one chose to admit to any wrongdoing.

"Towny, since you insist on being a coward, stand up," Yero said this in a voice so cold it lowered the temperature in the room.

Towny stood up on shaky legs and feebly stated his denial, "I don't know what you're talking about, Y.O."

He was so scared that sweat was popping up on his forehead.

"So you're going to keep lying?" Yero asked with a smirk on his otherwise expressionless face.

Towny knew his cousin Bolo wouldn't rat him out, so he figured Yero was fishing. He wondered what made him suspicious. *I could've sworn I was being careful*, he thought dismally.

"I don't know what you're talking about," he reiterated his denial, this time in a firmer voice.

"Dy, call Skittles up," Yero said without taking his eyes off of Towny.

Dynasty called her cousin ASAP.

"What's up, bitch?" Skittles answered excitedly. "You got me on speakerphone?" he asked when he heard the echo.

"Shut up, hoe. Yero wants you," Dynasty said, waiting to see the drama unfold.

"Oh, what's up, cousin?" Skittles asked.

"You got ya boy there with you?" Yero asked, still staring at Towny, who was starting to sweat harder.

"He right here, tied up real nice," Skittles responded with a giggle.

"Put him on." Yero waited until he was on the phone before he continued. "Mellz, do you know who I am?" he asked.

"I've been told you're Yero, aka Y.O." he responded in a shaky voice.

Towny was visibly shaking now.

"How did you come to know about me?" Yero asked, still watching Towny.

"Through my man's cousin. Some nigga name Towny," Mellz said, willing to tell everything he knew in exchange for his life.

Towny wondered if he should pull his gun and go out like a 'G'.

"And what did Towny tell you about me?" Yero asked calmly.

To anyone who didn't know him, he would appear calm and collected, but he was anything but. The whole room was captivated by what they were hearing. Jah and Jay-O looked at each other and shook their heads, denying any knowledge of it.

"He said you were a sucker who was fronting like he was built like that when you wasn't no street nigga. He told us you wouldn't miss the work he was giving us. He basically said you were pussy who had the connect."

Mellz was embellishing a little bit, but he was trying to live. Survival of the fittest, or in this case, of the best liar.

"Yo, that nigga lying," Towny said in a voice that lacked conviction.

"How much of my work did he give you?" Yero asked, drilling a hole in Towny with his eyes.

"A kilo of heroin and he was planning on hitting us off again soon," Mellz said, feeling that he was telling them what they wanted to hear.

"Man, I was just seeing if them niggas could hustle before I brought it to you," Towny said to Yero.

He didn't know that his death certificate was already signed.

This man a bitch, Dynasty thought angrily as she stared at Towny.

Dis mon is a pussy bwoy, Suai thought as she watched how Towny was sweating and fidgeting as he tried to lie his way out of dying.

"Skittles, get at me when you take care of that rat," Yero said before turning to smile at Towny.

The people in the room were starting to get a glimpse at the method behind his madness.

"A'ight, cousin," Skittles said over a begging Mellz in the background.

He had heard what Yero said and knew he was going to die. His voice was abruptly cut off when Skittles hung up.

"Let me murder this snake, bro," Dynasty said before pulling out her gun.

"Jay-O, did you know and or participate in this?" Yero asked, ignoring his sister.

He still hadn't removed his gaze from Towny, even though Towny was looking at everything but him.

"Nah, man," Jay-O said, shaking his head sadly.

He couldn't believe Towny tried some shit like this and kept him in the dark.

"What about you, Jah?" Yero asked calmly.

"Hell nah," Jah said heatedly.

He was mad Towny didn't turn him on. *That's why his stupid ass got caught*, he thought angrily.

"You have a gun, Towny?" Yero asked, even though he already knew that he did.

Towny was so scared that he couldn't get his voice to work, so he nodded.

"Give it to Jay-O," he ordered.

Towny was confused by the order, but he did as he was told.

"What am I supposed to do with this?" Jay-O asked.

He was just confused about what was happening. He stood up because he wanted to be ready for whatever.

Dynasty looked at her brother and wondered what he was doing. Everybody knew that Towny, Jay-O, and Jah were as thick as thieves. They had all grown up together.

"This supposed to be your man, but it's been revealed that he is a snake. He didn't even put you on and this supposed to be your brother from another mother. He violated, so kill him," Yero said like he was ordering him to cut the grass.

In reality, that's exactly what Yero was telling him to do— cut the grass.

Jay-O stared at Yero for a few seconds in disbelief before turning to face Towny. He raised the gun and pointed it at one of his best friends. Towny didn't open his mouth, but his eyes were begging Jay-O to let him live. Jah watched the scene unfold with an expressionless face. He was starting to realize how ruthless Yero really was. Dynasty was ready to pop any one of them niggas if they tried to turn on her brother. She looked at Suai and saw that she was prepared for the same eventuality. Jay-O saw the look in Towny's eyes and knew that he couldn't do it. They had grown up together, sleeping in the same beds, eating at the same tables, wearing each other's clothes. One fuck up couldn't erase a lifetime of good. He turned to Yero and stated flatly, "I can't do it."

"Give the gun to Jah. I respect your loyalty," Yero said calmly.

Jay-O didn't expect that response, but he gave Jah the gun and sat back down. He had no doubt that Jah would do the same.

"Kill the snake, Jah," Yero ordered.

He was a chess player, a grandmaster in his world, and he was about to let people know the stakes of playing this game with him across from them.

Jah stood up and pointed the gun at Towny with no hesitation. He also thought about all the things they had done growing up, from flipping bitches, stealing candy bars from the grocery store, smoking their first blunt together, to buying their first eight-balls together, but he felt like Towny threw all of that out the window when he made moves without letting him know what's up. So even though Towny was begging him to spare his life with his eyes, he pulled the trigger, twice.

"Oh shit!" P.R. shouted, shocked.

He didn't think that he was going to do it. Casper just chuckled.

"Man, are you crazy?" Jay-O shouted.

He jumped up and pushed Jah hard in his chest.

"You just killed our homeboy, nigga!" he grunted, ready to push him again but stopped when Jah swung the gun his way.

"Pipe down, nigga," Jah said seriously.

"Nigga should've put us on if he was our homeboy," he stated, letting everybody in the room know he was all about his paper.

Jay-O looked at Jah with a look of pure hatred. His mind was fucked up because he had just lost not one, but two friends—one because of death and the other because of betrayal.

"Man, fuck this shit," he said before storming out of the meeting.

"Nam . . ." Yero called out to the war veteran he had on his team. "Follow him and make sure he doesn't do anything worth dying over," he instructed.

Nam silently slipped out of the room.

"P.R. and Casper, deal with the body. Let this be a lesson to all with larceny in their hearts. I have eyes and ears everywhere. We are family and everyone will eat as long as we remember that. If you have a problem, speak up now." He looked around and waited for somebody to speak.

When silence ensued, he nodded.

"Meeting over," he said before leaving the room with Suai by his side.

Dynasty watched the reactions of everybody in the room after her brother had left and silently applauded his methods. She sometimes didn't agree with the way he did things, but the way he just manipulated the situation and the characters involved like a director on a movie set was brilliant. She noticed Jah was still staring down at the body of his dead homeboy with a look of regret on his face. She made a mental note to watch him closely. She was starting to realize that her brother was the most dangerous man she had ever met, and it wasn't even close.

Chapter 24

Beza was peeking out of the blinds in the living room to make sure she didn't get caught slipping in case Hollywood showed back up when she saw the police pull up. She took a deep breath and went to deal with them. For the next hour, she argued with them about pressing charges. She didn't want to, and they tried to make her. When she finally threatened to report harassment to their superiors, they acquiesced and left. When she was once again alone, she tried to call Niko.

***

"So we doing this or what?" Niko asked after he had finished running down his plans.

"Yeah, we're down," Chi Chi said, stealing one of Stari's French fries. "How are we going to split the profits?" he asked seriously.

Niko was about to answer but was stopped by the ringing of his cell phone.

"Hello?" he answered.

When they had arrived at the restaurant, he had turned his phone off so they could discuss business uninterrupted, but as he listened to Beza tell him what had happened, he regretted that decision. He felt his face tighten with anger.

"I'm on my way. Don't come out until you see me and my people in the Tahoes," he told her before hanging up.

He stood up, ready to go.

"What's up, Niko?" Stari asked when she saw her brother's face.

He rarely showed emotion, but when he did, she knew it was serious.

"These niggas down south don't know how to keep their hands to themselves," he said seriously. "I need to go pick B up because she's ready to go. Nigga put his hands on her one time and that's one time too many," he added as he revised his original plans in his head.

He was going to respect the game and not step on any toes as he moved his work, but shit just got real. Now he was going to get it how he lived—the hard way—and take what he wanted. He was about to treat Durham like he treated Brooklyn—'*My block*'.

Beza was in the bathroom, staring at her reflection. She couldn't believe that Hollywood had put his hands on her. She had seriously underestimated him, but she would never do that again. She had tried to use makeup to cover up the bruises, and she succeeded a little bit, but she couldn't do anything with the black eye she was sporting. She cursed and left the bathroom. Before entering the living room, she heard loud music coming from outside. Thinking that Hollywood had returned home, she ran to the front window and peeked out. When she saw the two Tahoes instead, she felt like crying tears of joy, but she grabbed her Jackie O-style Chanel shades and put them on to cover up her black eye before opening the front door and stepping outside.

Niko saw her step outside and hopped out of the truck. Chi Chi, Black Face, and Guardian got out also. He walked over and hugged her to him.

"I'm sorry, B," he whispered into her ear.

He felt bad for what happened to her because if his phone would've been on, he could've prevented it from happening.

"Where's your luggage?" he asked, ready to get missing before her ex showed up and shit became ugly.

"By the front door," Beza said, happy to be in his arms.

She leaned back and looked up at his face. Niko reached down and removed her sunglasses. Beza tried to put her head down, but he wouldn't allow her to feel ashamed in his presence. He clenched his jaw when he saw her black eye, evidence of Hollywood's brutality. He wanted to put his hands on that nigga so bad, but he calmed himself because unchecked anger was dangerous.

Beza saw the anger in his face and reached up to rub his cheek.

"Let's just go, please," she said.

She knew that if Hollywood showed up right then, he would be lucky to catch just a beatdown.

"G, come help me get this luggage into the truck," Niko yelled over his shoulder as he put her sunglasses back on. "Go get in the green Tahoe with my sisters," he told her.

"A'ight," Beza said.

She started to walk that way before she remembered her Gucci bookbag.

"Oh shit, hold up." She turned and jogged back into the condo to grab it.

When she came back out carrying it by the straps, Niko asked her what was in it. She held it up and smiled coyly.

"Let's just say that Hollywood paid for putting his hands on me."

Niko knew that the bookbag contained money, probably Hollywood's stash, and the hustler in him wanted to tell her to put it back, but he didn't.

Fuck that nigga, he thought angrily as he went to load the rest of her luggage.

Chapter 25
(Six Months Later)

"Stand in line before I sell you nothing," Trez told a junkie who was trying to cut line.

"I'm not taking no shorts on this *Blackout*!" Revolver yelled to the line of junkies in front of him.

It was summertime 2023 and Bull City was on fire. Yero's control over the city was tighter than a virgin's pussy. His team had a stamp on their heroin called *Blackout* that had the junkies going crazy. The name came from the time they were testing it out and all of the junkies kept passing out. Trez and Revolver had a spot on Liberty Street in East Durham that was doing numbers. They grossed at least five racks a day and even though they were young, they were about their business. A couple of times in the past, a few older heads had tried to muscle them out of their spot. They thought that because of their age they were pussy, but they quickly put that notion to rest when a few niggas turned up missing for trying them. They had a whole team of young wolves who wouldn't hesitate to burn a nigga ass up. Yero had put them on, and they would hold him down by any means, point-blank, period!

"What you want, player?" Trez asked an older junkie he didn't recognize standing in front of him.

"Let me get a bundle, young blood," the junkie said.

"You got a hundred, old head?" Trez asked.

The main reason he liked dealing with heroin more than crack was because the junkies didn't usually come with shorts. Crackheads might have six dollars for a ten-dollar rock, fifteen for a dub, but a heroin addict, nine times out of ten, will have all their money.

The junkie pulled a wrinkled Ben Franklin out of his pocket and handed it to him. Trez spread the bill out and checked it for identifying marks that could be used to jail him if the alphabet boys rolled up on him. When he was satisfied, he handed the junkie a bundle of Blackout. The man was about to walk off with his drugs until he noticed the stamp on the bundle.

"You don't have that Kiss Kiss stamp?" he asked seriously.

"Kiss Kiss," Revolver repeated with a puzzled look on his face when he overhead the junkie. "What the fuck is a Kiss Kiss?" he asked seriously.

"Kiss Kiss dat good shit, young blood," the junkie said, getting animated. "It be putting people on they ass. Word around town is its better than this Blackout," he added.

"Yo, old head, Blackout thing smoking around here," Trez said seriously.

"Naw, young blood, I want my money back," the junkie said, trying to give the bundle back.

"Fuck you mean . . . " Revolver said, screwing his face up . . . "Ain't no fucking refunds, nigga," he added seriously.

The junkies in line were quiet. They knew how Revolver got down and didn't want to attract his wrath.

"Look, young blood, I don't want no problems, but I didn't want this shit. I'm looking for Kiss Kiss," the old man said, holding up the bundle.

He made the mistake of taking a step towards Revolver. Trez didn't hesitate to react. He hit him in the face with a straight jab and knocked him on his ass.

"Fuck wrong with you?" he barked, looking down at the junkie who was on the ground holding his busted lip. "Don't ever disrespect me or my man again," he added seriously.

"Where the fuck they selling this Kiss Kiss shit?" Revolver asked.

He knew that Y.O. would want to know about somebody disrespecting him by pushing a rival stamp on his territory.

"Look, I'll take this and go," the junkie said as he tried to get up off of the ground.

Click clack! The sound of a gun being cocked made the old man freeze.

"Where the fuck they selling it?" Revolver asked.

The look on his face let the junkie know that he wouldn't hesitate to shoot him.

"The Mac. I heard it was McDougal Projects," the junkie said quickly.

"You sure?" Trez asked seriously.

"The Mac, young blood," the junkie said, scrambling up off the ground.

"Now get the fuck out of here," Revolver said before kicking the junkie in his ass.

"Your nosey-ass baby mama still stay in the projects?" Trez asked Revolver.

"Yeah," he said as he pulled out his phone. "We gonna find out what's up right now."

He knew Y.O. would bless them for the information, so he hoped his baby mama knew what was up. Whoever was disrespecting would soon get a rude awakening.

***

Jah pulled up in the front of Towny's baby mother's house on Rock Street in the west end and sat in the car for a few minutes, wondering how she would receive him. He hadn't seen her since he had killed Towny. He couldn't bring himself to go to his funeral, so he didn't know how she would act. He planned on paying his condolences to both Ashley and Towny's mother, Sheila, because it had been six months since he had seen either of them, and he needed to make sure they didn't suspect him for killing Towny. No one had said anything to him, but one could never be too careful.

For a few months, he had been worried about Jay-O because he had disappeared and didn't contact anybody. Yero knew what was up with him, but that didn't ease his mind at all because he saw the look in Jay-O's eyes when he had killed their friend, and the hatred there let him know he would try to get back, but didn't know when. Jay-O was back hustling for Yero, acting like nothing had happened, but they hadn't spoken to each other since the murder. Regardless of what it appeared to be, he knew what it was when they atoned for what he did. Clearing his mind, he climbed out of his new Dodge Charger and made his way up to the front door. He knocked and waited for someone to answer. A few seconds later, he heard her padding towards the door.

"Who is it?"

"It's Jah."

The door opened and Ashley was standing there with a frown on her face. He was about to say something when she broke out into a huge smile.

"Boy, where you been? Come here," she said before grabbing him into a hug. "Why haven't you been to see me and your niece?" she asked as she let him into the house.

Jah felt that familiar feeling of regret wash over him, but as was his custom, he pushed it out of his mind. *What's done is done*, he thought sadly.

"I've been stressed out, Ash," he said as he stepped into the house. "You still looking good, though," he told her as he looked at the tight velour pants she was wearing with a wife-beater. He noticed that she didn't have a bra on either.

"Boy, I'm not even dressed," she said self-consciously. "My sister has my daughter, so I'm using this free time to get some cleaning done," she added as she walked past him and into the living room.

Jah followed behind her, staring at her big ass bounce around in her pants. He remembered Towny used to brag about how she didn't wear panties and wondered if she had any on now.

"How you been holding up?" he asked sincerely.

Ashley took a deep breath as she gathered her thoughts. She looked up at him with unshed tears in her eyes.

"It's been hard, especially for Anitra, but what can we do but carry on," she said sadly.

"What the police saying?" he asked, unmoved by her emotional display.

Ashley's tears dried up quickly as she thought about how nonchalant the police were being about catching Towny's killer. She hated the police.

"Another nigga dead is no big deal to them," she said bitterly.

Jah wanted to smile, but he kept a somber expression on his face.

"Let's change the subject before I get mad all over again," she said, walking over to the entertainment system and turning on some music. "Sit down until I finish vacuuming the floor," she told him as she started cleaning up again.

Jah sat down and watched her as she moved around the living room. He felt his dick harden as he watched her bend over to pick something up off of the floor. He had always admired her. She wasn't a dime by anyone's standards, but she wasn't ugly either. What gave her sex appeal was her body. She had a big ass, a small waist, and a nice set of breasts. She could give a nigga an erection without even trying, like she was doing now.

"Oh shit, this my song!" she screamed as she ran over to turn the volume up on the Bluetooth speaker.

Ice Spice's '*In Ha Mood*' was blasting out of the speakers.

"Come dance with me," she said before grabbing his hands and pulling him up off of the couch.

Jah tried to keep some distance between them so she wouldn't feel his erection, but she grabbed him by his waist and pulled him up on her ass. He knew she could feel his dick because it was sitting right between her ass cheeks, and she was slow-grinding on him. He reached around and found out firsthand that she didn't wear panties. Before he knew it, he had her riding him reverse cowgirl, and he was beating the pussy up.

"Oh my God, it's been so long. Oh fuck . . . me harder," she screamed as she bounced up and down on the dick.

Jah stood up and bent her over the coffee table. He spread her ass cheeks and started long-stroking her. He was hitting spots he knew another nigga had never hit before. Ashley couldn't remember the last time she had been fucked so good. It crossed her mind that she was trifling for fucking her deceased baby daddy's friend, but that thought quickly vanished as her orgasm hit her full force, like a tsunami hitting a third-world country.

Jah felt his nut exploding out of his dick and pulled out. He shot his kids all between her juicy ass cheeks. He even smacked his dick against her butt just because he could.

"Clean me up with that mouth I've heard so much about," he told her arrogantly.

Ashley turned around and hungrily gobbled his dick up. The taste of her own pussy only turned her on more as she sucked him to another orgasm.

"Damn, you trying to kill me, girl," Jah said as he tried to catch his breath.

He fixed his clothes, flopped onto the couch, and waited for his heart rate to return to normal.

Ashley giggled. "You want to hop into the shower with me?" she asked, ready for round two.

"Naw, you go ahead. I need to recuperate," he said seriously.

She had just fucked the shit out of him.

"All right, I'll be about twenty minutes at the most," she said, disappointed he wasn't joining her.

She rushed off to the bathroom. Jah waited until he heard the shower running before he peeled off five hundred-dollar bills and sat them on the coffee table. He scribbled his cell phone number down and left the house. He was on his way to visit a woman who had helped raise him, a woman he had been calling his aunt all of his life: Towny's mother. If he got the same reaction out of her as he did Ashley, he would fulfill a childhood fantasy. His sympathy came with hard dick. *Sheila Mara Harris, here I come*, he thought as he pulled off.

***

Guardian, Black Face, and Red Star were posted up at City Flavor's tattoo parlor across the street from the old Northgate Mall, smoking a few blunts. Since they had started moving Kiss Kiss, it was one of the only spots they felt comfortable being in because it was owned by one of their people from up top. When they had first put Kiss Kiss on the streets, they had expected Y.O. and his people to retaliate, but nothing happened to any of their spots, and they started showing their faces a little more. Money was coming fast. Fuck whoever didn't like it.

"Oh shit, check out this whip," Black Face said, pointing towards the street.

"Check the boss move out that Chinese mu'fucka pulling," Red Star said excitedly.

Guardian looked up and noticed the car. Cars were a passion of his, so he knew exactly what kind of car it was: the new Ferrari F430 Spider, 4.3-liter V8 engine, 483 horsepower, 0–60 in 4.2 seconds, top speed 192 mph, 6-speed automatic with manual gear shifter. Base price: $199,000. It was a cherry-red drop-top with black racing stripes down the middle. He saw that the car had the top down in the middle of traffic, the driver getting head from the female in the passenger seat. Everyone could see her head bobbing up and down in his lap like she was trying to catch apples. Everybody was tuned in to the porn show going down in the exotic car. The driver looked over at them, saluted, and smirked before pulling off at the green light.

"Now that was some pimp shit," Red Star said, feeling the boss move.

"I need to find me a country bitch to do some shit like that," Black Face said as he eyed a couple of females eyeing him.

Guardian tuned them out as he stared in the direction the Ferrari had disappeared in. Something about the female in the car was familiar to him. He couldn't put his finger on it, but he couldn't shake it.

"Guardian, G . . . " He looked up to see Black Face and Red Star staring at him like he was crazy.

"What's up?" he asked, wondering why they were looking at him like that.

"Son, I just called your name twice," Black Face said with a laugh. "You was zoned the fuck out," he added, chuckling.

"That pimp shit had him gone," Red Star cracked.

Guardian smiled and shrugged. He looked in the direction the Ferrari drove off in one last time before he put it out of his mind. He knew it wasn't who he thought it was anyway.

***

Consuela felt Ichino's dick jerk and knew he was on the verge of climax. A second later, she was swallowing her favorite dessert: his semen.

"Oh my God, I can't believe you asked me to do that," she said, licking her voluptuous lips after she sat up.

She felt exhilarated; she felt young when she did things she didn't even know she was capable of doing, like having sex in public. She looked at his dick, still wet from her oral talents, getting hard again, and licked her lips. She wanted to suck him off again.

Ichino saw where she was staring and smiled.

"Suck my dick and shut up. Go slow this time because we are going for a drive," he said as he switched gears and got onto the freeway.

Consuela eagerly did as she was told. She found out that she loved having an audience. Neither of them noticed the black Mercedes-Benz tailing them. Ichino was so caught up in his manipulations that he was getting sloppy and careless. He felt invincible, and his arrogance blinded him to the fact that he was only a man. He couldn't fathom being outsmarted. He planned for every contingency, and his unpredictability was his greatest asset, but he missed one important detail, and it could be the difference between life and death.

Chapter 26

Captain Henderson snatched off his tie as he stormed out of Atlanta Police Headquarters, possibly for the last time. He couldn't believe they had suspended him after everything he had done and accomplished for the city, even saving the life of the mayor. The streets were safer because of him, but they had suspended him indefinitely with pay because powers in high places thought that he was too emotionally involved when it came to any investigation concerning the Alvarez twins, and it was effectively causing him to lose sight of the bigger picture. For the last six months, Internal Affairs had him under investigation because an anonymous source had reported that he was unstable and purposely jeopardizing cases because he was unstable. Through sources of his own, he had found out that Reggie Eduardo had been the one to blow the whistle on him. When he had gone to see him about it, he was suddenly unavailable. While he was under investigation, he put all of his energy into building a case against the twins because he could see that the deck was stacked against him. He knew time was now his enemy, so he used all of his resources to bring the twins down, but it seemed as if they had gone underground. They hadn't been seen in or around Atlanta since they had made bond after the 'failed assassination attempt' on Peachtree Street. His time had run out the day he was summoned to attend a meeting with Internal Affairs and his union rep. As soon as he walked into the room, he knew that he was going to be suspended; it was written all over their somber, fearsome faces as he sat there listening to their bullshit. After the verdict was handed down, he stormed out cursing and threatening revenge. Probably not the best exit he could've had, but hindsight was twenty-twenty. Now he was without a job. They had taken his gun and badge, and he felt naked without his constant companions. He looked at his watch and saw that it was two o'clock in the afternoon. It was a little early to start drinking, but he didn't have to work the next day, so he went to find the closest watering hole to numb his brain.

After sitting in a bar downtown for hours trying to drain his problems away, he decided to go home. After settling his tab, he stepped outside and saw that the sun had gone down. He made it to his car and sat inside for a few minutes trying to catch his bearings. He wasn't sloppy drunk, but he was over the legal limit and he was feeling it. When he finally collected himself, he pulled out and drove home. He tried to figure out what he was going to do with all of his free time. His life revolved around police work, but they had taken that from him, and it was all because of the Alvarez twins. The anger he was now feeling sobered him up a little bit as he thought about ways to bring them down once and for all. Just because he was suspended didn't mean he would stop doing his job. Nobody else seemed inclined to do anything about the twins, so he would handle it himself. When he pulled into his driveway, he sat there for a few minutes staring at his dark house and realized just how desolate his life really was. He was a divorcee with no kids, and before that night, he didn't have any regrets. Now he had more than a few. He got out of his car and trudged up the walkway towards his front door. He walked past the piles of leaves he had been meaning to bag up and set by the curb for weeks now and nodded. He really didn't have a life outside of police work. He stopped walking; his instincts were telling him that something wasn't right. He heard a noise behind him and spun around. When he saw a figure clad in all black, he reached for his service pistol, but his heart skipped a beat when he realized that he no longer had his gun. Realizing his doom, his survival instincts kicked in and he rushed his assailant, but was stopped dead in his tracks when he was hit with a cow prod.

"Night, night," Taboo whispered as he slid to the ground unconscious.

She pulled a two-way radio out of her pocket and made contact with her partner in crime, her brother Teck.

"Let's go," she told him.

Teck pulled up in a U-Haul and helped load the body into the back. He had a meeting he couldn't afford to miss.

***

Stari and Taji were eating in the food court at Southpoint Mall as they waited on Chi Chi, Khaos, and Show Off to finish shopping.

"These niggas better hurry up. The mall is about to close," Taji said before eating a French fry.

She looked at her watch and nodded.

"Isn't that them two niggas from the club awhile back who bodied them clowns on the dance floor?" she asked, ignoring her sister's complaining as she pointed to the two men she was referring to coming out of Foot Locker shoe store.

Taji was annoyed that her sister was ignoring her, but she turned to look at where she was pointing and got excited. Annoyance forgotten.

"Yeah, that's my boo-boo," she said before waving to get their attention.

"Bitch ain't seen this nigga in six months and he her boo-boo," Stari mumbled to herself, but she couldn't deny that she had been wanting to see her gangsta ever since that night.

Casper caught movement out of the corner of his eye and turned to see a female waving her arm at him.

"Ain't them the shorties from the Star Bar last year?" he asked P.R. when he recognized her.

P.R. looked and saw that it was indeed the two sisters from the club that night. He had forgotten all about them that night after they deaded TyJay's bitch ass, but now that they were within sight, he was remembering the body and face of the one he was dancing with, and he wouldn't mind tapping that.

"Yeah, that's them," he said. "Let's go see what's up. The mall about to close anyway," he added as he looked at his watch.

"What's good, shorty?" Casper asked when they made it over to their table.

"You, if you can remember my name," Taji challenged as she looked him up and down.

He still looked as good as she remembered.

"Stari and Taji. How can we forget y'all?" P.R. asked with a smile.

He knew that Casper was terrible with names and didn't want to fuck up a good thing by calling her someone else.

"What's our names?" he challenged them right back.

"How could I forget my gangsta Papi," Stari said flirting. "I've never visited Puerto Rico, but I wouldn't mind sightseeing," she added with a mischievous smile.

P.R. smiled at her double entendre. He tossed her his cellphone.

"You know what to do," he told her.

Stari smiled and put her number into his phone. She loved his aggressiveness. She looked over and saw her sister doing the same thing with Casper.

"I see you been shopping," she said as she gave him his phone back.

"What size shoe you wear?" P.R. asked, looking at her little feet encased in a pair of Air Jordan 4s.

"Why? You going to buy me some kicks?" she asked playfully.

Before P.R. could respond, they were interrupted.

"She don't need no kicks, son," Chi Chi said seriously as he walked up to the table.

He didn't bother to hide his distaste for the two men. P.R. looked at the man who had spoken out of turn and the two goons with him and immediately knew that they were from out of town. That 'son' shit was a dead giveaway, and a major no-no.

"First of all, you don't have any kids around here, so miss me with that 'son' shit, and second of all, I didn't ask you shit, *son*." He put extra emphasis on the 'son' to let him know it was disrespect intended.

Chi Chi smirked and nodded. "Let's go, Stari," he ordered.

Stari looked at him like he was crazy.

"This your man?" P.R. asked her with a smirk on his face.

"No, but we're going to go before this shit escalates into something serious because it's nothing right now," she said, grabbing her shopping bags as she stood up. "Just call me," she told him before rolling her eyes at Chi Chi as she walked past him.

"You owe me some kicks," Taji said to Casper before she followed her sister.

She looked back over her shoulder and told him not to disappear on her again.

"I got you, beautiful," Casper said without even looking at her because his eyes were trained on the niggas who could become victims if they weren't careful.

He could feel the tension in the air, and he was in a different zone. Fuck a bitch when it was time to eat.

"Be aware, duke," Chi Chi said before following Stari and Taji out of the mall.

"Fuck you two clowns staring at?" Casper barked at Khaos and Show Off.

He reached for his gun on his waist, forgetting for a second where he was, but P.R. stopped him.

"Chill, bro," he told him when Casper looked his way.

He knew Casper didn't mind catching a body anywhere, but they had to be smart.

"We in the mall," he warned.

Casper nodded and calmed his beast, a little.

"You about that gangsta shit?" Khaos asked rhetorically. "You better be when I catch you," he added seriously.

"I'm here now, pussy. I don't run, bitch nigga, and I'm ready to go to hell or jail. What about you?" Casper spat.

He already couldn't stand New York niggas, and this nigga was putting himself on his death list. Khaos started towards him, but Show Off held him back. People in the food court were starting to stare at them.

"Let's go, kid. Fuck these niggas," Show Off said, wanting to get it popping too, but he could wait.

Khaos stared at Casper for a few more seconds before snatching away from Show Off and stalking off. Show Off made the gun symbol with his free hand and pointed it at them before backing away. He didn't dare turn his back on unknown foes.

"Them niggas going to see me," Casper said seriously after they were gone.

"We'll see them dog," P.R. said, staring where they had exited the mall. "Trust me on that," he added quietly.

***

Desiree was twenty years old, living check to check in McDougal Projects. She was the legal guardian for her fourteen-year-old brother Buddy, who was her heart, because their parents were both in prison. She tried her best to make sure he had everything he wanted and needed, but it was hard when she was doing it by herself. She struggled to provide, or at least she did until she met Calvin 'Eat 'Em Up' Jenkins. She was working part-time at the Foot Locker shoe store when he walked in, laughing all loud with a few of his homeboys. At first, she was turned off by their boisterous display, but when he opened his mouth to talk to her, he had her attention.

"Yo, ma, can we get some help over here?" he shouted out.

"What can I help you with?" she asked when she walked over to him. "And my name ain't no ma, either," she added sassily.

"Well, what is your name, ma?" he asked as he looked her up and down.

He smiled at her, showing off his dimples. Desiree didn't want to admit it, but he was sexy.

"My name is Desiree," Desiree said, smiling despite herself. "What's yours?" she asked.

"Eat 'Em Up," he said, his dimples making another appearance.

"I'm serious," she said, thinking that he was playing games.

"Me too."

He knew she would think he was lying.

"Why they call you that?" she asked, intrigued by him more and more by the second.

"Let's see—" he said, counting the reasons on his fingers— "I eat beef. I eat drama. I eat . . . " he trailed off and smiled the smile she was starting to love.

Ever since that day, she was a goner. He sexed her right and took care of her and her little brother. He had moved in with her, and she was loving it. When he first asked her to trap out of her spot, she was against it because she knew Y.O. and his people had shit on lock, but after he popped a Rhino pill and gave her eight orgasms back-to-back, it was hard to deny him anything. So she gave in and let him use her apartment to set up shop. He made her quit her job and had her organizing the operation. She even had Buddy helping her. Eat 'Em Up didn't want his face to be seen that much, so her and Buddy served a lot of the customers, and they were doing a lot of serving. Eat 'Em Up's definition of a 'little hustling' was distorted. They were getting so much traffic they could barely get any sleep, but the money was great. She and Buddy were reaping the benefits. One look at their upgraded apartment and closets could tell you that.

"Desi, come upstairs!" Eat 'Em Up yelled from upstairs.

Desiree walked into the living room where Buddy was playing his *PlayStation 5*.

"What you playing?" she asked, trying to spark conversation with him.

Since she had gotten with Eat 'Em Up, there was a strain on their relationship and she didn't like it.

"*Call of Duty,*" Buddy replied blandly.

He never took his eyes off the television. Desiree sighed. She wanted to stay and talk, but she knew Eat 'Em Up wanted to fuck, and she wanted the dick so bad she couldn't wrap her mind around how gone she was. What made her feel bad was that she knew Buddy felt like she was neglecting him for her man. *I'll make it up to him*, she thought firmly.

"Make sure you take care of the customers, okay?"

"Okay," Buddy said again, not looking her way.

Desiree sighed before rushing up the stairs. She stopped off in the bathroom and stripped naked. She sprayed some strawberry blush body spray all over her body to make sure she smelled good. Eat 'Em Up lived up to his name. He left no part of her body untouched.

"You called me, daddy," Desiree said as she posed in the doorway of the bedroom they shared.

Eat 'Em Up looked up and felt his dick stand to attention. That's why he loved fucking Desiree. She was down for whatever. He wasted no time stripping out of his clothes.

"Come get your dick," he said as he stroked himself.

Desiree licked her lips and did as she was told.

Chapter 27

Captain Henderson groggily opened his eyes and shook to clear his vision. He looked down and saw that he was naked and duct-taped to a wooden chair. He looked around and noticed that he was inside some type of warehouse. He only saw one door, and there was a small generator sitting in front of him with wires running from it. He followed the wires and saw that he had cable clamps attached to his genitals. The implications of what someone was about to do to him really started to set in and made him try even harder to break free. Sweating heavily, he finally stopped and tried to think of who would go through the trouble of kidnapping him instead of just killing him in his front yard. The only people he could think of were the Alvarez twins. Just as he finished that thought, he heard the one door he had seen earlier opened. He looked that way and saw the bane of his existence walking towards him.

"Look who is up, Loca," Precious said sarcastically. "Sleeping Beauty."

Tiphany didn't respond as she stared a hole into Captain Henderson, who was defiantly returning her gaze.

"I'm not going to play games with you, puto," she told him coldly as they stopped in front of him. "Who tried to hit us?" she asked seriously.

Captain Henderson smiled wickedly. He knew sooner or later that they would come, but he expected it much sooner. They wanted information from him. Well, they wouldn't get it—not if he could help it.

"Fuck you, conniving whore slut," he spat in Spanish.

Tiphany smiled as she bent to adjust the current on the generator to an amperage low enough to knock him out, nothing more. She didn't want to kill him yet.

"I was hoping you played hard ball," she said as she sent the current into his body, knocking him unconscious just like she knew it would.

She turned and stared at her sister with a smirk on her face. Precious rolled her eyes.

"Bitch, you'll get paid. Just don't waste too much time torturing this puto," she said sourly.

They had made a bet and she lost. She had betted that he would break before they did anything to him, but he lost her fifty stacks with his stubbornness.

"Oh, it won't take long before he breaks," Tiphany said, hoping for the exact opposite.

She wanted him to hold out for as long as he could because she had some tricks she wanted to try out. She walked up to him and smacked him hard in the face.

"Wake up, puto. We're just getting started."

***

Buddy was so into his video game that it took him a few minutes to hear somebody knocking on the back door. Grumbling, he put the game on pause and went to answer the door. Thinking it was some customers, he opened the door without thinking of asking who it was first. When he saw the masked gunmen, he tried to close the door, but they pushed it open, causing him to fall to the floor. He tried to get up but was smacked with the gun and knocked back down to the floor. The gash that opened up over his eye was bleeding profusely and running into his eyes, temporarily blinding him. He tried to get up again, but this time he was knocked unconscious. The masked gunmen stepped over his body and checked the downstairs area. When they found no one else downstairs, they crept up the stairs. When they reached the top, they heard the rhythmic squeaking of a bed and telltale moaning that came from fucking. They knew they had caught their mark slipping, literally with his pants down.

***

"Harder, baby, harder!" Desiree screamed out as Eat 'Em Up pounded her pussy.

He had her legs bent back to where her knees were touching her shoulders and was digging her out. Eat 'Em Up was in his zone. He was watching his dick as it disappeared in and out of her pussy. She was so wet it was driving him crazy. Their relationship had started out as strictly business for him, but over the last couple of months, he had started developing feelings for her. He felt her pussy clenching around his dick and knew she was coming up on her third orgasm. He was trying to break their record of eight. He looked up into her face and saw her eyes go wide with fear. He looked over his shoulder and saw the two masked gunmen standing there with pistols pointed in their direction. He glanced over at his gun lying on the nightstand beside the bed and knew he would never be able to reach it before they killed him. He had been caught slipping.

"You thought this shit was sweet," one of the gunmen said as they walked up to him.

They put their guns down and proceeded to beat his ass.

"Stop, please stop!" Desiree screamed at them as she used the sheet to cover her nakedness.

She didn't even want to imagine what they might've done to her little brother.

"Shut the fuck up, Desiree," one of the gunmen said to her as they continued to beat the shit out of her boyfriend.

Desiree shut her mouth in shock when he called her name. *How does he know me?* she questioned herself as she tried to place his voice. She stared in horror as they beat her man bloody.

Eat 'Em Up tried to fight back, but he was no match for the both of them. He would take his ass-whooping like a champ as long as he kept his life.

"Where the money and the work, Desiree?" the same gunman said her name again as his partner continued the beatdown.

Desiree pointed to the closet. She hoped they didn't try to do anything to her. She wanted to ask about her brother, but she was too afraid to talk. The gunmen bagged up the work and money in a duffel bag.

"You should've known betta than to let an outta-towner move out of your spot. Let this be a lesson," one of the gunmen said before they ran out of the room.

As soon as they left, Desiree rushed over to Eat 'Em Up.

"You okay, baby?" she asked as tears flowed down her face.

Eat 'Em Up could only moan as he felt the damage done to himself. He knew at least three ribs were broken, along with his jaw. Desiree grabbed the gun off of the nightstand and rushed out of the room. She didn't even care that she was naked as she made it downstairs. When she entered the kitchen and saw her heart, her little brother, lying in a puddle of blood, she felt a part of her die. She rushed to open the back door and saw the two gunmen running away. With tears in her eyes, she raised the gun in her hand and started firing wildly at the two retreating figures.

Trez heard the shot and looked back just in time to see Revolver fall to the ground. He looked and saw that Desiree was standing in the back door shooting at them. He raised his gun and fired her way until he emptied the clip. He wasn't trying to hit her, but she was firing on them. When he saw her stumble back off the doorway, he ran over to Revolver and helped him up.

"Who shot me, dog?" Revolver asked as they jogged the rest of the way to their getaway car.

He was hit in the shoulder, and it was painful.

"Don't worry about it. Let's go," Trez said as he helped Revolver into the whip.

He pulled off and disappeared into the night. Trez's only thought as he sped off was getting his friend to a doctor. The sound of sirens and gunshots were an everyday occurrence in the projects, so nobody paid any attention to them. Durham was a warzone; a concerned citizen was likely to become a statistic.

Desiree was shot in the chest, and she knew she was dying. She heard sirens in the distance, but she knew they would never make it to her in time. She could already feel her life force draining out of her. She crawled over to her little brother, leaving a trail of blood in her wake, and collapsed on top of him. She cried because she didn't protect him in life, but she vowed to protect him wherever they ended up. She shuddered and left the earth the same way she entered it—naked. She had lived with hope of stability for her family in her heart, but she died with her eyes open and never saw death coming.

Chapter 28

Police Chief Dayton was looking around in nervous anticipation. He had been invited to the Governor's Mansion to have a private dinner with the beautiful Eileen Jackson. When he had first received the invitation, he had been wary, so he had placed a call to the Governor's staff and was told that the meeting was mandatory. He was told that the Governor wanted to build relationships with the police chiefs of the major cities in her state. So he was sitting in a private dining room waiting for her to make an appearance. The reason he was nervous was because the meeting would consist of only the two of them. He had been under the impression that the meeting would be attended by all of the police chiefs until he arrived and was told otherwise. He was pulled out of his reverie by the sound of a door opening up. He looked up just as Governor Jackson strode into the room. She smiled at him, and he felt his heart palpitate. She was beautiful by any man's standards, but she wasn't his cup of tea. Her smile seemed predatory to him, and he felt she had a hidden agenda.

"Police Chief Dayton, nice to meet you," Eileen said with her politician's smile as she held out her hand for him to shake.

"The pleasure is all mine," he said smoothly as he stood up and shook her hand.

He did well to hide his nervousness in her presence. He didn't hide it well enough because Eileen was able to see right through his faux calmness. She had worked around enough powerful men to know she made him nervous. She made note of it and let it go. She would take advantage of it later when she needed to.

"I hope you like what my cook has prepared for us," she said, sitting down as the servers entered with their food.

"It smells delicious," Police Chief Dayton said, grabbing his glass of wine as soon as it was filled and took a sip.

He felt his nerves calm instantly and took another sip. They made idle chit-chat during the meal and caught up on frivolous details. As soon as the servers had cleared the table and left the room, Eileen got down to business. She picked up a piece of paper lying on the table and cleared her throat.

"Let's talk about the rash of crime your city has been experiencing over the last year," she said as she locked eyes with him after placing the piece of paper face down on the table.

Police Chief Dayton eyed the piece of paper warily. He wondered what it was. All of a sudden, his nervousness returned in force, and he couldn't quite meet her gaze. He cleared his throat.

"I don't know exactly what you mean," he said lamely.

"So you mean to tell me your city is under control?" she asked aggressively.

Her time as a district attorney taught her how to ask questions and get answers—the answers she wanted. Chief Dayton shifted uncomfortably in his seat.

"We have our fair share of crime just like any major city. Nothing but gangbangers mostly," he said, shrugged.

"Do you know Yero Owens?" she asked pointedly.

She watched as his face paled at the mention of that name. Chief Dayton felt beads of sweat pop up on his forehead when he heard that name. His mind flashed back to the pictures he had safely tucked away in his safe at home and wondered if she knew. He decided to deny any knowledge of Yero Owens, aka Y.O.

"I've never heard of him."

"Are you sure?" she asked, picking up the piece of paper again as she looked at him.

She saw how he was nervously eyeing the paper in her hands and knew he was lying.

"This report says different," she said, waving the piece of paper at him mockingly.

She didn't have to know for sure because his predicament was hers; that she knew for a fact. Chief Dayton closed his eyes and took a deep breath. He refused to say anything that would incriminate him. He imagined that she had officers waiting just outside ready to arrest him if he admitted to the truth, so he remained silent.

Eileen saw the look on his face and softened a little. She knew his expression mirrored her own. They were both in a situation controlled by Yero.

"Chief Dayton, look at me," she ordered softly.

Chief Dayton heard the compassion in her voice and slowly opened his eyes.

"Does he have something incriminating hanging over your head?" she asked quietly.

Chief Dayton's heart was beating so hard he thought she might be able to hear it. He still thought she was trying to set him up despite the look of sympathy she was giving him, so he kept his silence.

"If I told you he had me in the same predicament, would it ease your fears?" she asked seriously.

She was gambling, but what is life without risks? Chief Dayton stared at her incredulously. Her words were intended to soothe his fears, but they did the exact opposite. If Yero had the Governor in his pocket, then he was much more dangerous than he thought. His fear was now bordering on hysteria.

"Yes, it's time. He's blackmailing me also."

Eileen looked into his eyes as she said this and received her confirmation that Yero was indeed blackmailing him too.

How many more do you have under your control, Mr. Owens? she silently questioned herself. "If we work together, we can bring him down, or should I say take him out . . . " she let her words sink in before she continued . . . "I have a plan that can free us, but I need you with me on this. If you agree, I will let you know what that plan is. Do you agree?" she asked seriously.

She was taking one of the biggest risks of not just her career, but of her life. Chief Dayton didn't want to hope that there was a way out of his situation, but this was the Governor of North Carolina talking to him. How could he refuse? After weighing the pros and cons in his mind, he nodded. Eileen silently let out the breath she had been holding as he considered her proposal. She proceeded to lay out her plan as she sat the piece of paper back face down on the table. He didn't have to know that she had been reading from her weekly financial report.

***

Shapphire was sitting at her desk in her office at the church on the phone, soliciting donations from many wealthy people she kept on speed dial when she heard a knock on her office door. She grew irritated because she had specifically told Rosario to make sure she wasn't bothered. With a frown on her face, she put her call on hold and told her unwelcome guest to come in. Her expression quickly changed to one of delight when she saw who walked through her door. She hung up the phone without hesitation. She stood up, walked around her desk, and gave her surprise visitor a hug.

"Ichino, long time no see."

***

Ya Ya was starting to feel depressed. Earlier that day, she had robbed Jah for ten thousand dollars from his stash spot, packed up a few clothes and essentials, and left home, never to return. Jah was out running the streets, and her mother was out doing her, so she took her chances and left. The first place she had gone was Beza's spot, but when she got there, Hollywood cursed her out and slammed the door in her face. A neighbor, recognizing her as Beza's friend, told her that Beza had gotten into an altercation with Hollywood last year and moved out. Ya Ya asked her if she had a new number or address for Beza, only to be told that she didn't know. She missed her best friend dearly. Jah had made sure she didn't talk to Beza after catching them with those New York niggas that day. He had even taken her cell phone. She had bought a new prepaid phone until she got settled in somewhere, but she didn't have anyone to call. Beza was her only friend, and she didn't have her new number. She couldn't even contact her on social media because she couldn't log into her accounts. So she was pacing back and forth in front of the Greyhound bus station, trying to decide whether or not to buy a ticket and just ride until she found somewhere to start over, because she knew that going back home was not an option. Just as she made up her mind to get a room and think it over for a few nights, someone grabbed her by the elbow. She spun around ready to fight but caught herself when she saw who it was.

"Boy, you almost caught a fade," she said, laughing nervously.

"Chill, Laila Ali," Guardian said, laughing along with her. "I haven't seen you in a minute," he told her, noticing the packed bags around her.

Ya Ya saw where he was looking and nodded.

"It's a long story," she said quietly.

Guardian used his finger to lift her head up.

"I have time, beautiful," he told her as he locked eyes with her.

Something in his eyes touched her, and had Ya Ya telling him everything that had transpired over the last year.

"He even fucked my mother where I could hear them," she said as tears flowed from her eyes.

"Beza been with my brother," Guardian said as he wiped the tears from her face. "I'll take you to her, but I need to know something first," he added as he stared into her eyes intently.

"What is it?" she asked quietly as she lost herself in his dark brown orbs.

"Are you done with this nigga for good?" he asked seriously.

He needed to know she wouldn't go running back to this clown once he let her into his life.

"Fuck that motherfucker," she spat vehemently in Spanish.

She would die before she went back to Jah.

"Death before dishonor," Guardian said seriously.

He wanted her to know there was only one way out if she took that step with him.

"Death before dishonor," she repeated just as seriously.

She was ready—ready for something new, something different.

"Let's ride then, beautiful," he said before putting her bags into his car, which had been illegally parked at the curb since the moment he had seen her.

For the first time in a long time, Ya Ya truly smiled. Life might just turn out to be worth living for.

***

Captain Henderson wearily opened his eyes and looked at the twins, who were both standing in front of him with frowns on their faces. For two days now, they had been torturing him, trying to find out who had put the hit out on them, but he refused to break, to their complete frustration.

Tiphany was one of the most twisted, sadistic people he had ever met. She had used methods of torture on him that he had never heard of before. She had put a plastic bag over his head and waterboarded him. When she saw that wasn't working, she switched to a method called a 'thousand cuts'. She took a salt shaker and shook the substance into the wounds, causing him to scream until his voice was raw. Then she took a bottle of rubbing alcohol and poured it all over his body. It was a burn so intense he passed out from the pain. She kept waking him up and repeating the process. The pain was unlike anything he had ever experienced. He couldn't take it anymore. He was ready to go wherever he was going to end up. They had won. He was defeated.

"Ichino . . . Ichino Tanaka," he whispered before passing out again.

Tiphany pulled her pistol out and unloaded the clip into his face.

"Fucking pussy," she spat when her gun was empty.

The sisters looked at each other with the same furious expressions on their faces. They knew who Ichino Tanaka was, just like they knew of anyone in their line of work with a name. The fact that he had tried to assassinate them was a direct violation in itself. The mistake on his part was that he didn't succeed, sealing his own fate.

"He's dead," they both said in unison.

***

"Yo, it's been two days since Eat 'Em Up got touched, and we've been sitting here twiddling our mu'fuckin' thumbs. I'm ready to dead some niggas," Show Off said seriously.

The images of his homeboy wrapped up like a mummy lying in the hospital wouldn't leave his head. When they visited Eat 'Em Up at Duke Regional to find out what had happened, he almost went out that night to search for retribution, but he knew that he was in a new jungle and out of his element. So he bided his time along with the rest of the *Ghetto Gunners*, but two days was too long, and he let it be known.

"Yeah, son, niggas gotta feel it," Chi Chi said as he locked eyes with Niko.

The *Ghetto Gunners* were already down one member when they came down south. Now they were down two. Just like them *Forty* niggas, somebody was going to pay for it. Niko could feel their anger, but they were also not thinking clearly due to elevated emotions. He figured they were lucky that Eat 'Em Up wasn't dead. He was used to send a message.

"If we go to war with this nigga in his city, we'll be wiped out," he told them seriously. "We don't know enough about him and his operation to go in blind. I'm all for get back, but I value life over foolishness. Recklessness will get you killed," he added as he tried to get them to see reason.

Khaos was posted by the window listening, and he wasn't feeling shit Niko was saying. That's why he never liked the nigga. He was always on some cerebral shit. The *Ghetto Gunners* could handle their own. They didn't need permission. Chi Chi knew Niko was right, but somebody had to feel it.

"What's the plan?" he asked, wanting to know how he was looking at it.

"Eat 'Em Up was a message. The nigga Y.O. basically saying 'I let you eat despite your disrespect, but now you're doing too much.' We were eating so lovely it had to be putting a dent in his pockets. So he flexed. He didn't even shut down all of our spots, but he letting us know it can and will get ugly," Niko said.

He knew they were feeling him because they were nodding.

"Your girl know this nigga, right?" Black Face asked, nodding at Beza, who was sitting quietly beside Niko.

"Yeah, I know him," she said.

She knew exactly how deadly Y.O. and his team were.

"Give us the run down then," Red Star told her.

Beza looked at Niko to see what he wanted her to do. She didn't want to, but she would if he wanted to. Niko knew what she was asking with her eyes, and he understood, so he would leave the discussion up to her. He could do his own DNA if it came down to that.

"Do you, ma," he told her.

Before Beza could say anything, the front door was opened and in walked Guardian carrying two duffle bags, but that wasn't what had her attention. Ya Ya, her best friend, her sister, walked in right behind him. She jumped up and grabbed her into a hug.

"Girl, I've missed you," she whispered, fighting the tears that were threatening to fall from her eyes.

"I've missed you too, girl. You don't even know the half," Ya Ya whispered back.

Guardian looked at his brother and let him know with his eyes that he would put him up on game later.

"Here go the rest of the money from the spots." He dropped the two duffle bags at the feet of his two sisters.

"I'm tired of counting money," Stari complained as she opened the bag and grabbed a stack of money.

"Yeah, just like you're tired of shopping," Chi Chi quipped.

"Whatever, nigga," she said, laughing as she put the stack into the money counter.

"So you going to tell us or what, Beza?" Show Off asked.

He wanted to know what she knew about the infamous Yero. Beza looked at Ya Ya, who was sitting beside Guardian looking happy, and decided to let them know what they were dealing with. The only reason she had been hesitant before was because she had thought Ya Ya was still with Jah, and she didn't want to do or say anything to put her in danger, but now that they were together again, safe and sound, she would let them know that Yero was nothing to play with, especially in Bull City. She had seen and heard enough to know just how dangerous they were. They might not like hearing the truth, but the truth shall set you free.

Chapter 29

Jay-O was cooped up in a hotel room losing his mind. He felt like he was going crazy. It started the day he watched Jah murder their homeboy over some bullshit, and he didn't do anything to stop him. He was scared to sleep because Towny had started visiting his dreams, accusing him of turning his back on him among other things. It all had to mean something, but he couldn't figure out what. He was stressed out, and he couldn't take the visits from his dead homeboy much longer, so he started snorting powder to stay up as long as he could. The drugs mixed with the anger and resentment he was feeling wasn't a good combination. He rarely slept, so his visits from Towny had all but stopped; instead, he had acquired two new friends, and they both were making good points about what he should do next. He just didn't know who to listen to. He started doing some more lines as his two friends started arguing.

"You dog, you need to get at them niggas, especially Jah," the demon on his left shoulder said into his ear.

"No, Jay-O, you need to forgive," the angel on his right shoulder countered.

"Shut yo' bitch-ass up," the demon shouted to the angel.

"God bless you," the angel said seriously.

"Bless this," the demon said as he stuck up his middle finger.

"Satan, I rebuke you," the angel said crossly.

Jay-O continued to feed his nose as he listened to them go back and forth. He didn't know what he was going to do, but if he didn't do something soon, he was going to end up killing himself.

***

Kandy was coming out of the bathroom when she ran into Ceaz, who was standing in front of her with a gun in his hand and a frown on his face.

"Damn, Joe, you scared me," she said with a nervous chuckle.

"Who was you talking to?" he asked as he stared at the cell phone in her hand.

Kandy immediately knew that she was on shaky ground. Ever since Bless had been killed in the shootout at the funeral, Ceaz had become extremely paranoid. He kept reading the newspaper articles on the incident every day like he could somehow change what had transpired by rereading it over and over again. She had been talking to Dynasty, but she wasn't about to admit that to him, especially not with a gun in her face.

"I was talking to customer service. My phone been acting up since we've been in Delaware," she said.

She held her breath, waiting to see if he bought her story.

"Hit redial and put it on speaker," he said seriously.

"Joe, you tripping," Kandy said, trying to walk past him.

Ceaz grabbed her around the neck and slammed her against the bathroom door. He put his gun in her face and growled.

"Bitch, I said hit redial and put it on speaker!"

Kandy saw the look in his eyes and knew he would kill her if she refused to do what he wanted, so she did it.

"Press zero if you want to talk to a live representative. Press one if you want to buy special features for your plan . . ." the automated voice said after she hit redial.

Kandy stared at Ceaz defiantly until he let her go.

"I'm sorry, Kandy, but this shit has me fucked up. I need to get some air. I'll be back," Ceaz said before tucking his gun into his waist and running out of the hotel room.

When the door slammed shut behind him, she ran to the window to make sure he was really leaving. When she saw his car leaving, she called Dynasty back. If Dynasty hadn't told her to always call another number after talking to her, she would be dead right now. Ceaz was a lit fuse, and she didn't want to be around when he blew.

***

Yero and Suai were riding in one of his many hoopties when they ran into some traffic on Fayetteville Street. Yero saw niggas up ahead running from car to car and knew what was up.

"Did you set up something on this strip?" he asked Suai, already knowing that she didn't.

"No," she answered.

She knew her man knew his operation up and down, left and right, so if he was asking that question, then someone was violating and was about to be dealt with. She took her gun out of her purse and put it in her lap. She was ready for whatever.

Yero kept quiet as they followed the traffic until they were by the action. He had the area around the old Fayetteville Street projects jumping, but not this area. When he saw a nigga running up to his window, he pulled his fitted low and cracked the window a little.

"What you need?" the dealer asked, trying to see inside the car.

The 5% tint was making it hard to do so without getting all up on the car, and he wasn't about to do that until he saw some money.

"What's the stamp you carrying?" Yero asked.

"You know it's that Kiss Kiss. Now what you want? I got money to make," the dealer said, sounding anxious.

"Give me a bundle." Yero held a hundred-dollar bill out the window.

The dealer all of a sudden had a bad feeling about this. Selling to this nigga when he couldn't really see his face was making him nervous. He might be the police. Yero peeped the nervousness and smirked.

"What? My money ain't no good?" he asked, waving the Franklin.

The dealer couldn't turn down the hundred-dollar sale, so he grabbed the bill, checked it for any identifying marks, then handed him the bundle. When he did, the window was down a little more, allowing him to see inside the car. *This nigga don't look like he use,* the dealer thought. His knees buckled when he saw the gun pointed at him.

"You should've followed your gut instincts," Yero said before pulling the trigger, hitting him in the stomach.

He got out of the car and started shooting up the block. Suai followed suit and started picking niggas off.

"This shit is shut the fuck down! This is my block! Fuck wrong with you niggas? Fuck is Kiss Kiss? This is not a mu'fuckin' Chris Brown video!" he shouted as niggas scattered.

He heard sirens in the distance and ordered Suai back into the car. He hopped back into the driver's seat and pulled off, blending into traffic. His point had been made.

***

Khaos was looking out of the window, tuning out the conversations around him, when he thought he saw something move in the shadows of the night. He peered into the darkness intently, trying to see if something or someone was out there. When he didn't see anything, he turned around and tried to pay attention to the bullshit being talked about in his presence.

"Fuck them niggas straight up," Black Face said seriously. "My gun go off," he added with a snarl.

Before anyone could respond, the front door and the back door were kicked in simultaneously.

"Freeze! Freeze! Hands up now!" Detective Jerome Davis shouted as he rushed into the living room.

He had an AR-15 automatic rifle in his hands. At least ten officers rushed in behind him. Khaos was trying to get to his pistol on his waist but stopped moving when a rifle was pointed at his chest.

"Try it," the officer said, daring him to move again.

"Everybody stand the fuck up!" Detective Davis ordered. "Search them," he told his officers. "Which one of y'all mu'fuckas is Niko?" he asked, looking directly at Niko with a smirk on his face as his officers searched them.

After stripping them of their guns, they searched the house. Niko kept his peace because it was obvious to everyone in the room that he knew exactly who he was.

"I have a message for you from Mr. Owens . . . " Detective Davis smiled at the shock on some of their faces.

He was enjoying himself.

"He said you're violating by moving work on his territory without his permission, and the whole city, the whole state is his territory. He's done his homework on you and your people, and he sends his condolences for your loss. He's only having a message sent because he respects your hustle. You know the rules to this game. The only reason you're still alive is because he's allowed it. War and money don't mix. He's being lenient, or I wouldn't be just talking to you—" he let that sink in before he continued— "He wants to meet you and your people. He says you have people in common. He's about his money, but disrespect will be handled violently if it continues. You now know what it is. The next move is yours. Grab these two duffel bags and let's be out," he told his officers.

He followed them to the back door but stopped before leaving and turned around. He pulled an envelope from his pocket and held it up.

"I almost forgot . . . " he said, tossing it onto the coffee table. "If you were smart—and I assume that you are—you'll meet with him. If you choose not to . . . " he shrugged and disappeared into the darkness.

"This nigga got the police on his team," Show Off said in awe.

He had only seen shit like that in movies.

"That's some shit Papa would've done if he was alive," Stari said, reminiscent.

"Check these photos out," Guardian said as he spread the pictures from the envelope onto the coffee table. "This nigga had us under surveillance." He was incredulous as he sorted through the different pictures of them in different locations.

"Fuck them pictures," Chi Chi said angrily. "What we going to do about this nigga taking our money?" he asked seriously.

"The money is inconsequential to the bigger picture. He don't want our money. We can get that back," Niko said, still thinking about what the officer had said.

"You going to meet him?" Taji asked.

She knew how her brother thought things out.

"Why not?" Niko asked rhetorically.

"He could have had us killed or locked up for a very long time, but he sent a message. It could be beneficial for us in more ways than one. If he wanted us dead, we'd be dead. Money is the motivation," he added seriously.

"Where are we supposed to meet this nigga?" Black Face asked. "Pigs didn't give us no directions," he added.

"Here go the directions," Guardian said, holding up a piece of paper he just found stuck inside of the envelope the pictures came in. "It says that the meeting is set up for two days from now," he said as he read from the paper.

"Well, fuck it. We all going," Chi Chi said seriously. "I most definitely want to meet this kid."

Chapter 30

Precious was standing on the balcony of the hotel room she was sharing with her sister at the Marriott on Capital Boulevard in Raleigh, sipping a glass of her wine as she watched the sunrise. She had a lot on her mind, and the revelation her twin had dropped on her the other day was at the forefront.

"That bitch nigga Y.O. fucking with that fish-eating Tanaka," Tiphany said with death dancing in her eyes.

"You sure?" she remembered asking.

She was reeling. *Was he in on the setup from the beginning?* she questioned herself silently. *What about Tangie? She turned him on to us.* The questions were swirling in her mind.

"Am I sure?" Tiphany repeated with a laugh. "That nigga in on it. Don't go soft on me now, P," she warned.

"If he was in on it, then he's going to die too, in the most painful way, but Loca, be sure on this." Precious had wanted to be 100% positive.

"I'm sure now, but I'll get you the proof," Tiphany said before leaving.

That was two days ago. She turned and picked up the photos her sister had dropped in her lap the night before.

"You dirty rat motherfucker," she whispered as she stared at a picture of Yero meeting with some of Ichino's henchmen.

"You ready?" Tiphany asked as she stepped out onto the balcony.

She was dressed for warfare in all-black with two Glock 21s on her hips. Precious stood, staring at her sister for a few seconds, wondering why shit always went bad. *Disloyal niggas,* she thought sourly.

"Let's ride."

***

Consuela had her bag packed, ready to spend a lovely weekend with Ichino. When she came home last night, she noticed that her front door had been replaced with a new one. She assumed that her children and their friends had done something and fixed it before she could see it, but she noticed it right away. She had been with Ichino for the past three days, so she hadn't seen her kids. Over the past couple of weeks, she had been living in her own world. A world that Ichino built for her, and that was by design. Guilt was a constant feeling whenever she was with Ichino because she knew he had killed her husband and her children's father. So she avoided them to a certain degree because being around her kids intensified her guilt. Ichino was so demanding that it helped keep her mind off of them. He made her feel young, alive, and she was addicted to that feeling. That's why she was up early, trying to sneak out of the house to meet Ichino before her kids or their friends got up. She was almost out of the door when she heard her youngest child call her.

"Madre," Guardian called out as he walked into the living room. "Where are you going this early?" he asked as he hugged her.

"Me and the ladies from church going on a spa retreat," Consuela said as she hugged him back.

She hated to lie, but it was necessary in this instance.

"You really have adjusted to the country life," Guardian said, laughing as he stepped back out of her embrace. "I'm glad you're happy," he told her sincerely.

"Thank you, baby," she said, kissing him on his cheek. "My friends at the church have helped me a great deal," she told him with a straight face.

"Well, don't let me hold you up," he said, hugging her again. "Be safe, Madre," he whispered into her ear before letting her go.

"I will, baby. I'll see you later," she said, turning and rushing out of the house before he could see the tears in her eyes.

The sincerity in his voice had touched her heart, and she had to go before she broke down.

"Was that Madre?" Stari yawned as she walked past Guardian and into the kitchen.

"Yeah, she's going on a trip with her church friends," Guardian said as he went to hop into the shower.

For some reason, the image of that cherry-red Ferrari wouldn't leave his mind.

***

"Ye really gwan do dis?" Suai asked Yero.

"Why did you think I was playing?" he asked, looking over at her as he ate his eggs.

"Mem thought ye was playin'," she said, wondering why he was so adamant about this meeting.

She looked over at Dynasty for some help.

"Why you want to meet these niggas?" she asked her brother.

She trusted her only sibling, but she didn't agree with this move.

"Look . . . " Yero said seriously as he stood up.

He looked at the only two women in the world he trusted and sighed.

"Have I ever steered either of you wrong?" he asked quietly.

They both shook.

"Then trust me on this. I have a feeling about this, and if y'all not feeling it, then stay home." He walked out of the room.

He didn't have time for the bullshit because he had too much on his mind. Whether they were with it or not, he was going to the meeting.

Suai and Dynasty looked at each other and shook in exasperation. They didn't know why he wanted to meet with these New York niggas, but they would be there when he did. Staying home wasn't an option.

Chapter 31

Guardian was sitting in the woods in some country-ass town called Creedmoor, watching a two-story house that sat on some farmland. He looked around at the cows, chickens, pigs, goats, and horses, and shook in amazement. The only animals he saw in New York were the sewer rats, stray cats, feral dogs, and the horses the police rode. He was confused as to why his mother was there. That morning, when he hugged her, he had slipped an AirTag into her purse because over the last couple of months he had noticed a lot of changes in his mother's behavior. From the days-long absences to the mood swings and the skittish looks, she was hiding something. So he decided to get to the bottom of it. While his siblings were getting ready for their meeting with Yero, he had slipped out and was on the highway tracking his mother. After an hour, he ended up in the country, wondering what his mother was doing in that house and with whom. He took the binoculars out of his bag and trained them on the house. There was only one car, so he knew that the church trip was a lie. He figured she was with a man and didn't want them to know, but he had a bad feeling in the pit of his stomach. He still had that Ferrari stuck in his mind, but he knew what he was thinking wasn't right. Determined to get to the bottom of it, he pulled out his gun and trudged across the field stealthily until he was standing at the back door. He reached up and tried the doorknob. Surprisingly, the door opened and he was able to slip inside. After searching downstairs and finding no one, he crept upstairs. The closer he got to the top, he heard the telltale sound of sexual activity, and he was forced to stop when he clearly heard his mother saying things he wasn't supposed to hear. His anger rose inside of his body so fast and steady that he couldn't control his actions. Before he knew what was happening, he had kicked the bedroom door open.

***

"Oh my God, this dick is so good!" Consuela screamed as she bounced up and down on Ichino's dick.

She couldn't believe how good she was feeling. When Ichino had pulled up to the farmhouse, she was confused at first until he told her they would be completely alone . . . no security or anyone else for the whole weekend. Then she was excited. Ichino had really been showing her a different side of him, and it was making her fall in love with him all over again.

"Who am I?" Ichino groaned as he grabbed her hips and thrust up into her.

"Daddy," Consuela moaned as he hit her spot.

"Who do you belong to?" he asked as he reached up and grabbed her around her neck.

He loved that she did anything he asked her to do. She never denied him.

"I belong to you, Daddy." Consuela couldn't believe how good she was feeling.

She was on the verge of another orgasm, and it was so intense.

"Who's my bitch?" Ichino felt his climax fast approaching.

"I'm your bitch, Daddy!" Consuela screamed as her orgasm hit her like a tidal wave.

"Well, get up and suck Daddy's dick," Ichino ordered.

He groaned as her mouth wrapped around his dick. He knew that by the time he was through with her, she would never disobey him again.

***

Niko and his people pulled into an abandoned warehouse in the middle of nowhere. He saw the group of people standing in the middle of the empty warehouse. He didn't see a point in wasting time, so he hopped out, followed by Khaos, Black Face, and Show Off. Chi Chi hopped out and caught up to them. Red Star got out also, but he took his time catching up with them. Stari and Taji also took their time.

"You know me from somewhere?" Yero asked when they were face-to-face.

He didn't waste time with formalities. He didn't know why he spoke in Spanish, but it felt right.

"I was about to ask you the same," Niko replied in Spanish as he sized him up.

He recognized him from that day he got into it with Jah and his peoples. He was the one sitting at the light in the hooptie staring at him. *Looks can be deceiving,* he thought wryly.

Yero was doing his own sizing up. He couldn't shake the feeling that he was supposed to know the man, but he didn't know why he was supposed to know him or where they were supposed to have met before. He could feel his people's eyes on him, but he didn't give a fuck. He was about to say something when Rosario came over the two-way again.

"That broad Tangie on her way in."

"What the fuck that bitch doing here?" Dynasty asked, frowning. "This shit don't smell right," she added seriously.

Yero felt the same way, but he kept it to himself. It wasn't long before they heard Tangie's mouth.

"Hello! Hello!" she called out.

They could hear her heels click-clacking on the warehouse floor as she made her way towards them.

"Oh. There you are," she said when she finally spotted Yero. "Why did you tell me to meet you here, Y.O.?" she asked as she eyed everybody in attendance.

When she caught Dynasty grilling her, she rolled her eyes and turned her attention back to Yero, who was looking confused.

"I didn't tell you to meet me anywhere," he said seriously.

Now it was Tangie's turn to look confused.

"You left me a message to meet you here," she said seriously.

Yero knew he never called her, so he knew that something wasn't right. He looked over at Niko and saw a confused expression on his face. He was about to turn his attention back to Tangie when he saw the red dot dancing on Niko's chest. He looked down at his own chest and saw the same telltale dot.

"Everybody down! Snipers!" he screamed as he dived to the ground.

***

Consuela had just swallowed Ichino's load when she heard the bedroom door being kicked in.

"Oh my God! Oh my God!" she kept muttering as she grabbed the sheet to cover her nakedness.

The sight of her youngest son standing there with tears flowing down his face and a gun pointed in their direction broke her heart.

"Baby, please put the gun down. I can explain," she begged as she started crying also.

"How in the fuck can you explain this, Madre?" Guardian asked angrily. "You sneaking off to fuck this gook behind our backs. You told us the Japanese killed our father, but you sleeping with one," he added in disbelief.

Then he felt his blood go cold with his next question.

"Is this the mu'fucka who killed Papi?" he asked coldly as he trained his gun on the Japanese man, who was still lying there naked, staring at him with a nonchalant attitude like he wasn't worried.

"No, no, no! Please, Guardian, don't shoot him!" Consuela screamed as she threw her body across Ichino's as if to shield him with her own. "Let me explain, please, baby," she pleaded.

"Why are you protecting Papi's killer, Madre?" Guardian asked, confused at her actions. "Why won't you let me avenge Papa's death by killing this raw-fish-eating mu'fucka?" he asked as his anger threatened to overpower him.

Consuela looked at her youngest son and knew that the truth would devastate him, possibly forever, but she knew that the only way out of this situation would be by telling him her deepest, darkest secret. She looked him in the eyes and did just that.

"The reason I can't let you kill him, Guardian, is . . . " she took a deep breath and continued . . . "is because he's your father."

***

Yero looked up and saw men dressed in black tactical gear falling out of the ceiling on ziplines with automatic weapons slung across their chests. Once they landed, they were surrounded and ordered to stand up. He stood and brushed himself off. He could see the questions in everyone's eyes around him, but no one was likely to speak out of turn when automatic rifles were pointed at them.

***

Beza and Ya Ya were cowering on the floor of the Yukon, scared to death.

"What the fuck is going on?" Beza whispered.

"I don't know, but you betta pray they don't come search this truck," Ya Ya whispered back.

She had her eyes closed. Beza closed her eyes also and sent up a quick prayer.

***

It sounded like a thousand men marching towards them. Yero looked up and saw Precious and Tiphany leading a contingent of men towards them. With a confused look on his face, he asked,

"What's going on?"

"Nigga, don't act all confused now," Tiphany said angrily. "Your bitch-ass working with that snake Tanaka," she spat.

"Bitch, ye betta watch ye mouth," Suai said seriously.

"Fuck you, bitch," Tiphany said, smirking at her.

"Ye real tough wit' de gun in ye hand." Suai was ready to get busy.

Any disrespect to her man was disrespect to her. Yero held up his hand and she fell silent.

"It's not what you think," he said, thinking they were salty about him doing business with another supplier.

They left him out to dry with no word, so he didn't understand their actions.

"What are we supposed to think when you're partners with the man who tried to kill us?" Precious asked, watching his facial expression.

"What!" he said, incredulous at what she had just revealed.

He knew that Ichino was a rival of theirs, but he had no clue that he had tried to kill them, or he would've killed the sushi-eater a long time ago. He now knew why they came ready for war.

"I was only dealing with him to kill two birds with one stone. He was supplying me with work at dirt-cheap prices while you two went underground, and y'all didn't exactly put me up on game before you disappeared, so what was I to do? When you got situated, I was going to dirt-nap him because he violated for the only time by putting his hands on me and mine. I was just biding my time until I heard from either of you," he told them seriously.

Precious was convinced that he was telling the truth and was about to tell her sister as much when she heard footsteps behind them, alerting her to new and unexpected visitors. She spun around and gasped.

"Papi!" she screamed.

Tiphany was beyond furious and she let it be known.

"What the fuck are you doing here?" she asked their father angrily.

She hated that he was always into their business like they couldn't handle theirs. They didn't need a babysitter.

Stari and Taji couldn't believe their eyes. They started crying and rushed into the arms of their father.

"Papi, you're alive!" Stari cried as she clung to his neck.

Taji was crying so hard she couldn't talk.

"What the fuck is going on?" Tiphany asked rhetorically as she looked on.

Precious was staring in disbelief. Niko stared at his father walking towards him in disbelief. He couldn't believe that he was alive. Despite the fact that he was walking with a cane and a noticeable limp, he looked the exact same. He turned his attention to the man walking alongside his father, his most trusted companion, his godfather and namesake Niko, and wondered what the fuck was going on. He was confused by the situation, so he decided to let it play out.

Yero looked at the two well-dressed men in front of him and felt everything click into place. The face in front of him was almost a mirror image of his own.

"Tangie, Tiphany, Precious, Stari, Taji, and Niko, meet your brother and sister Yero and Dynasty," Manny said as he stared at his oldest son.

Yero and Niko looked at each other and nodded. To some degree, they both had felt it in their hearts that they shared the same blood, but it was shocking to hear that they were brothers. Nothing in life happens without reason, so they took it for what it was: a blessing. As far as their father was concerned, it was a totally different story. Yero looked into the eyes identical to his own and said, "Fuck you."

WAS BLOOD REALLY THICKER THAN WATER?

To Be Continued . . .

Lock Down Publications and Ca$h Presents
Assisted Publishing Packages

Due to an increase in the price of services we have increased our prices. The prices below reflect the price increase as of 11/1/24.

BASIC PACKAGE **$699** Editing Cover Design Formatting	UPGRADED PACKAGE **$1000** Typing Editing Cover Design Formatting Upload eBooks to Amazon Upload Paperback to Amazon
ADVANCE PACKAGE **$1,400** Typing Editing (line editing/content) Cover Design Formatting Copyright Registration Proofreading Upload eBooks to Amazon Upload Paperback to Amazon	LDP SUPREME PACKAGE **$1,700** Typing Editing (line editing/content) Cover Design Formatting Copyright Registration Proofreading Set up Amazon Account Upload eBooks to Amazon Upload Paperback to Amazon Advertise on LDP's Amazon and Facebook Page

***

Other services available upon request.
Additional charges may apply

Lock Down Publications
P.O. Box 944
Stockbridge, GA 30281-9998
Phone: 470 303-9761
Email: lockdownpublications@gmail.com

Submission Guideline

Submit the first three chapters of your completed manuscript to ldpsubmissions@gmail.com. In the subject line add **Your Book's Title**. The manuscript must be in a Word Doc file and sent as an attachment. Document should be in Times New Roman, double spaced, and in size 12 font. Also, provide your synopsis and full contact information. If sending multiple submissions, they must each be in a separate email.

Have a story but no way to send it electronically? You can still submit to LDP/Ca$h Presents. Send in the first three chapters, written or typed, of your completed manuscript to:

LDP: Submissions Dept
P.O. Box 944
Stockbridge, GA 30281-9998

DO NOT send original manuscript. Must be a duplicate.
Provide your synopsis and a cover letter containing your full contact information.

Thanks for considering LDP and Ca$h Presents.

NEW RELEASES

BLOODLINE OF A SAVAGE 1-3
THESE VICIOUS STREETS 1-3
RELENTLESS GOON 1-3
BY PRINCE A. TAUHID

THE BUTTERFLY MAFIA 1-3
BY FUMIYA PAYNE

A THUG'S STREET PRINCESS 1&2
BY MEESHA

CITY OF SMOKE 3
BY MOLOTTI

GET IT IN SLUGS 1 &2
BY B. STALL

STANDING ON HER BUSINESS 1&2
BY DG SANTANA

STEPPERS 1,2&3
THE REAL BADDIES OF CHI-RAQ
BY KING RIO

THE LANE 1&2
BY KEN-KEN SPENCE

THUG OF SPADES 1&2
LOVE IN THE TRENCHES 2
CORNER BOYS
BY COREY ROBINSON

TIL DEATH 3
BY ARYANNA

THE BIRTH OF A GANGSTER 4
BY DELMONT PLAYER

PRODUCT OF THE STREETS 1-3
BY DEMOND "MONEY" ANDERSON

NO TIME FOR ERROR
BY KEESE

MONEY HUNGRY DEMONS 1-2
BY TRANAY ADAMS

HUB CITY MENACE 1-3
BY J. WHITE

A THUGGISH PASSION 1&2
LAND OF DA HOOLIGANZ 1-4
KILLAZ ON STANDBY 1&2
BY IRA B.

FO'EVA ROLLIN 1&2
BY ASSA RAYMOND BAKER

THE LEVEL UP 1&3
BY LUXURY KING

Coming Soon from Lock Down Publications/Ca$h Presents

IF YOU CROSS ME ONCE 6
ANGEL V
By Anthony Fields

A THUGS STREET PRINCESS 3
By Meesha

CORNER BOYS 2
By Corey Robinson

THA TAKEOVER
By Keith Chandler

BETRAYAL OF A G 2
By Ray Vinci

SAVAGE FAMILY EMPIRE 1&2
SOULLESS GOON 1,2&3
THE DIRTY SIDE OF MONEY 1,2&3
By Prince

FOR MY ENEMY'S SAKE
AMBITIONS OF A SLIDER
FRESH OFF DA PORCH
By IRA B.

BY THE TRUCKLOAD 1-4
TIPPIN' THE SCALES 1-3
BAD BITCHES WIT GUNZ 3
PROBLEM SOLVED 2
By Christopher "Diesel" Hornezes

Available Now

RESTRAINING ORDER 1 & 2
By **CA$H & Coffee**

LOVE KNOWS NO BOUNDARIES 1-3
By **Coffee**

RAISED AS A GOON I, II, III & IV
BRED BY THE SLUMS I, II, III
BLAST FOR ME I & II
ROTTEN TO THE CORE I II III
A BRONX TALE I, II, III
DUFFLE BAG CARTEL I II III IV V VI
HEARTLESS GOON I II III IV V
A SAVAGE DOPEBOY I II
DRUG LORDS I II III
CUTTHROAT MAFIA I II
KING OF THE TRENCHES
By **Ghost**

LAY IT DOWN I & II
LAST OF A DYING BREED I II
BLOOD STAINS OF A SHOTTA I & II III
By **Jamaica**

LOYAL TO THE GAME I II III
LIFE OF SIN I, II III
By **TJ & Jelissa**

IF LOVING HIM IS WRONG…I & II
LOVE ME EVEN WHEN IT HURTS I II III
By **Jelissa**

PUSH IT TO THE LIMIT
By **Bre' Hayes**

BLOODY COMMAS I & II
SKI MASK CARTEL I, II & III
KING OF NEW YORK I II, III IV V
RISE TO POWER I II III
COKE KINGS I II III IV V
BORN HEARTLESS I II III IV
KING OF THE TRAP I II
By **T.J. Edwards**

WHEN THE STREETS CLAP BACK I & II III
THE HEART OF A SAVAGE I II III IV
MONEY MAFIA I II
LOYAL TO THE SOIL I II III
By **Jibril Williams**

A DISTINGUISHED THUG STOLE MY HEART I II & III
LOVE SHOULDN'T HURT I II III IV
RENEGADE BOYS 1-4
PAID IN KARMA 1-3
SAVAGE STORMS 1-3
AN UNFORESEEN LOVE 1-3
BABY, I'M WINTERTIME COLD 1-3
A THUG'S STREET PRINCESS 1&2
By **Meesha**

A GANGSTER'S CODE 1-3
A GANGSTER'S SYN 1-3
THE SAVAGE LIFE 1-3
CHAINED TO THE STREETS 1-3
BLOOD ON THE MONEY 1-3
A GANGSTA'S PAIN 1-3
BEAUTIFUL LIES AND UGLY TRUTHS
CHURCH IN THESE STREETS
By **J-Blunt**

CUM FOR ME 1-8
An LDP Erotica Collaboration

BLOOD OF A BOSS 1-5
SHADOWS OF THE GAME
TRAP BASTARD
By **Askari**

THE STREETS BLEED MURDER 1-3
THE HEART OF A GANGSTA 1-3
By **Jerry Jackson**

WHEN A GOOD GIRL GOES BAD
By **Adrienne**

THE COST OF LOYALTY 1-3
By **Kweli**

BRIDE OF A HUSTLA 1-3
THE FETTI GIRLS 1-3
CORRUPTED BY A GANGSTA 1-4
BLINDED BY HIS LOVE
THE PRICE YOU PAY FOR LOVE 1-3
DOPE GIRL MAGIC 1-3
By **Destiny Skai**

A KINGPIN'S AMBITION
A KINGPIN'S AMBITION II
I MURDER FOR THE DOUGH
By **Ambitious**

TRUE SAVAGE 1-7
DOPE BOY MAGIC 1-3
MIDNIGHT CARTEL 1-3
CITY OF KINGZ 1&2
NIGHTMARE ON SILENT AVE
THE PLUG OF LIL MEXICO 1&2
CLASSIC CITY
By **Chris Green**

A GANGSTER'S REVENGE 1-4
THE BOSS MAN'S DAUGHTERS 1-5
A SAVAGE LOVE 1&2
BAE BELONGS TO ME 1&2
A HUSTLER'S DECEIT 1-3
WHAT BAD BITCHES DO 1-3
SOUL OF A MONSTER 1-3
KILL ZONE
A DOPE BOY'S QUEEN 1-3
TIL DEATH 1-3
IMMA DIE BOUT MINE 1-6
DYING FOR LIKES
By **Aryanna**

A DOPEBOY'S PRAYER
By **Eddie "Wolf" Lee**

THE KING CARTEL 1-3
By **Frank Gresham**

THESE NIGGAS AIN'T LOYAL 1-3
By **Nikki Tee**

GANGSTA SHYT 1-3
By **CATO**

THE ULTIMATE BETRAYAL
By **Phoenix**

BOSS'N UP 1-3
By **Royal Nicole**

I LOVE YOU TO DEATH
By **Destiny J**

I RIDE FOR MY HITTA
I STILL RIDE FOR MY HITTA
By **Misty Holt**

LOVE & CHASIN' PAPER
By **Qay Crockett**

TO DIE IN VAIN
SINS OF A HUSTLA
By **ASAD**

BROOKLYN HUSTLAZ
By **Boogsy Morina**

BROOKLYN ON LOCK 1 & 2
By **Sonovia**

GANGSTA CITY
By **Teddy Duke**

A DRUG KING AND HIS DIAMOND 1-3
A DOPEMAN'S RICHES
HER MAN, MINE'S TOO 1&2
CASH MONEY HO'S
THE WIFEY I USED TO BE 1&2
PRETTY GIRLS DO NASTY THINGS
By **Nicole Goosby**

LIPSTICK KILLAH 1-3
CRIME OF PASSION 1-3
FRIEND OR FOE 1-3
By **Mimi**

TRAPHOUSE KING 1-3
KINGPIN KILLAZ 1-3
STREET KINGS 1&2
PAID IN BLOOD 1&2
CARTEL KILLAZ 1-3
DOPE GODS 1&2
By **Hood Rich**

THE STREETS ARE CALLING
By **Duquie Wilson**

STEADY MOBBN' 1-3
THE STREETS STAINED MY SOUL 1-3
By **Marcellus Allen**

WHO SHOT YA 1-3
SON OF A DOPE FIEND 1-4
HEAVEN GOT A GHETTO 1&2
SKI MASK MONEY 1&2
By **Renta**

GORILLAZ IN THE BAY 1-4
TEARS OF A GANGSTA 1/&2
3X KRAZY 1&2
STRAIGHT BEAST MODE 1&2
By **DE'KARI**

TRIGGADALE 1-3
MURDA WAS THE CASE 1-3
By **Elijah R. Freeman**

SLAUGHTER GANG 1-3
RUTHLESS HEART 1-3
By **Willie Slaughter**

GOD BLESS THE TRAPPERS 1-3
THESE SCANDALOUS STREETS 1-3
FEAR MY GANGSTA 1-5
THESE STREETS DON'T LOVE NOBODY 1-2
BURY ME A G 1-5
A GANGSTA'S EMPIRE 1-4
THE DOPEMAN'S BODYGAURD 1&2
THE REALEST KILLAZ 1-3
THE LAST OF THE OGS 1-3
By **Tranay Adams**

MARRIED TO A BOSS 1-3
By **Destiny Skai & Chris Green**

KINGZ OF THE GAME 1-7
CRIME BOSS 1-4
By **Playa Ray**

FUK SHYT
By **Blakk Diamond**

DON'T F#CK WITH MY HEART 1&2
By **Linnea**

ADDICTED TO THE DRAMA 1-3
IN THE ARM OF HIS BOSS
By **Jamila**

LOYALTY AIN'T PROMISED 1&2
By **Keith Williams**

YAYO 1-4
A SHOOTER'S AMBITION 1&2
BRED IN THE GAME
By **S. Allen**

TRAP GOD 1-3
RICH $AVAGE 1-3
MONEY IN THE GRAVE 1-3
CARTEL MONEY 1&2
By **Martell Troublesome Bolden**

FOREVER GANGSTA 1&2
GLOCKS ON SATIN SHEETS 1&2
By **Adrian Dulan**

TOE TAGZ 1-4
LEVELS TO THIS SHYT 1&2
IT'S JUST ME AND YOU
By **Ah'Million**

KINGPIN DREAMS 1-3
RAN OFF ON DA PLUG
By **Paper Boi Rari**

THE STREETS MADE ME 1-3
By **Larry D. Wright**

CONFESSIONS OF A GANGSTA 1-4
CONFESSIONS OF A JACKBOY 1-3
CONFESSIONS OF A HITMAN
CONFESSIONS OF A DOPE BOY
By **Nicholas Lock**

I'M NOTHING WITHOUT HIS LOVE
SINS OF A THUG
TO THE THUG I LOVED BEFORE
A GANGSTA SAVED XMAS
IN A HUSTLER I TRUST
By **Monet Dragun**

QUIET MONEY 1-3
THUG LIFE 1-3
EXTENDED CLIP 1&2
A GANGSTA'S PARADISE
By **Trai'Quan**

CAUGHT UP IN THE LIFE 1-3
THE STREETS NEVER LET GO 1-3
By **Robert Baptiste**

NEW TO THE GAME 1-3
MONEY, MURDER & MEMORIES 1-3
By **Malik D. Rice**

CREAM 2-3
THE STREETS WILL TALK
By **Yolanda Moore**

THE STREETS WILL NEVER CLOSE 1-3
By **K'ajji**

LIFE OF A SAVAGE 1-4
A GANGSTA'S QUR'AN 1-4
MURDA SEASON 1-3
GANGLAND CARTEL 1-3
CHI'RAQ GANGSTAS 1-4
KILLERS ON ELM STREET 1-3
JACK BOYZ N DA BRONX 1-3
A DOPEBOY'S DREAM 1-3
JACK BOYS VS DOPE BOYS 1-3
COKE GIRLZ
COKE BOYS
SOSA GANG 1&2
BRONX SAVAGES
BODYMORE KINGPINS
BLOOD OF A GOON
By **Romell Tukes**

CONCRETE KILLA 1-3
VICIOUS LOYALTY 1-3
BLOODY MONEY BAGS
By **Kingpen**

THE ULTIMATE SACRIFICE 1-6
KHADIFI
IF YOU CROSS ME ONCE 1-3
ANGEL 1-4
IN THE BLINK OF AN EYE
By **Anthony Fields**

THE LIFE OF A HOOD STAR
By **Ca$h & Rashia Wilson**

NIGHTMARES OF A HUSTLA 1-3
BLOOD AND GAMES 1&2
By **King Dream**

GHOST MOB
By **Stilloan Robinson**

HARD AND RUTHLESS 1&2
MOB TOWN 251
THE BILLIONAIRE BENTLEYS 1-3
REAL G'S MOVE IN SILENCE
By **Von Diesel**

MOB TIES 1-7
SOUL OF A HUSTLER, HEART OF A KILLER 1-3
GORILLAZ IN THE TRENCHES
OOPS CRY TOO 1&2
THE DAUGHTER OF A CARTEL BOSS
By **SayNoMore**

BODYMORE MURDERLAND 1-3
THE BIRTH OF A GANGSTER 1-4
By **Delmont Player**

FOR THE LOVE OF A BOSS 1&2
By **C. D. Blue**

KILLA KOUNTY 1-5
TENDER
By **Khufu**

MOBBED UP 1-4
THE BRICK MAN 1-5
THE COCAINE PRINCESS 1-10
STEPPERS 1-3
SUPER GREMLIN 1-4
A GANGSTA'S SON
By **King Rio**

MONEY GAME 1&2
By **Smoove Dolla**

A GANGSTA'S KARMA 1-5
By **FLAME**

KING OF THE TRENCHES 1-3
By **GHOST & TRANAY ADAMS**

BAD BITCHES WIT GUNZ 1&2
PROBLEM SOLVED
By **"Christopher Diesel" Hornezes**

QUEEN OF THE ZOO 1&2
By **Black Migo**

GRIMEY WAYS 1-3
BETRAYAL OF A G
By **Ray Vinci**

XMAS WITH AN ATL SHOOTER
By **Ca$h & Destiny Skai**

KING KILLA 1&2
By **Vincent "Vitto" Holloway**

BETRAYAL OF A THUG 1&2
By **Fre$h**

COUNTDOWN OF A KILLA 1&2
SEX, MURDER AND GOD 1&2
GUNS DOWN, BOTTOMS UP 1&2
By **Lo-Life**

THE MURDER QUEENS 1-7
By **Michael Gallon**

FOR THE LOVE OF BLOOD 1-4
By **Jamel Mitchell**

HOOD CONSIGLIERE 1&2
NO TIME FOR ERROR
By **Keese**

PROTÉGÉ OF A LEGEND 1,2&3
LOVE IN THE TRENCHES 1&2
By **Corey Robinson**

THE PLUG'S RUTHLESS DAUGHTER 1&2
By **Tony Daniels**

BORN IN THE GRAVE 1-3
CRIME PAYS
By **Self Made Tay**

MOAN IN MY MOUTH
By **XTASY**

TORN BETWEEN A GANGSTER AND A GENTLEMAN
By **J-BLUNT & Miss Kim**

LOYALTY IS EVERYTHING 1-3
CITY OF SMOKE 1-3
By **Molotti**

HERE TODAY GONE TOMORROW 1&2
By **Fly Rock**

WOMEN LIE MEN LIE 1-4
FIFTY SHADES OF SNOW 1-3
STACK BEFORE YOU SPLURGE
GIRLS FALL LIKE DOMINOES
NAÏVE TO THE STREETS
By **ROY MILLIGAN**

PILLOW PRINCESS
By **S. Hawkins**

THE BUTTERFLY MAFIA 1-3
SALUTE MY SAVAGERY 1&2
By **Fumiya Payne**

THE LANE 1&2
By Ken-Ken Spence

THE PUSSY TRAP 1-5
By **Nene Capri**

DIRTY DNA
By **Blaque**

SANCTIFIED AND HORNY
by **XTASY**

BOOKS BY LDP'S CEO, CA$H

TRUST IN NO MAN
TRUST IN NO MAN 2
TRUST IN NO MAN 3
BONDED BY BLOOD
SHORTY GOT A THUG
THUGS CRY
THUGS CRY 2
THUGS CRY 3
TRUST NO BITCH
TRUST NO BITCH 2
TRUST NO BITCH 3
TIL MY CASKET DROPS
RESTRAINING ORDER
RESTRAINING ORDER 2
IN LOVE WITH A CONVICT
LIFE OF A HOOD STAR
XMAS WITH AN ATL SHOOTER